THE SOUND THAT FOUND ME

JILLIAN MARIE

PERFECT PROSE PRESS LLC

Published by Perfect Prose Press LLC
Ladera Ranch, California

Cover design by Saara Helkala
Interior design by Autumn Morgan

ISBN-13: 979-8-9986254-4-2
First Edition

Digital Edition, March 2026.
ISBN: 979-8-9986254-5-9

Printed in the United States of America.

www.booksbyjillianmarie.com

To the ones still listening for something more. Keep your heart open. It will find you.

READER NOTE

Your mental health and emotional well-being are important to me. For a full list of content warnings and potential triggers, please flip to the "Content Warning" page in the back of the book.

PROLOGUE
HEATHER

Punta Cana, August 2001

The ocean was warm enough that it felt like hands. Hands and heat and wanting.

Salt clung to my lips, my hair, my skin. Waves lifted and lowered us in slow, heavy pulses, like the sea was breathing around us. His fingers found my waist beneath the surface—steady, sure—pulling me closer until his body pressed fully into mine.

"This week," he whispered, his mouth hovering a breath from mine, "has been everything."

"It's been surreal," I said, though it didn't feel like enough.

Then he kissed me.

His lips were warm and insistent. His body molded to mine, heat rushing through me so fast it stole my breath. I wrapped my arms around his neck, sliding my fingers into his dark, wet curls. He held me like he was afraid I'd float away—when the truth was, I was terrified I never would.

The world narrowed to the slow drag of water, the taste

of salt on his mouth, the frantic ache of knowing this was ending.

I was sixteen. He was the boy I'd known for six days. And somewhere between the sand and the salt and his mouth on mine, everything felt suspended in that moment. I already knew: I was never walking off this island the same.

For the first time in my life, I wasn't just noticed—I was seen. And I saw him too, not as a beautiful boy or a passing summer story, but as something that would stay with me long after this moment became only a memory.

Earlier that day, my life had looked ordinary—at least, as ordinary as anything got with my family.

My mom—Cheryl for the week—was on husband number three and glowing, insisting Punta Cana was "alignment." Ben, my older brother, spent the trip in his Duke hat and quiet superiority. Tory, fifteen and sharper than anyone guessed, lived for virgin piña coladas and signs from the universe.

And me? Somewhere in the middle.

We were leaving before sunrise. Dresses drying on chairs, half-packed bags, sunburn stinging my shoulders. My long, nearly black hair frizzed thick around my face, freckles blooming across my nose. Tory turned golden. I turned pink.

That afternoon, on our so-called excursion, my mom insisted we "experience the real culture," but all I felt was a soft dread curling in my chest.

This was ending.

Not just the trip.

Him.

Bradley.

He wasn't my boyfriend. We weren't anything defined—just two people who kept finding each other like magnets.

He was here with his aunt and uncle and their three boys—Jared, the goofy flirt; Tommy, the steady older-brother type; Brett, the quiet observer. The family—loud, loyal, impossible to miss.

But Bradley... he had something else. Something I didn't have a name for then, except it drew me in without effort.

Being with him felt like standing in the one place where everything stopped shifting, where I didn't have to brace for what came next.

Later that night, after everyone drifted back to their rooms—even Tory calling it early—I knew I wasn't sleeping. I put on a simple white dress, and I slipped into the warm night.

Bradley stood outside the beach club, music spilling into the palm trees, colored lights bleeding across the sand. His dark curls stuck to his forehead, his sun-faded T-shirt clinging to his lean frame. His green eyes caught the lantern light, as if they held their own glow.

When he saw me, his smile was warm like he'd been waiting.

"Wanna go stargazing?" he murmured, his arm slipping easily around my waist.

"Yeah," I said. "I'd love that."

We walked until the resort faded behind us, waves crashing louder as the darkness opened up. We dropped our sandals on the edge of the sand.

He stopped where the foam fizzed around our toes.

"I don't want to go home," I said.

He turned fully toward me. "I was just thinking the same thing."

He reached up and tucked a strand of hair behind my ear, his touch sending a shiver down my spine.

I hugged my arms around myself. "Home is always changing for me. Another place, another man my mom swears will be permanent. I swallowed. "She's always talking about alignment and crystals and following the air—like if the air shifts, we're supposed to shift with it."

I looked at him, "But what if I don't want to believe that every time the air changes, I have to change too?"

His expression tightened, something protective passing through his eyes.

"I'm sorry you don't have that kind of stability," he said. "Everyone should."

I picked at the edge of my dress.

He studied me, then gently linked his pinky in mine.

"You don't have to," he said. "Not with me."

I wanted to believe him. I smiled, twirling my fingers in my hair, trying not to let the hope in his words show too much.

After a beat, he added, "My uncle's already planning my whole life. College. A major. Something practical. He says music's just a hobby."

"But it's not," I said.

He shook his head. "Music is my life." After a moment, he said quietly, "Just because my dad got lost in the dark side of rock and roll doesn't mean I will."

Our fingers interlaced. He lifted my hand and pressed a soft kiss into it—like a promise sealed between us.

"I know it's only been a few days," he said, "but being

around you feels in tune. Like the noise finally drops out and everything sounds the way it's supposed to."

I couldn't stop the cheesy grin on my face. "I have to admit, being with you was a lot of firsts for me, and I was out of my comfort zone. But somehow you made it all feel genuine and special."

We stood there, the water brushing our feet, both of us knowing the same thing without having to say it: neither of us was ready to leave what we'd found.

"I was wondering... could I get your number before you go?" he asked.

Relief flooded through me. "I was hoping you'd ask."

I handed him a folded scrap of paper I had tucked in my bralette—my home number, my screen name, a tiny cat doodle. His mouth pulled into a smile.

"Mookie?" he asked.

"My cat."

"I like it," he said, tucking it carefully into his back pocket.

He studied me for a moment. "You ever gone skinny-dipping?"

I laughed. "For real?"

"If we're doing something unforgettable... "

I pulled my dress down, letting it fall, stepped out of my underwear, and slipped my bralette off. My heart pounded everywhere at once. He stared—wide-eyed, moonlight catching in green.

"Coming?" I asked.

Then I ran into the water.

Warmth wrapped around me. Waves lifted and pulled— his lips on my lips, his hands on me, skin to skin. Everything else disappeared.

Then the sky opened. Warm rain fell in heavy sheets.

We shrieked and sprinted toward shore, drenched and laughing. Pulling damp clothes on was almost impossible; the fabric clung stubbornly, leaving us laughing. My dress clung to me; his shorts were soaked.

"Oh my," through laughter— "We're going to catch a cold."

A grin, rain in his eyes. "It'll be worth it."

Thunder rolled low as we slowed near the walkway, the night shrinking to the two of us and the sound of water on stone.

He fell into step beside me, close enough that our shoulders brushed.

"I wanted tonight to be remembered." He ran a hand through his wet hair. "I'm sorry it wasn't smoother."

I smiled. "I think the best parts are always the ones you don't plan, and for the record, I will remember it."

We reached my door. Neither of us moved.

"I'll see you again," he said, voice rough.

"I hope so."

"You will." A promise in his voice. "I'll find you."

A tear slipped down my cheek. He caught it with his thumb, slow and gentle.

"I don't want this to end," I whispered.

He didn't answer; instead, he leaned down and kissed me.

Slow. Deep. Like it hurt to pull away.

Rain blurred my vision.

"This week was unforgettable," he said.

"It was everything," I breathed.

Then he reached into his pocket and pressed something into my palm.

A small guitar pick. Worn smooth at the edges.

"So you don't forget me," he said, his expression soft and unguarded.

I took the pick and smoothed my thumb over it, as if it were the most prized jewel I'd ever held.

And I knew—heart pounding hard enough to ache—that this was the before-or-after line. Not just of the trip.

Of me.

Years later, I would still feel that rain and taste the salt on my lips and think:

That was the night everything shifted.

The night I started belonging to a song I hadn't even heard yet.

1

FIFTEEN YEARS LATER

HEATHER

I t was a spring day in Chicago, the kind where Lake Michigan couldn't decide if it wanted to blow mist or let the sun through. The sidewalks along Michigan Avenue were still damp from the morning drizzle, but the air felt almost warm. Hopeful. Fake hopeful.

And I was late. As usual.

I wove around a couple walking a Yorkie in a raincoat, muttering, "Sorry, sorry," as I jogged across Superior Street in heels not designed for dodging buses and cabs. My tote bag was sliding off my shoulder, sketch folders bent inside, and I could already hear Tripp in my head: *Punctuality is a form of respect, Heather.*

Time in fashion didn't work like normal time. You didn't live in April. You lived in next October. Scarves. Layers. Textiles. My love language. No one in my world cared if you were five, ten, twenty minutes behind, not when you were juggling fittings in River North and fabric samples from Milan, as long as you delivered something beautiful.

Tripp cared. He always cared.

The Peninsula glowed at the corner like quiet money. I'd

walked from River North, figuring it was close enough, until my heels reminded me otherwise. Polished black cars lined the curb outside the revolving doors. The doorman had better posture than most elected officials. I caught a glimpse of myself in the glass before I went in—black dress, trench, hair I'd tried to smooth in the reflection of a shop window and promptly lost to the lake humidity somewhere near Chicago Avenue.

Not terrible. Not Gold Coast perfect, either.

Inside was soft lighting and elegance. A hostess in a sleek black pant suit glanced up, and before I could even say Tripp's last name, her face changed.

"Oh," she said, like she'd been told to watch for me. "Ms. Brown."

That threw me for half a beat. Only doctors and land-lords ever called me Ms. Brown.

"Right this way."

I followed her past the main dining room, deeper, toward a private space in the back. My heart did a weird, uneven kick. Tripp said dinner. He hadn't said private room.

Still, a part of me smiled. This was such a Tripp thing to do. Always thoughtful, always bigger than necessary, the kind of man who made grand gestures. It reminded me why I fell for him in the first place, even if it sometimes made me nervous.

"Let me take your coat," she said before opening the doors. The sound hit first—laughter, glass, a woman's voice saying, "There she is," like I was late to my own party.

There were at least twenty people inside.

Champagne flutes were already poured. Candles, low and white, ran the length of an impossible table. Pale blush flowers and greens, like a bridal magazine spread. Everyone —literally everyone—turned and looked at me.

For a moment, I honestly thought I'd walked into the wrong room.

Tripp stood at the far end of the table in a navy suit, white shirt, no tie. He'd taken off his glasses, which meant he cared about the photos. When he saw me, his smile softened—clean, composed, and a little proud, like he'd been waiting for this moment. And just like that, some of my irritation evaporated. For a breath, before the noise reached me again, it felt like the room belonged to only us.

"Heather," he said, like a toast.

My throat went dry.

Nico, my best friend, was there. He lifted two fingers in a wiggle-wave from the corner, expression somewhere between electric and about to combust.

Tory sat next to him, already holding a glass of champagne. She mouthed, *Surprise,* and widened her eyes in that *are you okay* way only a sister can pull off without moving her face.

I wasn't sure if I was okay. I was confused... That was the only word that fit.

Jessica Walton, my client, was there, of course. Blonde, glowing, Gold Coast gloss, like she'd been lit by a softbox. Her husband, Clint, had one arm around her chair and the other around Tripp's shoulder, like this was also somehow his win.

But aside from those three?

Everyone else was... not mine.

I searched Tripp's face, waiting for him to explain.

To tell me what this was.

Tripp's mother sat near the center. Pearls. Cream silk blouse. A smile you couldn't quite read all the way through. Next to her, his father, wearing a watch that probably cost the same as a Lake Forest mortgage. Two of his college friends in suits that fit like they'd been tailored at Trunk Club before it went too mainstream. A couple I'd met once at a charity gala, whose names I was already scrambling to remember and failing.

"Heather," Tripp said again, and this time he lifted his glass. "Come here."

People pulled back, forming a loose half-circle. My legs felt like they were still walking and also like they'd detached from my body.

I tried to smile. I think I did.

"Hi," I whispered when I finally reached him, because what else do you say when you walk into something you did not know was happening?

He leaned in and kissed my cheek. He smelled like his soap—clean, expensive aftershave, a little sharp. His hand slipped into mine, warm and steady, and for a second I felt anchored. Then he let go.

"I'm going to make this brief," he told the room, voice projecting like he'd done this before. "Because anyone who knows Heather knows she hates a scene."

The room laughed. He smiled like he'd earned it.

"Heather," he said, turning back to me, and there it was —that softness he only ever had when it was just us. "You are the most unexpected thing that's ever happened to me. You are chaos wrapped in silk."

Gentle laughter moved through the room.

"And I mean that in the most flattering way," he added.

His mother tilted her head, smiling like she knew exactly what he meant.

My face warmed.

My heartbeat climbed into my throat.

Then Tripp reached into his jacket.

Oh my God.

No.

He wasn't—

He was.

He dropped to one knee.

For a suspended second, the room fell away. The candlelight, the clink of glass, the soft gasp I heard from Tory. Nico whispered, "Oh my God, babe," like the moment itself might shatter if he spoke any louder.

Tripp lifted the ring. Even in the dimness, it caught the light.

"Heather Lee Brown," he said—and here his voice wavered just slightly, like this was the only part he hadn't been able to rehearse—"will you marry me?"

When our eyes met, something inside me steadied.

The nerves. The shock. The spinning rush of everything. All of it fell quiet.

All I could see was him—the man who always knew what he wanted, who made plans and followed through. And in that stillness, I felt myself reaching for that same certainty.

For the first time, I wanted to believe that this—this moment, this man—might be what forever was supposed to look like.

Every eye in the room swung to me.

My mouth opened.

The expectation in the air felt physical, like a weight on my skin. His mother's hands were folded at her chest. Jessica's phone was angled discreetly down for the photo. A waiter in the corner hovered with a silver tray of more champagne, as if he'd been given a cue.

Tripp was looking up at me with that earnest, hopeful face. A piece of hair had fallen forward at his hairline. That tiny, human imperfection hit me right in the sternum.

He loves you, I told myself. *He chose you. He thinks you belong here.*

"Yes," I heard myself say.

The room broke. Applause, chairs scraping, people closing in. Someone slid a glass into my free hand. Someone kissed my cheek. I couldn't track the voices—congratulations, welcome to the family—just perfume and clinking glass and light.

The ring went on before I'd really processed it. Sparkly. Heavy. Big.

Tripp stood and kissed me, and the whole room applauded like we were onstage.

For a minute, I let myself lean into him and breathe.

Safe, I told myself. Stable. Someone who files his taxes early and never forgets your coffee order and can talk to your landlord without sounding scared.

When the noise thinned for half a second, Tory slid in and grabbed both my hands.

Her eyes were bright. "Hey," she whispered. "Deep breaths, okay?"

My laugh was a little shaky. "Were you—did you know?"

"Not really," she said. "He told me yesterday. Kind of sprang it on me."

"Yesterday," I repeated. "That's it?"

"Yeah." Tory shrugged, the red fabric slipping off one shoulder, her big brown eyes looking up at me, her brown hair falling in soft waves that looked like Nico had definitely blown it out before this.

I swallowed. "Was Mom invited?"

Tory made a face. "Not sure, but I don't think she would have gotten the message on such short notice; she is traveling in Bali with Keith."

"That's right. And Ben?"

"I called him. He said Steph has been wiped her pregnancy with our little niece. He didn't want to travel right now."

I nodded. "Dad?"

"He couldn't get a flight out last minute either," she said softly. "He said to tell you he loves you, and he would call you first thing in the morning."

First thing in the morning for my dad meant sometime after he was done working and after Sports.

I nodded, but something in my chest dipped.

Not because of who wasn't in the room.

Because of who was.

Everyone here had known.

Everyone here had been planned for.

My family didn't have the chance to come in for this, other than Tory, who lives here.

And I told myself not to make it into something—not tonight, not now.

Across the table, Tripp's mother leaned in to whisper to a woman draped in Chanel, both of them looking briefly at me like I was a very nice acquisition. Tripp's father clapped him on the back. Someone said something about summer in Lake Geneva. Someone else said we should book the Drake Hotel, "before dates disappear."

"Hey," Tory said under her breath. "You okay?"

"I'm fine," I said automatically.

And I almost was. Because this was… beautiful. It was. The flowers, the champagne, the way Tripp had talked about me, the ring catching the light when I moved my hand. It felt like a movie. It felt like what adults who had their lives together did when they were ready for their next chapter.

It also felt like I'd walked into someone else's movie.

Tripp reappeared and slid his arm around my waist, pulling me gently against him. He kissed my temple and looked down at me with that private pride.

"Mrs. Kensington," he murmured against my hair.

For a split second, I let myself smile. The way he said it. Like it was already decided. Like I was already his.

His mother approached then, composed, perfect posture.

"Heather," she said, taking both my hands. Up close, she smelled like soft powder and money. Her smile didn't waver. "Welcome to the family, dear."

There was some kindness in it. There was also something else, humming just underneath.

"Thank you," I said.

She leaned in and kissed my cheek. "Tripp will make a wonderful husband."

I laughed softly because that felt like the correct answer.

When she pulled back, her eyes flicked down—quick—to my ring, to my shoulders, to the way I was standing.

I wasn't sure if I was a pass or a fail for her. I always sensed she wished Tripp ended up with someone from their social network.

A waiter swept by with fresh champagne. Someone across the room called Tripp's name. He squeezed my waist and was already turning toward them, already mid-conversation about August weekends and guest lists.

And just like that, I was standing in a room full of people toasting my future.

People who knew his middle name, his prep school, and his favorite Scotch. People who did not know me. I looked down at my hand. The diamond was flawless. The band was covered in more diamonds. I told myself the weight I felt was just the ring.

2

SAFE AND SPARKLY

HEATHER

The next morning, the ring felt heavier than it had the night before.

I'd lift my hand to push my hair out of my face and catch a flash of light, then jolt like something was on me. By the third time it happened, Tripp was openly amused.

"That reaction does not inspire confidence," he said, leaning against the kitchen counter in his Yale Law School T-shirt, watching me like he watches numbers.

"It's large," I said.

"It's platinum," he said, like that answered it.

He was in his Ralph Lauren slippers, hair still damp from his shower, glasses on. No suit yet. This was my favorite version of him, not the one who filled out a tux like he'd been born inside it, but the one who padded around in expensive sweats he'd had monogrammed and didn't think twice about.

Neither of us had to rush this morning; he'd pushed his first meeting, and I'd emailed my assistant to move a fitting.

His apartment, technically, until we "merged our lives,"

as he'd said last night, was spotless. Marble counters. Slate-gray cabinets. Fresh lilies on the table in a narrow glass vase. The lilies hadn't been there when I fell asleep.

"Did you have flowers delivered at six in the morning?" I asked.

"Mother sent them," he said, resting one hand on the counter beside the vase. The morning light caught the rim of his glasses, softening his usually sharp features. "They were already here when I got up."

I poured the last of my coffee, watching it swirl in the cup. *Figures.*

There wasn't a single dish in the sink. Not a sock on the floor. Not a takeout container in sight. Somehow, even the pile of mail looked curated, squared up by size and lined like we were about to photograph it for a lifestyle feature.

This was the thing about being with Tripp: nothing leaked. Nothing spilled. Nothing frayed.

"Okay," he said, folding his arms. "Eight-letter word. 'One who cannot delegate.'"

I blinked at him. "You're doing crosswords at eight in the morning, and you're judging my ring reaction?"

"It's eight-oh-six," he said. "And yes."

I plucked the folded paper from the counter and skimmed the clues. "Control freak," I said.

"That's two words."

"You didn't say it had to be one," I said, leaning against the counter across from him.

"'Control freak' is also eight and five," he said mildly. "Try again."

"Autocrat," I said.

He looked down at the boxes, then up at me, and smiled. "There she is."

That was the part I liked. The way he talked to me like I was quick. The way he expected me to keep up.

Most guys I'd dated before him had gone one of two ways: too impressed by what I did ("You're in fashion? That's so hot."), or weirdly threatened by the fact that I had my own thing and didn't need them to rescue me.

Tripp wasn't threatened. Tripp admired competence almost to the point of worship. If he could label it, file it, and define it, he could relax. And he loved that I had a craft he didn't understand but respected.

And—maybe more than that—he liked taking care of the parts of life I never had time to get a handle on.

"We have dinner next week at Jessica and Clint's, Wednesday at seven," he said, refilling his coffee. "She texted me last night to confirm because you didn't answer her."

I winced. "I was busy saying yes to your entire bloodline."

"And at three you're meeting that buyer from Bergdorf," he went on. "And you promised Nico you'd send him photos of the new muslin fits by tonight, or he's going to, quote, 'combust in a tragic salon fire.'"

I laughed. "You took notes?"

He tapped his temple. "Catalogued."

This was another thing: he kept my moving parts straight. All of them. My brain was mood boards, and fabric sourcing, and fittings that ran long. Bills that were always semi-handled. His brain was... grids. Systems. Calendars. Next steps. He made chaos feel like a plan.

With Tripp, I didn't have to be the girl calculating if rent cleared before fabric invoices. With Tripp, I could just design.

"Okay," he said lightly, adjusting his glasses, "your turn. Pop quiz. What's my nine-thirty?"

"Call with someone who ends their name with the third and... you're yelling at someone about a fund?"

He snorted. "Close enough."

He reached past me and straightened the stack of mail again. He didn't even seem aware he was doing it, but I watched his fingers neaten the edges, line them up, square, square, square.

You are in control here, I thought. You are safe here.

His phone buzzed face down on the counter. He didn't pick it up right away. That always made me feel weirdly chosen, like I was important enough to make a man ignore work, even for a minute.

"So," he said, and his voice shifted—softer, "Are you happy?" The question caught me.

I looked at him. "Yes," I said, and it wasn't a lie.

He searched my face, like he was fact-checking me.

I lifted my left hand a little. "It just still feels... surreal."

He smiled at that. Really smiled. The real one, the one where his mouth curves more on one side, and the tension leaves around his eyes.

"Good," he said quietly.

Then, like a switch had flipped, he kissed my forehead, slid his coffee mug into the sink (then rinsed it and placed it in the dishwasher, obviously), and headed to the bedroom to get ready.

I stayed where I was, sipping my coffee slowly as I skimmed a few work emails.

When he came back, he was tugging at his tie. I crossed the room to finish the job—either the fashion designer in me or maybe this was the wife-to-be stepping in.

"Also," he added, "I moved your sketchbooks into the

office so the cleaning crew doesn't shift anything. And I told them not to touch the dress form in the guest room. They'll be here at noon."

Cleaning crew. Flowers that appeared before sunrise. Calendars I didn't have to manage. A future with a man who said "we" like it already existed.

All I had to do was show up and make beautiful things.

That sounded, in theory, like everything I'd ever wanted.

"Tripp?" I asked.

"Hm?" He was in front of the hall mirror now, knotting his tie with practiced hands.

"Last night," I said slowly, "did you... Did you tell your parents they could invite everyone?"

He met my eyes in the mirror. "You didn't like it."

"I didn't say that."

He gave the tiniest smile. "You didn't have to."

He turned then, leaning one shoulder into the doorway, tie half-done, glasses on, that analytic Tripp look back in place. "It mattered to them," he said simply. "It mattered to me." Then, after a beat, "And you said yes."

I exhaled. "Yeah," I said. "I did."

He stepped forward, took my left hand, and kissed my ring like it was an oath.

"Get used to it, Brown," he murmured against my knuckles. "You're mine now."

Something in my chest fluttered. Something else... tightened.

He let my hand go, finished his tie, grabbed his briefcase, and brushed a quick kiss over my mouth.

"Dinner with my parents tonight," he said.

"I was planning to hang with Tory," I said.

"Well, when you become the Mrs., dinner with my parents is mandatory."

Mandatory. I thought to myself. I never had mandatory dinners with my family, Cheryl didn't really live on a schedule.

"You are welcome to dinner tomorrow night with Tory, Nico, and his debut boyfriend," I said, knowing he wouldn't come.

"Dancing in Boystown is not my scene," he said, adjusting the cuffs on his sleeves.

Sometimes I wondered if my life "wasn't his scene".

"Bye, my future bride." He planted a small kiss on my cheek.

"Bye, have a good day," I said. Like that was exactly what he would want to hear every morning as the future Mrs. Kensington.

The door clicked shut.

Silence settled over the apartment like a hotel lobby early in the morning: still, temperature-controlled, expensive.

I looked around the house. Everything was in its place. Perfect. Curated. My sketchbook waited on the desk, open to a half-formed silhouette I'd started and abandoned sometime around 2 a.m.

I tried to imagine myself here. *Living* here. Was I too messy for this apartment? Did Tripp even know I had a messy side? He'd only been to my place a handful of times. He'd preferred his space, so I just came here.

The lilies on the table were opening more in the light.

I held my left hand up and watched the ring throw fractured brightness across the marble.

This is what being chosen feels like, I told myself. This is what secure looks like. Everything was in its place. Including me.

3

BRAVE

HEATHER

After Tripp left, I went to my one and only drawer, the small space he'd cleared months ago and never expanded. Inside was a pair of pajamas, a soft white tee, one pair of clean underwear, and a single pair of pants. Enough for a night here and there, never enough to really belong.

This was why we didn't do many spontaneous date nights or sleepovers.

I considered slipping back into the dress I'd changed into after work yesterday—the one Tripp had asked me to wear for dinner—but it felt too formal. Instead, I pulled on the trousers from my drawer, tucked in the white tee, and added the blazer I'd worn yesterday to pull it all together. Not perfect, but passable.

I swiped on some lip gloss, pulled my hair into a low bun, and headed to work.

The light streamed through the loft windows of Rowan & Wolfe, glinting off rolls of fabric stacked like soft sculptures in the corners. The space smelled like muslin, coffee, and the faintest trace of jasmine from Alena's diffuser. It was the kind of place that felt lived in—unpolished and layered with ideas.

Tisha Rowan and Jackie Wolfe had started the label together. They were my bosses once; now they are my partners. Alena kept everything running—half office assistant, half miracle worker.

In the back, the hum of the machines was steady as Lidia and Marta worked through fittings for a mother-of-the-bride gown. The sound was comforting, the quiet choreography of women who knew what they were doing.

On my desk sat a framed photo of Tory and me in Punta Cana—two tiny figures high above the ocean, parasailing against a sweep of sky so blue it looked unreal. You couldn't even make out our faces from that far away, just the arc of the parachute and the thin rope trailing down to the boat.

I remembered gripping the harness so tightly my hands ached, convinced I might fall—or pee my pants. Tory was laughing, arms spread wide, hair whipping in the wind, completely free.

I'd kept that photo there to remind myself to be brave. Later that night, I told that curly-haired boy with the olive green eyes how scared I'd been. He'd smiled and said, "You did it—and you lived to tell the tale."

It had made me feel tethered in a way I hadn't known I needed.

"Knock, knock."

Alena's voice pulled me back. She stood in the doorway balancing two coffees, curls half-pinned, a pencil still tucked behind one ear. There was a faint smudge of graphite on her cheekbone that somehow made her look even more like herself.

"Brought you the good stuff," she said, stepping inside.

She set one cup beside my sketches, the steam curling between us.

"Thank you," I said, wrapping my hands around it even though it was too hot to hold.

"Oh my God," she said suddenly, pointing. "Is that what I think it is?"

It took me a second to realize she meant the ring.

"Oh." I looked down at my hand, turning it slightly so the diamond caught the morning light. It flashed sharp and brilliant, almost blinding against the gray tabletop. "Yeah."

Her mouth fell open. "You're engaged?"

"I am engaged." The words felt strange in my mouth, too big for the smallness of the studio.

Alena gasped and crossed to me, grabbing my hand before I could tuck it away. "Holy hell, Heather. That thing could have its own zip code."

I laughed, tucking a piece of hair behind my ear.

She leaned her hip against my desk, eyes still on the ring. "Was it everything you wanted?"

"It was... beautiful," I said, my voice catching on the word in a way that felt half-true, half-careful. "He really went all out."

Her smile held, but her eyes shifted from the ring to my face. "How did he propose?"

"At the Peninsula," I said. "A private room. Close friends. Family."

"Sounds like you were surprised."

I tried to meet her eyes and couldn't quite hold them.

"It was sweet," I said. Too quickly. "Definitely unexpected."

She studied me for a moment, her expression softening. "You okay?"

I nodded, forcing another small laugh. "Yeah. I mean, yes. Just—processing."

"That's allowed," she said.

Alena's strawberry-blonde hair fell forward as she tilted her head, her small upturned nose giving her something quietly thoughtful. "It's a lot to take in."

"It is," I admitted, and something in my chest eased at the honesty.

She exhaled and nudged the corner of my sketchpad with one finger. "Well—congratulations. That explains why you came in late."

I smiled. "Yep, we wanted to soak in the moment."

She squeezed my shoulder before heading for the door. "We'll toast later. You deserve it."

When she was gone, I exhaled, the room settling back into the sound of sewing machines and quiet focus. My ring caught the light, scattering tiny prisms across my desk—one landing right on the photo of Tory and me, high above the water.

Be brave, I thought.

It had worked once before.

4

______

FAJITAS AND FLASHBACKS

HEATHER

By the time I got home, the rain had picked up; it beat steadily against the windows like background noise the city couldn't turn off.

I dropped my bag on the counter, kicked off my shoes, and peeled off the blazer I'd been wearing since morning. My shoulders ached from the day, from pretending everything was fine, from the weight of something gleaming on my hand.

From the hallway came the rush of the shower. Tory was probably taking an hour-long "therapy session," as she called them.

The blender sat on the counter beside a half-cut pineapple. That meant piña coladas. Fajita Fridays, her weekly invention to "celebrate survival."

I walked to my room and slipped the ring off my finger. It felt like it had been suffocating me all day, and when it came off, my skin pulsed where it sat, leaving a faint red indent marking the place it had belonged. It was as if I'd been claimed by something heavier than it looked. I carried it over to my dresser and set it in my jewelry box between a tangled gold chain, a pair of hoops, and the pick Bradley gave me. I traced my thumb along the edge of it, the small nick that he made with his teeth still there. Before I started to let my mind go down memory lane, I put it back where it belonged and closed the lid.

When I popped out my contacts and switched to glasses, the world blurred, then refocused. I didn't look like a woman newly engaged. More like someone who'd borrowed the role for a day. The mirror gave me back a version of myself I almost recognized—hair still damp from the Spring rain, frizzy; faint mascara smudge under one eye; lips bare except for the gloss I'd swiped on hours ago. My freckles stood out more without foundation, my expression softer, almost uncertain.

By the time I'd pulled on my comfiest sweatshirt and drawstring sweatpants, the shower had stopped. I could still smell the faint trace of Tory's shampoo drifting down the hallway, something citrusy.

I padded barefoot to the kitchen and opened the box of fajita mix, checking what she'd already set out. Bell peppers. Limes. A mess of cilantro on the cutting board.

Tory appeared a minute later, towel-drying her dark curls, wearing an oversized NYU sweatshirt and leggings. Her skin was still pink from the heat of the shower, her energy big enough to fill the room.

"Happy Friday," she said, walking over to the kitchen. "Survived another week in fashion?"

"Barely," I said, smiling. "You?"

"PR life, baby. Fridays are either about pretending to work or recovering from pretending to work. Today we celebrated with an early lunch that accidentally turned into the weekend."

I laughed. "Remind me why I didn't go into PR again?"

"Because you like stress and deadlines," she teased, pulling the rum toward her. "I like free drinks and an expense account."

She tossed pineapple chunks into the blender, added coconut milk and ice, and turned it on. The low roar drowned out the rain for a moment.

While she worked, I sliced the peppers she'd already set out. The scent of cilantro and lime filled the kitchen. The rhythmic chop of the knife, the rain, the blender—it all blended into a quiet, familiar soundtrack.

Tory poured two glasses and set one beside me. She leaned against the counter, eyes glinting.

"So," Tory said, wiping her hands on a dish towel, "how are you feeling about last night?" Her expression softened. "Does it feel right for you?"

I looked down at the pan, watching the peppers and onions catch a bit of color. "I want it to," I said finally. "He's steady. Predictable in the best way. He doesn't forget things or flake or make me feel like I'm waiting around for him to choose."

Tory's mouth curved slightly. "Predictable," she repeated, a little wryly.

I hesitated, stirring the vegetables. "I guess I'm still a little shocked. But we've been together for almost two years, so it shouldn't feel surprising. He's thirty-four, I'm thirty-one—it feels like the right time." I don't know why I felt like I was convincing myself.

Leaning against the counter, Tory tilted her head, her hair still wet from her shower. "If sweater vests and sending your future kids to the most overpriced schools in the city is your dream, then yeah, you're right on track."

I laughed, shaking my head. "You make him sound like a brochure for responsible living."

She smirked. "I just always pictured you with someone a little less... pressed."

"He's stable," I said, too quickly. "He's good to me. You know how many guys our age are still figuring life out? Tripp knows what he wants."

"I'm sure he does." Her voice was gentle now. "But having it together doesn't mean it fits you."

Tory lifted her drink and took a sip. "God, this tastes like Punta Cana," she said, smiling. "Remember that trip? I was fifteen, you were sixteen, and we thought we were the most stealth people on the beach."

I laughed, the scent of coconut in the air taking me back. "Oh my God, yes. We smuggled those piña coladas from the swim-up bar and thought no one noticed."

"Ben definitely noticed," she said, twisting a piece of damp hair around her finger. "He hovered like a lifeguard with a clipboard—so self-righteous before he left for Duke."

"Right? He wouldn't shut up about it. Classes, dorms, basketball—he was unbearable."

"Guess it worked out," Tory said. "He met Steph in his Sophomore English class."

"And now they're having their first baby," I said with a squeal.

"Wild," she murmured. "That trip feels like forever ago."

"It does," I said softly. "Sometimes it feels like we left versions of ourselves there we never really got back."

Her gaze sharpened slightly, a teasing glint in her brown eyes. "You mean you left someone there."

I tried to play dumb. "What? Who?"

"The boy," she said. "Tan skin, messy curls. You danced with him for hours. Your first kiss, your first love."

I smiled, heat blooming in my cheeks. "Feels like a million years ago?"

"You came back to the room barefoot with sand in your hair," she teased. "Something about skinny dipping."

I took a big sip of my drink. Trying not to think about his hand warm against mine as the rest of the world blurred away.

He was the first boy I ever danced with closer than arm's length. The first boy who made me forget who I was supposed to be.

Even now, I could still hear that song—the one that made everything start to shift.

My phone buzzed on the counter, snapping me out of it.

"Sorry," I said, setting my glass down.

A text from Tripp lit up the screen.

TRIPP

Mom's not too happy about your absence tonight. Promise me you'll call her tomorrow and start making plans to look at wedding venues.

Efficient, even in text form.

"Everything okay?" Tory asked, flipping a tortilla.

"Yeah." I set the phone face down. "Just Tripp."

The word *wedding* hung there, heavy as the rain outside.

While the vegetables softened, Tory set plates on the counter. "Does Mom know yet?"

"Not yet. I was going to call her today, but... the day got away from me."

Tory gave a knowing look. "You're stalling."

"I'm not," I said, though I kind of was. "She's only met Tripp once, and you know how she is."

"With the crystals and sage?" Her eyebrow flared up.

I laughed. "Last time she saw him, she said his aura

didn't blend with mine. Something about his energy being too... beige."

Tory grinned. "That's one way to say dull."

"She said it wasn't *bad,* just 'imbalanced.' Then she burned sage in our kitchen for three hours."

Tory snorted.

I tossed her a napkin. "You're terrible. Tripp is good to me."

"I am not saying he isn't."

We sat across from each other at the counter, plates steaming between us, lime and char filling the air. For a while, we just ate and laughed, the quiet comfort of Friday night settling in.

Eventually, we poured the last of the piña coladas and got a little drunk, laughing until our cheeks hurt. For a few fleeting hours, it was easy—just two sisters in a small apartment, pretending life wasn't shifting underneath them.

The ring, the parents, the wedding—all of it faded.

But the boy from Punta Cana lingered anyway, quiet and uninvited.

5

RABBIT RABBIT
HEATHER

I must've fallen asleep with the lamp still on.

The air was thick with the scent of coconut and lime from the night before, but when I closed my eyes, it shifted—salt, warmth, laughter. The city fell away. The sound became the ocean.

I was back in Punta Cana. Under the stars. Hearing the waves crash in the dark, like the ocean woke up after everyone else had gone to sleep.

Bradley was beside me, stretched out in the sand, pointing toward the sky. "That one's the Little Dipper," he said, guiding my hand until our fingers overlapped.

His laugh still lived somewhere in me—the low, easy kind that made you want to keep saying stupid things just to hear it again. I'd told him I never really understood the stars until that night, and he smiled, brushing my hair away from my face with a touch that made my chest ache.

That was the moment before our first kiss—my first real kiss.

I'd only kissed one other boy, under the bleachers, back in freshman year. Kyle Fisher.

He tasted like Dr Pepper and desperation, and I remember thinking, Is that it?

But with Bradley, it was different. His lips taught me what kissing was supposed to feel like—slow, certain, like breathing in rhythm with someone else. I fit against him like I'd been waiting for that shape all along. A rush of something wild moved through me, dizzy and perfect. When we finally came up for air, he smiled, his forehead resting against mine.

"Heather," he said, voice still rough from kissing, "I don't usually say stuff like this, but if I did, I'd want this... You."

My mouth curved before I could stop it, "That was cheesy," I said.

"Maybe." He smirked. "But I'm serious."

"I hope I don't wake up and remember this as just a dream." My honesty slipped out.

He smiled, a quiet one that reached his eyes, and kissed me again. The stars above us seemed to pulse, the whole sky humming like it might keep our secret.

Something buzzed. Ugh—my phone. I woke up and the dream dissolved, replaced by the pale morning light slipping through my curtains. My throat was dry; my head thudded faintly from too much rum and too little sleep. The buzzing kept going.

Mom.

I debated sending her to voicemail, but I already knew that would only lead to more calls. I sighed and hit answer.

"Hi, Mom."

"Heatherbug!" Her voice was bright, far too bright for the hour. "It's the first of the month! Did you say rabbit rabbit yet?"

I closed my eyes. "You just reminded me."

We said it together, the way we always had when I was little—a superstition to start the month off right.

"Thanks for the reminder," I said, half annoyed, half touched.

I squinted at the screen. "You *just* got back from Bali, didn't you?"

"Oh, sweetheart, time is a construct."

"Tell that to my REM cycle."

"So, what have you been up to lately, bug?"

"Actually, Mom... I have to tell you something important."

"Oh no. Please don't tell me you're getting the flu shot. I told you that's a hoax."

I rubbed my forehead. "It's not medical. I—I'm engaged."

Silence, then: "I'm sorry, I thought you just said 'engaged'?"

"I did. To Tripp."

"The man who took five phone calls in forty-five minutes?"

"He has a really demanding job." *She should be congratulating me, not questioning me.*

"Heatherbug..."

"Mom, please. I don't need judgment, herbs, oils, or any other kind of witchcraft. Just your support. Of me."

She exhaled dramatically. "I will bite my tongue. But Heatherbug, the energy you choose is the life you live. Choose one that glows, not just one that looks good on paper."

"I *am* happy, Mom."

"I know you *think* you are. But happiness and comfort aren't the same thing."

I sit up, tucking a strand of hair behind my ear. "Why does everyone assume comfort's a bad thing? Maybe I'm just tired of chaos. Maybe I want something simple."

"You've never been simple," she said gently. "You've always chased things that made your heart race."

She said it like it was love, not criticism—and that almost made it worse because she wasn't wrong.

"Remember when you went to Paris for that study abroad trimester? You called me from the airport crying because you were scared to go—but you did. And when you came home, you'd blossomed. I just don't want you to lose that spark, Bug."

I didn't know how to explain that the thing making my heart race lately wasn't adventure. It was relief. It was someone else choosing for me, so I could stop choosing wrong.

"I'm still that person," I said, though I wasn't sure if I believed it. "Just... grown up."

She laughed softly. "Just promise me you'll listen if your soul starts whispering for something more."

"Mom, I promise, I am okay."

"Okay, dear." Her tone brightened again. "Now, I'm going to call Ben and remind him it's the first of the month. Love you, Bug."

"Love you too."

When I hung up, I stared at the phone, half laughing, half ready to throw it. I should've let it ring. I'd been content floating in that dream, even if it hurt. Because it always did.

It was so good until it was suddenly nothing at all.

Somewhere down the hall, I heard Tory moving around in the kitchen—cabinet doors, the clink of a mug. I pulled the covers back and groaned, the weight of the dream still clinging to me.

The smell of fresh coffee hit before I even made it out of bed. Morning light spilled through the kitchen window, catching dust motes in the air. The hardwood was cool beneath my bare feet. Tory stood at the counter, hair pulled into a messy ponytail, her running shoes half-laced.

"Morning," she said, glancing up with a grin. "*Rabbit rabbit.*"

"I was just about to tell you Mom would be calling," I said, yawning.

"I already texted her. Said mine at midnight." She stretched, then bent to tie her laces. "I'm heading out for a run."

"I don't know how you can do that after all those piña coladas," I said, pouring myself coffee.

"That's exactly why I need to run." She straightened, tossing her ponytail back. "You sure you don't want to come? Little sisterly cardio bonding?"

"Not a chance."

Tory grinned. "Did you tell her?"

I blow on my coffee. "About the engagement? Yeah. It went about as well as you'd expect."

"Meaning?"

"Meaning she told me to choose something that glows."

Tory smirked, grabbing her phone. "That sounds about right. Mom's allergic to normal."

"Apparently, stability is an illness now."

She laughed, slinging her jacket over her arm. "Don't forget dinner tonight with Nico and his new boyfriend, Marcus."

"I'll be there. He's pressuring me to come in for a blowout before. Says I need to look 'presentable for introductions.'"

"You probably do." She winked. "You could use a little shine."

I made a face. "Rude."

"That's why you love me."

She disappeared out the door, the sound of her sneakers fading down the hall.

The apartment fell quiet again—just the hum of the fridge, the light coming through the window.

I carried my mug to the table and opened my sketch-book, something I hadn't done in months unless it was work-related.

For a moment, I just stared at the blank page. Then my pencil started moving.

I drew the sky first, the stars scattered unevenly across it. Then the line of the ocean. Then him. *Bradley.*

I used to do this all the time—sketch him so I wouldn't forget the details: the curls that fell over his forehead, the way one dimple showed deeper than the other when he smiled. I hadn't drawn him in years. Maybe because remembering him hurt in a way that forgetting never could.

But this morning, it all came back easily. The lines, the shadows, the feeling.

Each curve of my pencil brought him closer, as if memory had muscle memory too.

I didn't notice how long I sat there until the coffee went cold beside me.

When I finally looked down, the page was full of stars, water, and Bradley smiling up from the paper like he'd been waiting for me to remember.

I traced the edge of the drawing with my finger, the graphite smudging slightly beneath my touch.

He was still there. Maybe he always would be.

6

THE SOUND OF ALMOST
HEATHER

The curling iron hissed as Nico tugged another section of my hair around the barrel. The scent of heat and hairspray mixed with the faint trace of his Le Labo cologne.

He was in his element—focused, meticulous, moving with quiet precision in his black frames that made him look like an adorable art professor. His thick, coal-dark hair swept to one side, perfectly in place; lashes for days; skin perfectly tan, like the sun had signed off on him personally.

"So," he said, "Marcus is meeting us for dinner and dancing. I told him to wear something subtle."

He smirked at his own sarcasm.

"I can't wait to meet him," I said, smiling into the mirror.

Before he could respond, I heard the lyrics of a song.

I hadn't noticed it playing before, but something about the voice made my entire body jolt. My breath caught. My hands went clammy against my thighs. I blinked at my reflection, but the room started to blur.

The lyrics were simple, soft—

You wore white, and I knew I was doomed...
You smiled like you forgot me, and I smiled like I
    knew.

No. It couldn't be.

"Heather?" Nico's gaze met mine in the mirror. His voice sounded far away. "You okay? You look like you just saw a ghost."

My mouth went dry. "Who sings this?"

He glanced toward the front of the salon. "Some new band—Midnight City, I think? Everyone's obsessed. The guitarist's supposed to be hot as sin."

My pulse pounded in my ears. "Can you turn it up?"

He laughed. "Turn it up? Babe, are you—"

"Please."

He shrugged and nodded toward the receptionist, who raised the volume a little.

The voice filled the room. That rasp—steady, soulful, a little rough around the edges. It wasn't a copy of Bradley's voice.

It *was* Bradley's voice—gruffer, stronger. The kind of sound that carried years inside it.

The floor seemed to shift. My chest tightened until breathing felt like work.

I barely noticed Tory walk in until she was beside us, latte in hand. "What happened?" she asked, scanning our faces. "Why does she look like she just realized Tripp irons his underwear?"

"I don't know," Nico said, eyes wide. "This song came on, and she went full mannequin."

I turned to Tory. My throat felt raw. "It's him."

She froze. "No."

I nodded once. "It's him. I know that voice."

She set her drink down slowly. "Heather—"

"I'm not crazy. Listen."

The song hit the chorus, and even Tory's face changed—like she could hear it too, the echo of a memory that wasn't hers but she'd lived close enough to feel.

"Okay," Nico cut in, waving his comb. "Someone please explain before I call a medic."

Tory pulled out her phone, already searching. "Midnight City," she muttered. "New band. Just dropped an album..." She stopped. Her breath caught. Then she turned the screen toward me.

There he was.

Wavy hair falling over one eye. That same smile. A guitar slung over his shoulder like it had grown there.

Bradley. Older and sharper, but still entirely him.

The world seemed to tilt. I grabbed the chair to steady myself.

"The lead singer, Bradley," Tory told Nico quietly, "was Heather's first love. They met in Punta Cana when we were teenagers."

Nico's brow shot up. "Okay, plot twist. But please tell me she at least slept with this hunk."

I shook my head. "We didn't sleep together. He was my first real kiss. He got my number, my AOL screen name, and then... nothing. He never contacted me."

"AOL?" Nico gasped. "Oh, sweetie, this was pre-Instagram trauma. Ancient history."

"She was heartbroken," Tory said. "I mean, they actually seemed in love, crazy, right?"

He softened. "Still—ghost move. Radio silence after a week in paradise? Trash."

Tory gave him a look. "It wrecked her. I don't think Heather really opened up to anyone after that."

My eyes stayed fixed on the photo.

Every trace of him had been packed away, like a box I shoved to the back of the closet and promised myself I'd never open.

But now, somehow—after all this time—I'd dreamed about him last night, sketched him this morning, and now I was hearing him.

The same voice, older but still his.

It made my skin prickle, like the universe was winking at me.

Mom's voice floated through my head: *Listen if your soul starts whispering.*

I didn't know what to believe.

Only that the song felt like it was meant for me.

Nico finished the last curl and misted me with hairspray. "There." He gave a satisfied nod, smiling in the mirror.

My pulse was spiraling.

I stared at the photo on Tory's phone, at the name below it—

Midnight City–"The Sound of Almost."

Almost. God, even the title felt like a jab.

Nico clapped his hands. "Alright, heartbreakers. We've got dinner reservations and a dance floor waiting. Marcus is going to die when he sees you."

I smiled, automatic and hollow. "Can't wait."

But the words of the song looped through my head as we walked out to hail a cab—

> *You wore white, and I knew I was doomed...*
> *You smiled like you forgot me, and I smiled like I*
> > *knew.*

We met Marcus at Bavette's in River North—dim and

golden, with the low hum of conversation blending into the soft rasp of jazz spilling from the speakers. The ceilings were low, the light warm and flattering, every surface glowing with reflections from glass and brass. The air smelled of steak, butter, and something faintly sweet—bourbon maybe, or the caramelized onions drifting in from the kitchen.

Marcus was the kind of man Nico's always pictured himself ending up with—steadfast, gracious, easy to be around. He was on the shorter side, with a round, open face and eyes that smiled before he did. His voice was calm and unhurried, each word landing with quiet confidence. Marcus was the calm, and Nico was the spark. They just worked—like peanut butter and jelly, opposites that somehow made perfect sense together.

I hated to admit I was distracted all evening. I laughed when something was funny. I chimed in at the right moments, but my mind kept drifting back to that song. To him.

By the time the check came, Nico was practically vibrating, ready to dance. There was no getting out of it. He and Tory lived for the dance floor, and if I tried to bail, I'd never hear the end of it.

So, off we went to Boystown—to Minibar, our old faithful. The place was pulsing with colored lights and beats you could feel in your chest. I followed them in, weaving through the crowd, already wondering how early I could slip out without being disowned. Maybe I could claim a headache. Maybe they'd be too busy to notice.

All I really wanted to do was go home, crawl into bed, and Google the shit out of Bradley.

The club was warm and loud, a blur of bodies and bass. The beat pressed into my chest, but I couldn't lose myself in it. Not even Patrón could wash the ache out of me tonight.

Tory and Nico screamed lyrics to a remix while Marcus grinned beside them, spinning Nico under his arm. They looked happy, carefree. I used to know what that felt like.

Marcus leaned toward me over the music. "Nico tells me you just got engaged."

"I did. Two days ago. I'm still getting used to it."

He took my hand, studying the ring. "Whoa, that's a big old rock, girl. Where's this lad of yours?"

I laughed. "This isn't really Tripp's scene."

"Got it," he said, smiling kindly. "He's missing out."

Our drinks arrived, sweating on the table. We talked a little more—how he and Nico met, how much he adored Nico's mom, how welcome she made him feel. Marcus was grounded and sweet, the kind of man who could balance the messy in someone else's life.

Just when I was sinking into Marcus's stories, the song was on again, in a remix version. Once again, I could hear my mom's voice... *Heatherbug, don't fight what comes your way.* I needed to get out of this bar.

I leaned in to Marcus so he could hear me, "I'm going to hit the ladies' room."

When I checked my phone, I had a missed call from Tripp. I tried calling back, but it went straight to voicemail. He said he was staying in to catch up on work. I was relieved; I wasn't in the mood.

Back at the bar, Tory was ordering another round. Nico and Marcus were on the floor again, laughing, Nico's head tipped back at something Marcus said.

"Hey," Tory called over the music. "Did you hear Bradley's song in that remix?"

Of course I did.

Instead, I lied, "I must have missed it when I was in the bathroom."

"He is blowing up," Tory squealed, whipping her ponytail around.

"I think I'm going to head home. I've got a headache."

"Are you going home to Google?"

Busted, she knew me so well.

"No. It's just loud in here. The hangover from last night's catching up."

"Heather..." She gave me a look. "You don't have to fib to me."

"Fine. I can't stop thinking about that damn song."

She smiled. "Then go. Go Google."

"Is that wrong?"

"I think you've got some things left unsaid. And if you need answers, how can that be wrong?"

Was she right? Did I really need answers from fifteen years ago?

Nico and Marcus came back, both flushed and laughing. "We need Agua," Nico said dramatically.

"Don't be mad," I told him, "But I'm going to head out."

"I could never be mad at you," he said, fanning himself. "But that hair is too good to waste. Maybe swing by Superior Street instead?"

"No, going home... Marcus, it was so nice to meet you."

"Pleasure's all mine," he said, pulling me in for a hug.

I waved to Tory, and she just nodded with a smirk.

Outside, the air felt cool against my skin, carrying that faint city mix of rain and cigarettes. I hailed a cab and climbed in.

The thing was... I didn't even know Bradley's last name. Until now. Bradley Hart.

We never thought about telling each other. We were

teenagers. It was a vacation romance—a blink. But for me, it had echoed.

For him, I guess it was just a fling. We lived in different states, and even if we hadn't, what could have come of it?

I leaned my head against the window as the city blurred past, the lights streaking like memories. Somewhere out there, Bradley was a rising star—singing songs that were getting stuck in people's heads. In *my* head. His voice was warm, familiar, and impossible to forget.

7

THE KEYCARD
HEATHER

The next morning, I woke to the smell of coffee. Tory was already in the kitchen, hair twisted into a messy bun, dancing barefoot to a song I couldn't place. She looked far too cheerful for someone who'd had several Gin and Tonics and a tequila shot last night.

"Caffeine?" she asked, without turning.

"Please," I said, sliding into a chair.

She poured two mugs and passed one to me. "So. What did you find out?"

"Nothing," I said, wrapping my hands around the cup. "I chickened out."

"I figured," she said, grinning. "Which is why I took the liberty. My iPad's open. Want the rundown or the dramatic reveal?"

"Tory," I groaned. "I cried myself to sleep for weeks after I didn't hear from him. Then months. I checked AOL like it was a lifeline. But nothing ever came. This is ridiculous."

She looked at me for a moment, softer now. "I know," she said quietly. "You don't have to defend it. I thought you'd say that." She took a sip of her coffee, then added, "But I still did the dirty work. You get to decide what to do with it."

"There's nothing to do," I said, shaking my head. "I'm engaged. And Bradley—he clearly didn't care. He never even asked for my last name."

Tory tilted her head, studying me. "You were both kids, you didn't ask for his either."

"I know." A thin laugh escaped. "And this isn't some great romantic mystery. It's nostalgia. I'm marrying Tripp. That's the real story."

Tory arched a brow, the warmth returning to her voice. "Then maybe you should hear what I found before you close the book."

I gave her a flat look. "Ugh. Fine. Tell me."

"That's the spirit," she said, already reaching for her iPad.

She grinned. "He lives in L.A. Got discovered opening for some bluegrass band—Greensky or something. He's kind of a mystery. Barely any interviews, barely any presence. His Instagram's all press shots and promo stuff... except for one post."

She turned her iPad toward me.

It was a photo of a worn hotel keycard, resting in the center of his palm. The caption read: *Inspo for my next song.*

My stomach twisted—his keycard. From Punta Cana.

"Do you think it's possible he lost my—?"

"Yeah," Tory said softly, cutting me off. "I think it's possible he lost your number." I had told myself that, too—more than once. It was easier to believe than the alternative. It kept the romantic version of the story intact, the one my heart still wanted to protect.

"I don't know. Either way, this isn't fair to Tripp."

"Tripp doesn't have to know."

I stared at the screen. That damn keycard. Was this some kind of sign? Had he kept it all these years as a symbol of the trip—of *us*?

"He's playing in New York next weekend," she went on. "A little trip to visit Mom and Ben? You can't tell me that's not a sign."

"This is next-level crazy."

"Is it? You're not going to sleep until you have answers."

"It's too late."

"Which is exactly why we should go. Clean break or closure."

I sighed. "Even if I wanted to, how would we get in touch with him?"

Tory gave me a smug smile. "Enter: Marcus. He wants to set me up with his older brother, Joel, who just happens to be a creative consultant in the music industry."

"That doesn't mean anything."

"I'm also in PR and marketing. I can make it mean something. Oh, and I already agreed to the date. For you. You're welcome."

I opened my mouth to respond, but my phone buzzed on the counter.

"Tripp just texted," I said, reaching for it.

TRIPP

Morning, babe. Dinner tonight, RH?

Tory crossed her arms, watching me with a grin. "That doesn't answer the question about the concert."

"I'll think about it," I muttered.

"There's no time to think," she said, shaking her head.

"I don't know—it sounds ludicrous," I said, though part of me already wanted to go.

"Come on, Heather," she pressed, her tone teasing. "You

have to be curious. And just think of it as a night out with me."

I groaned, dropping my phone onto the table. "Fine."

Tory clapped her hands. "Victory!"

Before I could say anything else, another text came through.

NICO

Brunch?? Need to crush this hangover with some Bloody Marys.

"Nico wants to get brunch," I told her.

"Perfect," Tory said, already heading down the hall. "Let's go."

I stood, stretching. "I need to shower first."

Before stepping into the bathroom, I texted Tripp back.

HEATHER

Can we stay in? I'm pretty tired from late-night shenanigans with Tory and Nico.

TRIPP

We could do that. I'm heading out for a run. Come over around seven tonight.

HEATHER

Have a nice run. See you tonight. xo

I couldn't help feeling a bit guilty. Tripp bought me jewelry for my birthday, sent flowers when I had a bad day, and made reservations at the city's best restaurants. He was clean-cut and dependable. He cared about me. I shouldn't have been thinking about a boy I met on vacation a lifetime ago. I was going to tell Tory the plan was off.

But in the middle of my shower, my mind took over.

I was back on that jet ski, my arms wrapped around Bradley as we skimmed across the turquoise water. We'd found a secluded cove behind a line of rocks, shaded by palms and bathed in gold from the late-morning sun.

"Let's stop for a second," he said, easing us to a float.

My chin rested against his shoulder. He reached back, fingertips brushing my thigh before sliding up to my bikini waistband. One hand stayed on the handlebars, steadying us, while the other slipped inside me—slowly, deliberately.

"Is this okay?" He asked into my ear.

My breath hitched. "Yes." Was all I could mutter out.

My forehead dropped against his neck. When he added another finger, I melted into him, trembling as his mouth found the side of my throat. The world went still except for the sound of my own gasp and the water lapping softly around us.

A soft, breathless laugh slipped out of me—half shock, half surrender—and the smile he gave in return nearly unraveled me all over again. We rode back in silence, skimming across the water, the wind in our faces and something wide and impossible opening inside me.

8

OFF KEY

HEATHER

As I was leaving my apartment that evening, the reminder for my overnight at Tripp's popped up. The train rattled beneath me as the Red Line glided toward Fullerton. When it screeched to a stop, I stepped off with the aftershocks still in my legs and followed the crowd across the platform to the Brown Line. A familiar stale-coffee smell thickened as the doors closed behind me. Every time someone shifted, the scent thickened, sticking to my shoes.

When the train hissed to a stop, I nudged my tote higher on my shoulder and moved toward the doors. Fresh air always felt different after a packed car—sharper, cleaner, like a reset. Outside, the city held that late-Sunday quiet, light skimming off glass and steel while the wind softened around corners. I walked past cafés closing early, traffic fading behind me, until the Montgomery building rose into view. Tripp's building.

The doorman gave a polite nod as I flashed the key fob Tripp had gifted me for Christmas. A "symbol of trust," he'd said back then. Now I wondered if it had been a warm-up proposal.

The elevator mirrored my reflection back at me: wind-tangled hair, tired eyes, a designer's tote heavier than it should be. You love Tripp, I told myself. You're lucky. You're building a future. The doors opened onto the twenty-fourth floor before I could answer myself.

"Hey, honey," Tripp called from the kitchen, voice smooth and confident. "Sorry, just in here. I ordered sushi and apps from Japonais. Should be here any minute. Mind running down to grab it? They never make it up without a hassle."

I dropped my bag and forced a smile. "Sure."

"Thanks. I have to finish up this email."

The annoyance was small but real. After two train transfers, lugging a bag around, and a throbbing headache that hadn't quite faded since the weekend, the last thing I wanted was to play delivery girl. Still, it wasn't the time to bitch, I was headed on a secret mission to hear my first love's concert. Even if guilt carried me there.

Downstairs, the lobby glowed with warm marble light. A man in an immaculate coat held the leash of a tiny white dog wearing a Louis Vuitton collar and a pink T-shirt. I couldn't help but laugh softly.

The doorman glanced up. I tucked a strand of hair behind my ear, then twirled it around my finger, a nervous habit I'd never broken. Finally, the delivery guy appeared, scanning his receipt.

"Tripp Kensington?" he asked.

"That's me—well, I'm his girlfriend. I mean, fiancée." The word felt foreign on my tongue, like it belonged to someone else.

The doorman nodded toward me. The delivery man

handed over the bag, and I slipped him a tip. "Thanks so much."

"Congratulations," the doorman said flatly as I turned away.

"Sorry?"

"On your engagement," he replied.

"Oh. Right. Thank you." I smiled, the one you use when your mind is somewhere else and you're hoping no one notices.

Inside the elevator, my reflection wavered again in the brushed metal. I'm with Tripp. I love Tripp. So why did my chest feel tight, my thoughts too loud?

Back upstairs, I unpacked the sushi, washed my hands, and set the table. Tripp appeared, glasses on, a long-sleeved shirt that looked casually overpriced. His dark hair was swept back, neat as ever.

"Look at these rolls," he said. "Glad you're okay with sushi."

I nodded, forcing an easy grin. After dinner, Sunday-night football murmured in the background while I curled up on the couch. The lamp cast a honey-colored glow across his minimalist living room. I pulled out my sketchbook and began tracing lines for a new dress silhouette, the pencil gliding almost of its own will.

Tripp leaned over and kissed my cheek. "Maybe you could put that away for a bit," he teased. "I have something to show you."

I smiled. "Just finishing this thought." I closed the book anyway.

He opened a drawer and pulled out a glossy flyer. "Ta da. Take a look at this."

The photo showed a stately brownstone, tall, narrow,

perfectly restored, the kind of house that had probably seen more champagne than children.

"It's coming to market soon," he said, excitement lighting his face. "Near my parents'. We should jump on it. Close to Holy Name. The kids could go there. Mother would be nearby."

"The kids?" I repeated.

"Yes, our kids." He kissed me again, this time on the lips. His mouth felt dry against mine.

"Hang on," I murmured, reaching for my purse and pulling out a tube of ChapStick. I smeared it on, the faint scent of vanilla filling the space. "Okay, continue."

He smiled and handed me the flyer. "You could make it your own. Renovate however you want." He added, "Once you quit your job."

I blinked. *Quit my job?* The words slid under my skin like ice. My career was finally taking shape. For the first time, I was becoming someone in the game.

"I think I need the bathroom," I said quickly. "Maybe the sushi's catching up with me."

In the powder room, I let the faucet run and splashed cold water on my face. My reflection looked flushed, uncertain. I don't have to figure it out tonight.

When I came out, Tripp was straightening the pillows I'd leaned against. "You okay?"

"Yeah. Just tired." My voice sounded smaller than I meant it to. "I'm going to unpack, then get ready for bed."

I needed to distract myself from the bomb Tripp just exploded so nonchalantly. *Once you quit your job.*

He chuckled. "Unpack? Moving in already? Can you imagine Mother's reaction?"

I laughed softly. "Just swapping out what's in the drawer." *The only square footage I have been given up to this point.*

In the bedroom, I placed my clothes neatly inside his dresser. I had a skirt that wouldn't fit, and it would crease if I stuffed it in there.

"Hey, Tripp?"

"Yes, hun?" He emerged in his monogrammed pajamas, perfectly pressed even now.

"Would it be okay if I hung this skirt? I don't want it wrinkled."

"New fashion statement, slacks with a skirt?" he joked, pulling open his immaculate closet.

I rolled my eyes. "Two separate things."

He sighed theatrically, scanning his color-coordinated wardrobe as if one extra hanger might upend the system. He shifted a few shirts aside and made a space. "There. All good?"

"Very." I meant it. *Progress.*

A few minutes later, when I came out of the bathroom, he was already in bed, and my side of the bed was set up. Pillow fluffed, the heavy duvet folded back, replaced with the light blanket I always prefer.

"I set it up the way you like," he said, almost shyly. "You always sleep better like this."

My throat tightened. It was thoughtful. It was sweet. It was him trying.

I slid into bed. The blanket really did feel perfect.

He opened a crossword on his tablet. "Six-letter word meaning *abundance,*" he murmured.

"Plenty," I said automatically.

He smiled, a real one. "You're brilliant. You know that?"

Warmth spread through me. Tripp's compliments assured me that *I did* belong with him.

"Come here." He leaned in and kissed me, slow and tender.

I tried to deepen it, hoping something inside me would catch. Tripp laughed softly. "Ouch. Did you just bite me?"

"Maybe," I teased, though the spark wasn't there.

"Heather," he said gently, "you're going to be my wife. You don't have to be dirty."

I let out a quiet laugh, pretending his comment didn't make me pull inward. He kissed me again—slow and practiced. I matched his rhythm, careful not to push too hard, careful to be exactly the version of me he expected.

Tripp pushed his pajama bottoms down, reached for the bedside drawer, and slid on a condom. "Sails up," he joked.

He tugged my shorts off and settled between my legs. When he pushed inside me, I exhaled, letting my body move with his. It felt good, familiar, his hands warm on my hips, his breath brushing my cheek. And still... something inside me faltered. Why was I struggling to stay here, in this moment, with a man who loved me?

I tried to chase the feeling, to lose myself in him, but my mind betrayed me—flashes of another man breaking through. Bradley. His hands gripping my waist in the ocean. The taste of saltwater. The breathless way he'd said my name like it meant something.

My body reacted before I could stop it, a soft sound slipping from my throat.

"That's my girl," Tripp murmured, mistaking the noise. His pace stuttered; he finished quickly, collapsing against me with a satisfied sigh.

"I could really feel you tonight," he whispered, pressing a kiss to my shoulder. "Love you, Heather."

"Love you too," I said, my voice barely above a breath as I stared at the ceiling.

He rolled out of bed to take care of the condom, and when he crawled back in and rolled to his side, his breathing settling into sleep, I turned toward the window. The city lights blurred into gold and gray, the room too quiet, my chest too tight.

Guilt crept in first. Then shame.

Tripp wants a life with you, I told myself. *A home. Kids. Stability. Security.*

So why did my mind keep pulling somewhere else?

Why did the thought of Bradley, suddenly a potentially tangible idea, feel like a pulse I couldn't quiet?

And why—God, why—did I still want to go to that concert more than anything?

9

ONE BIG OFFER

HEATHER

Monday morning, I came in early to prep for my meeting; bolts of ivory crepe and whisper-soft organza spread across the worktable. I stacked sketches and measurements into a neat folder, my nerves and excitement twisting together.

At ten, Alena poked her head in, lipstick a perfect scarlet, coffee in hand. "You nervous?" she asked, nodding toward the Bloomingdale's appointment marked in bold ink on the calendar.

"Excited and nervous," I said, and meant it.

Alena smiled. "Don't forget who you are in there."

That used to be harder. I'd always assumed I'd end up in New York after school; it was the plan, the dream, the inevitability. But the city didn't open a single door for me. I tried every one—legacy houses, boutique studios, even the labels that would never look twice at an unknown assistant from the suburbs. Nothing. No interviews. No chances.

Chicago wasn't the dream.

It was the place that said yes.

I landed an internship at Rowan & Wolfe—barely paid,

barely stable, so barely getting by—right around the time Tory got into DePaul. It felt like the universe was nudging us in the same direction, so we went. Two sisters, one apartment with questionable winters and humid summers, starting over in a city we didn't know.

The turning point came the night Jessica walked in, frantic, two days before a charity gala, the gown she'd commissioned slipping off her shoulders after another crash diet. Jackie was swamped, Tisha was in Paris, and I—still technically an assistant—heard myself offer.

I stayed until two in the morning, restitched the bodice by hand, and added a sheer organza train that shimmered with every step. Jessica wore it. *Chicago Style* ran a feature on the look. And suddenly, her friends wanted me. Then their friends did too.

By fall, my client list rivaled designers twice my age. Jackie and Tisha treated me like a partner, not an extra pair of hands. My name began to mean something.

Now, Bloomingdale's wants to talk capsule lines—my silhouettes, my fabrics—at prices women like me can afford. Early thirties, working hard, craving luxury without apology.

The rest of the afternoon slipped into its own quiet rhythm. Alena popped in with questions about the winter line, and I pinned a hem for one of our regular clients who'd stopped by for a fitting. A courier arrived with fabric swatches from Lyon, and I spent an hour matching them to the sketches spread across my table. The studio smelled faintly of steamed silk and lavender starch. Outside the windows, the light had shifted—Chicago's kind of golden that turns everything soft for a minute before it fades.

I tucked one last swatch into a sample bag and closed

my laptop. For the first time all day, my pulse kicked up a little.

At 4:58, I checked the clock. My meeting was at five-thirty.

The next hour passed in a blur: a quick Uber ride downtown, a mirrored elevator, and a warm handshake from the VP of contemporary labels at Bloomingdale's on Michigan Avenue. The meeting flowed effortlessly. She understood the vision. She loved the story. She wanted more samples.

By the time we stood, something new buzzed through me—hope. Real, grounded, maybe-this-could-happen hope.

I stepped onto the sidewalk, and the city air met me like an exhale. Warmth rolled off the lake, carrying that soft, humid breeze that made the streetlights glow a little hazier. Traffic hummed along Michigan Avenue, tires whispering over dry pavement, mixing with bursts of laughter from people spilling out of late-night stores. My reflection flashed in a shop window—tired eyes, hopeful smile, folder in hand—and for once, I let myself feel proud.

It was 7:21. My dinner with Tripp was at 7:30. I was still in my pleated trousers, my hair in a low twist, my blouse too structured for dinner lighting. I texted quickly—*On my way* —and slid into a cab heading toward the Gibsons in the Gold Coast, one of Tripp's favorite spots.

Inside the restaurant, Tripp was already seated. To my surprise, so was his mother.

She wore head-to-toe Chanel—ivory tweed jacket, gold CC earrings, ballet flats with perfect bows. Her wine glass was half full, and her gaze sharp.

"Oh, good," she said, rising just enough to air kiss me. "We were just looking at calendars. Have a seat, darling."

I slid in beside Tripp, who looked vaguely guilty.

"I hope you don't mind," he said, taking a sip of his martini. "Mom wanted to talk venues."

"I was just telling him how lovely The Drake was for Reagan's wedding," she said. "We did everything there—the Gold Coast Room, the afterparty, even the brunch."

"Oh," I managed.

"I've also reached out to someone at The Langham, just to compare dates," she continued. "These things book quickly, you know. Vera Wang alone takes six to eight months minimum to make a dress."

My heart jumped. "Actually, I haven't even started looking yet."

"Well, we should get you in soon," she said, patting my hand. "You'll want something fitted. With your frame, it's the only way to go."

I took a breath. "I'd love for my mom and sister to be part of that. They'd want to join. I may design my own dress as well."

Her smile didn't flicker. "Of course. But perhaps we can start this weekend? Just to get a sense of silhouettes?"

"I won't be able to this weekend," I said, glancing at Tripp. "I'm going to visit my mom and brother in New York."

"Really?" he asked, surprised.

I nodded. "Just some time with the family. I haven't seen them in a while, and... Ben is about to become a dad. Things are going to get really busy for him." I let out a nervous laugh that I hoped passed as casual.

"Where will you stay?" his mother asked.

"My mom's," I said.

She sipped her wine. "You'll come back refreshed and ready to plan."

I smiled politely.

Thankfully, Tripp was able to switch the conversation and give his mother updates on the firm.

After dinner, we were outside, and Tripp gave me one of his pleading looks. "Come back with me?"

I shook my head. "I didn't bring anything."

He tilted his head. "You've got that drawer."

Something in me folded in on itself, smaller than the drawer itself.

A small smile tugged at my lips. "Not tonight."

He frowned slightly. "I work late tomorrow, but we have plans with Jessica and Clint on Thursday."

"Yes, it's in our shared calendar." I laughed

He didn't have a response for that—just a quiet exhale and a look I couldn't quite read.

"I should go," I said. "I've got a lot to do."

"Want me to get you an Uber or a cab?"

"I'm okay, I'll take the red line from here. It's nice out."

The thought of being alone for a little while felt fresher than the air itself.

I kissed him goodnight and stepped toward the corner, the city lights washing everything in a soft gold glow. A train rumbled in the distance, its sound threading through the undertone of traffic and late-night laughter.

As I waited on the platform, I felt tired and the faintest trace of doubt in both my relationship and myself.

For a moment, I thought about everything I hadn't said, how sometimes a drawer doesn't feel like enough space, how sometimes a wedding dress feels more like a costume, and how sometimes, even the right path can feel like the wrong story.

10

THE DM
HEATHER

The next evening, it was midweek, and I walked in the door to the sound of Fleetwood Mac and the unmistakable scent of Tory's perfume.

She was mid-glam—hair half curled, full makeup on, a cute black top paired with her favorite jeans.

"Ah, you look ravishing," I said, dropping my bag.

"I gotta look cool for this hunk. Look at his photo." She flashed me his Instagram. You could barely make out his face—it was mostly a business page—but from the jawline alone, he wasn't hard on the eyes.

"Marcus showed me a photo before I agreed," she added. "And yes, he's cute. Even if he wasn't, I would've gone out with a troll to find this information for you."

"Please don't go on this date just to dig for intel. You don't even know if they run in the same circle."

"I'm sure he knows his people."

"Even if he does, you should go to have a good time. What if this Joel is something special?"

"Then I'll be killing two birds with one stone," she said with a wink.

After she finished curling her last piece, she looked over at me. "I think I'm ready."

"You look incredible."

She smirked. "He'll definitely give me whatever information I need."

"Go have fun. And obviously text me if he ends up being a creep."

"He won't be a loser. Gay guys have the best taste in straight men. Marcus is adorable—cut from the same cloth."

"Kind of like us?" I teased.

She laughed.

"Have a good time and be careful," I said, getting a little motherly.

"Don't wait up. Love ya."

And just like that, she was off.

I had the apartment to myself for the night. I dug into the leftover Chinese from the other night—cold, but still satisfying. I curled up on the couch with the TV playing in the background, mostly for noise.

Without even thinking, I opened my phone and searched for Bradley Hart.

That stupid keycard photo is a ticking time bomb taunting me. Somehow, it made me think about his hands, how I loved his hands. It was ridiculous. Juvenile. I was engaged. I should be making a Pinterest board, picking out color schemes, and flowers. But here I was... spiraling over a memory.

I told myself it was curiosity. Nostalgia. Closure, maybe.

I tapped the DM button before I could talk myself out of it.

I stared at the message. It sounded... dumb. Too eager. Too transparent.

I should wait for Tory before doing something like this. But before I could change my mind, I hit send.

My heart instantly pounded. He'd probably never even see it. Tory said his PR person seemed to run his account. And honestly, he didn't seem like someone who lived on social media. I'd never been able to find any real "Bradleys from Ohio" either. Not without a last name. Not when you're chasing a memory.

I polished off the rest of the Lo Mein and checked my DMs five more times. Refresh. Refresh. Refresh. I was acting insane.

My phone buzzed. My heart skipped. It was Tory. I needed to calm down.

I smiled, knowing Tory was having fun made me happy. I put the phone down, and the second I did, a hollow feeling spread through my chest. The kind that comes when you know you have crossed a line you can't uncross. *Why did I send that message?*

At eleven, I was still awake. Still checking. Still nothing. Every time I refreshed, I told myself I didn't care. That it didn't mean anything. But every time I didn't see his name, something sank lower. It was pathetic how quickly old feelings could resurface.

Eventually, exhaustion won. I dozed off, dreaming of myself at sixteen, back in Punta Cana.

It was late afternoon, the sun starting to slip, the kind of hour where everything feels quieter without anyone trying. The hammock hung between two palms, the waves rolling in behind us. I didn't know how rare that feeling would become.

We lay in opposite directions, my feet near his head, his near mine, the fabric pulled tight between us. My sketchbook rested on my stomach, the page already smudged from where my hand kept dragging through the charcoal.

"Hold still," I said, already smiling. "I need to get that dimple just right."

"I don't think I have a dimple," he said, smiling, proving himself wrong.

"You definitely do."

He smiled wider, like he was testing it. "Then how'd I get it?"

I tipped my pencil, pretending to think. "An angel kissed you."

He blushed with the most adorable smirk, and everything beneath us swayed.

I kept drawing, wanting to remember the feeling of that moment, even though I didn't know yet how much it would matter.

I woke up in a sweat. The clock read 3:08 a.m. My pulse was racing, my forehead sweating like I'd just run from something I shouldn't have gone looking for.

I wondered if Tory was home. I got up to grab some water, quietly checking her door. It was shut. Phew.

Somewhere along the way, I'd become mildly obsessive because I opened Instagram again. Still nothing.

Sixteen-year-old me needed to grow up. And go back to bed. And stop waiting for a message that probably wasn't coming.

11

UNFORGETTABLE

HEATHER

I woke up before my alarm, tangled in sheets that felt like they were wrapped twice around me. My mouth was dry, my hair was doing something triangular, and I had that weird buzz in my chest, like maybe I'd forgotten something. Or maybe I hadn't.

I blinked at the ceiling, trying to hold onto whatever dream had jolted me awake. Something with water. His hands. That same wave crashing over me again.

I reached for my phone. Just habit, I told myself.

Nothing from Instagram. No notifications.

Just a couple of Snapchat stories from Nico: one of some Pomeranians in sunglasses. He had a sixth sense for my moods, slipping in little serotonin boosts throughout my day, disguised as fluff.

A text lit up my screen.

TRIPP

Clint and Jessica canceled. The twins have the stomach bug. I'm going to work late tonight, big case to prep for.

HEATHER

No problem. Miss you already.

Relief slipped through me in a quick, guilty wave. At least I could catch up on work before heading out.

TRIPP

You should watch Making a Murderer tonight. The way they build the case is insane.

HEATHER

I'll have to check it out.

I knew I wouldn't watch it.

TRIPP

Two words. Seven letters.

My throat tightened. His coded *love you* should've felt comforting.

Instead, all I could think about was that dimple, the keycard, and the sound of his voice—the one I desperately hoped was a message meant for me.

Guilt slid in, sharp as a pin.

HEATHER

Love you, too.

I tossed the phone onto the quilt and dragged myself out of bed.

Tory's door was still shut, her white noise machine doing its thing. No rescue text and sleeping in meant her date went well.

I showered fast, skipped washing my hair, and pulled it into a low bun. I was already running late. My makeup was passable. My outfit looked like I had my life together, which was the best thing about being in fashion. You could dress on trend, and no one would know if you were making questionable decisions. I made myself a quick to-go cup of coffee, hoping the buzz of caffeine would snap me into place.

On the subway, I stood pressed between a man who kept humming under his breath and a girl doing Wordle out loud. My phone sat heavy in my hand. I checked it again. Still nothing. Just the echo of my own ridiculous message hanging out in the void.

What was I thinking? Bradley. From a vacation. A lifetime ago.

By the time I got to Rowan & Wolfe, I was five minutes late and sweating. Alena didn't even glance up from her screen. Tisha waved her coffee at me from the studio as if nothing had happened. "You have a new client at twelve," she called. "A Gold Coaster."

"On it," I said, tugging my hair out of its messy bun. Funny how I could dress their world, marry into it, and still feel like I was crashing the party.

I dropped my bag and took a sip of my half-cold coffee. One last check before I get to work.

I opened Instagram, and everything in me stuttered to a stop.

@bradley.sound sent you a message.

My stomach flipped—hard—the way it does on a roller coaster when the track drops in the dark and you don't see it coming. Heat shot through my chest. My palms went slick. Adrenaline roared under my skin like I'd just been yanked into freefall.

His profile photo was a half-lit smirk, the kind that

pretended not to try while knowing exactly what it was doing. His bio was barely a heartbeat: *music/life.* One link to his tour.

The message preview glowed at the bottom of the screen.

Just a few words.

Not enough to explain a single thing.

More than enough to put my pulse in a chokehold.

I tapped it.

@BRADLEY.SOUND

Hey Heather! How could I forget you?:)

I'll leave you a pass at Will Call.

Want to come backstage and say hi after the show?

The room slid a little sideways. Backstage. A pass. *How could I forget you?* After all this time, he remembered me.

Something hot and dizzying flared through my chest, and I didn't know if it was excitement or fear. Maybe both.

I stared at the message long enough for the screen to dim. Then I reread it. Twice. Three times.

The past wasn't past at all. It had just knocked on my door.

I should text Tory. I should say something clever. I should close my mouth.

Instead, I just sat there, blinking, hands hovering over my keyboard while everyone around me went on with their day.

I didn't know what to do with the feeling.

Heat rushed through me, sharp and sudden, like my body remembered something my life had tried to forget.

Sixteen flickered through me—not who I was then, but who I'd been with him.

Except now I wasn't a girl in saltwater. I was a woman with a career and a ring big enough to blind me if I tilted my hand the wrong way.

This wasn't a daydream or a what-if. This was real—him, here, in my phone, within reach in a way I had never let myself imagine.

And the worst part was how my body reacted before my mind could catch up.

Nothing about this was safe.

A smile tugged at my mouth anyway—unwanted, unstoppable.

I grabbed my phone and texted Tory.

HEATHER

So...

I sent him a DM last night. He responded this morning.

Her text came through quickly.

TORY

WHAT THE ACTUAL F!!! I slept with Joel for no reason.

Just kidding. I didn't sleep with him. But he said he does know Bradley's people.

Looks like you didn't even need me.

I let out a laugh, one of those stupid ones you try to swallow in a quiet office. Alena peeked in.

"You good?" she mouthed.

I nodded and spun back to my desk, heart still racing.

HEATHER

> He's leaving a pass at Will Call. He wants to say hi after the show. What do I even say back? PS How was the date?

TORY

> Say yes, obviously. VIP, babe. This is fate. Don't overthink it. (But also screenshot everything immediately.) The date was really good... but let's stay on track.

I was just about to type something when another notification popped up.

@bradley.sound sent you a message.

I opened it fast.

@BRADLEY.SOUND

> Realized IG's not the best place for this.

> Here's my number. (310)-947-9210.

I stared at it, my hand hovering over the keyboard. Here he was offering up his phone number on a silver platter.

I did what any sane person would do. I screen-shot the message, sent it to Tory, and saved his number. Then I took a sip of coffee and bit my lip like something wild and impossible might happen.

HEATHER

> What do I even say back? I am also going to need more details about the date with Joel... good, sounds promising?

The bubbles popped up instantly.

TORY

Text him.

For the love of God.

CONFIRM IT.

HEATHER

Okay, I will. Don't spare the details on Joel.

I laughed, then exhaled. I wasn't ready yet. I needed to get through my day without combusting.

I tried to throw myself into work. I had sketch reviews due by five and a half-day tomorrow, which meant the to-do list was already four pages deep. Alena walked into my office and handed me a protein bar and a look that said please stop smiling like that, it's weirding people out.

By the time I was back in the groove—redlining sketches, tweaking a neckline, adding annotations—I had almost forgotten about my client at noon.

Alena appeared at my desk with an older woman who was thin and had a short, blown-out bob. "This is Muffy Sinclair. She's friends with Mrs. Kensington."

I wondered if this was a setup to have her friend spy on me.

"Oh, nice to see you," I said. "I believe we met at the engagement party—briefly."

"We did, dear. I wanted to see if you could make me a dress for an upcoming fundraiser I'm hosting for Epstein-Barr awareness."

"How compassionate. The event sounds lovely," I said. "Why don't you tell me what you're thinking, and I'll show you some samples."

Muffy's taste was conservative to the point of paralysis— old money with no evolution. At Rowan & Wolfe, we leaned edgier, modern. But my job was to make magic happen and keep Ms. Sinclair happy.

"Have you thought about where you'll have the big day?" she asked.

"It all happened so fast," I said. "Tripp and I haven't had a chance to sit down and discuss yet."

"You really need to get on these things. You don't want to be waiting three years."

I smiled and steered her toward the fabric wall, trying to ease her away from tweed and into something with a pulse. After we landed on a color and silk blend, I walked her over to Alena.

"Alena will take you back to our seamstress, Dani, for measurements. I'll mock up some sketches and send them your way next week."

"Okay, dear. Don't forget to book that venue soon. We can't wait for the wedding of the century."

I smiled again, forced but professional. "Will do. Nice seeing you, Ms. Sinclair."

Back at my desk, I exhaled. Amazing how Tripp's mother could weasel her way into my world without looking manipulative. I can just imagine Tripp defending Ms. Sinclair's bold yet direct statements, ones I'm sure were pushed upon me from Mrs. Kensington herself.

Work was a good distraction; it kept me from thinking about Bradley's message. Still, every time my phone lit up, my heart flipped like it was auditioning for Cirque du Soleil.

After what felt like a marathon of a workday, I was finally on my way home. The subway was crowded, the car smelled vaguely of sweat and someone's tuna salad, and I held onto the pole like it was the only thing tethering me to earth.

I pulled up the message again. Bradley's. The second

one, with his number. It felt too sacred to answer while being jostled between a college kid playing Candy Crush and a woman whispering affirmations into her AirPods. I texted Tory.

HEATHER

What do I say back to Bradley?

TORY

You say yes. Yes, I'll be there. Yes, I'd love a backstage pass. Yes, I'll come with my amazing and supportive sister, who may or may not be dying of secondhand anticipation.

I shouldn't even be doing this, I told myself. I wasn't thinking about Tripp's feelings—not in the real, consequential, life-building way. I wasn't thinking about the ring on my finger or the wedding plans his mother was already orchestrating. I was just thinking about that week. About Bradley's hands. About the way he said he remembered me.

When the train slowed at my stop, I stood and made my way toward the doors. The warm air hit as I climbed the concrete steps from the station, the city opening up again above me. I turned down Fletcher Street toward our walk-up. The trees along the block were just starting to fill in, that in-between stretch when summer was on the brink, and everything glowed a little longer.

I stopped for a moment, taking it in: the quiet, the faint drone of traffic, the soft amber of the streetlights against the brick. Then, without really thinking, I pulled out my phone. Bradley's message was still there. I opened it. Stared at the number. Paused. Checked it twice. Triple-checked. It felt like something I shouldn't be trusted to hold—like it could burn if I kept it too long.

I typed slowly.

HEATHER

Hi, Bradley. I would love to see you after the show. Can Tory come too? For old time's sake.

I stared at it. And before I could talk myself out of it—before I could spiral—I hit send.

12

THE UNNECESSARY COMMUTE
HEATHER

I woke up earlier than usual to pack and get everything ready before heading to New York for the weekend—first stop, Scarsdale, our hometown in the suburbs, just outside of the city. Mom insisted on a family dinner so she could feed us her "new recipes" and introduce us to whatever witchcraft she'd picked up in Bali. Tory and I had a midday flight. I needed to drop off sketches and wrap up a few things at the studio first.

Tripp had offered to have his driver take me to work so we could "spend time together" before I left. It was a sweet gesture, in theory. The car service arrived first, the driver already holding a coffee. I thanked him and slid into the back seat.

The city was waking up—the light soft and golden, the air already warming, the kind of morning that promised summer was close.

When we pulled up to Tripp's building in River North, he came down a few minutes later, perfectly pressed in a navy suit and striped tie. He didn't do casual Fridays—or anything casual, really.

"Morning," he said, leaning in to kiss my cheek before immediately glancing at his phone.

We had maybe ten to fifteen minutes together as the car merged into traffic. He asked if I had everything packed, but before I could answer, he was already on a call.

Words like *'client meeting'* and *'merger timeline'* filled the space between us.

I stared out the window, half-listening, half-counting the minutes. I'd cut an hour out of my morning to see him— skipped breakfast, rushed—all to sit beside someone who wasn't really here.

When his call ended, he adjusted his cufflinks and looked over at me.

"By the way, my mother wants to meet early next week. She wants to go over wedding details. She hired a wedding planner."

My stomach tightened. "She hired a wedding planner without us?"

"It's not a big deal. She thought it could take the stress out for you."

Before I could ask another question, his phone lit up again.

"I've got to take this," he said, already tapping his cell.

Of course you do.

When we reached his office at Willis Tower, the driver slowed to the curb. Tripp leaned over, kissed my cheek again, and said, "Text me when you get to your mom's. Love you."

"Will do. Love you too."

He disappeared into the revolving doors, swallowed by glass and steel and purpose.

The driver glanced at me in the rearview mirror.

"Next stop, Rowan & Wolfe?"

I nodded. "Yes, please."

As the car moved back into traffic, I took a sip of my coffee, now lukewarm. Guilt lingered, but underneath it was something heavier—a dull ache with nowhere to place itself.

By the time I got to Rowan & Wolfe, I was late from the detour with Tripp. Alena gave me a quick wave before getting back to work.

"Morning," I said, exhaling.

Tisha was walking out and waved her coffee. "I've got a downtown with a boutique buyer on Oak. Tell your mom I want her Bali recommendations!"

I smiled and walked over to Alena's desk, handing her a thick folder. "Here are the sketches for the new collection. Can you send these to the clients who've been waiting?"

"Already on it," she said. Then she lowered her voice. "Mrs. Kensington left a message—there's an opening at The Drake next June. She made it sound urgent."

I swallowed. "Can you let her know I'm buried in work before my flight?"

"You bet," Alena said gently.

As I walked toward my office, my mind spun harder. My future mother-in-law was practically fast-tracking the wedding of the century, and I couldn't even decide which overnight bag to bring. The pressure felt crushing—and yet my thoughts kept drifting backward, to somewhere warmer, easier.

To him.

I remembered one night at the resort when the kitchen had technically closed, and I'd mentioned craving pancakes. Bradley had grinned, disappeared, and come back with a plate stacked high—syrup, butter, the works.

"I'd make pancakes anytime you want," he'd said.

"I can't believe you pulled this off." I pointed my fork at him. "You and your charm."

"Snorkeling tomorrow?" he asked, leaning against the vacant tiki bar where we were sitting after hours.

"I wish," I said. "But it's Cheryl's big day. She and Keith are tying the knot."

He studied me for a second. "You don't seem that happy about it."

"I am," I said. "If it sticks. My mom can change her mind easily. My dad worked too much. Her second husband didn't work enough."

He didn't say anything right away. Just looked at me.

"Maybe the third one's the charm," he said, his jade eyes holding mine.

I had to look away before he could see too much of what that stirred up in me. Talking about my parents always made me do that.

"She's kind of like Goldilocks with husbands," I said, brushing it off.

His laugh pulled me out of the quiet place I'd gone. "Come here, Baby Bear."

He nudged my stool closer with his knee and smiled at me, then leaned in and kissed my lips.

"You taste like syrup," he said, laughing.

I giggled.

He grew a little softer then. "It's okay to be nervous about your mom's future. But remember—you've got your own future coming. You're going to do amazing things, Heather. That sketchbook? It's going to be worth millions."

I laughed. "And your voice is going to sell out Madison Square Garden."

He leaned back slightly, "I can picture you in the crowd, with *your sister on Jared's shoulders so she can see," he said jokingly. His voice shifted. "You make me believe I could get there."*

We sat under buzzing string lights, talking for hours—the kind of conversation that makes the world shrink to the space between two people. He told me about when his dad left, about his brilliant sister, about how his mom ran a bookstore and had the softest soul.

I felt myself really getting to know him, and I was opening up with a real person, not just through a drawing.

And he'd touched something in me I never admitted out loud.

My phone buzzed. I blinked at the clock.

10:53.

TORY

Meet you out front in five.

I grabbed my bag and sketches, gave Alena a quick wave, and headed toward the door.

The city suddenly felt louder, alive, pulsing with weekend energy. I tried to match its pace, but my heart was a mix of anticipation, guilt, and something restless.

Tonight, we'd be with family.

Tomorrow... everything else waited.

13

HEATHER

The first thing I did after we landed at LaGuardia was check my phone. Nothing. No missed call. No follow-up from the one person I was trying not to think about—but obviously couldn't stop thinking about.

I had messages from Tripp, Ben, and Nico.

TRIPP

Work dinner Thursday. Please refer to our shared calendar.

BEN

Let me know when you land. I'll circle around front.

NICO

I need a step-by-step. Love you!!!!

I shoved my phone into my bag and focused on the small wins: we had landed. Tory hadn't talked the entire flight (she slept with a sheet mask on). And I didn't throw up from nerves, though I came dangerously close every time I thought about what I was doing.

Tory blinked her eyes open, lashes fanned and flawless, hair somehow still in place. "Still no word from Bradley?"

"No, how can you tell?"

"You're not full 'happy Heather' yet." My eyebrows lifted, all fake confidence, even though my chest felt tight.

I laughed. "What does that even mean? I am happy."

"You're at, like, ninety percent. But he's probably busy. And I mean that—not in a he's-a-douche kind of way. He's literally getting ready to perform in front of thousands of people tomorrow."

I shook my head, pushing my hair back as I smiled despite myself.

Tory was grinning too, tapping out a text. I tilted my head.

"Is that Joel?"

She looked up. "Okay, he is a really good kisser. So... yes."

"You look like you are one hundred percent happy," I said with a smirk.

"We're focused on you," she said quickly, sliding her phone into her purse. "Alright, let's get our bags."

We stood and grabbed our carry-ons from the overhead bin, moving with the stream of passengers funneling toward the front. The jet bridge air hit first warm but breezy, carrying that faint, unmistakable mix of jet fuel, pretzels, and New York impatience.

Inside the terminal, everything felt sharper. Brighter. Faster. New York didn't yawn its way through the afternoon; it buzzed. Even at 3 p.m., people moved like they were chasing something important.

We followed the signs through Terminal B, rolling our bags past families reuniting, suits on phone calls, and travelers power-walking as if missing a train to destiny. Outside, the pickup lane was a symphony of honking taxis, rolling luggage, and a dozen people calling, "I'm at Zone 4, where are you?"

I called Ben.

"We're at Terminal B, Level 2—Zone 4," I said, raising my voice over a bus pulling away.

A few minutes later, his silver Honda Pilot pulled up, his full *I'm a suburban dad now* transformation complete.

Steph sat in the passenger seat, her blonde hair pulled back, blue eyes tired but bright, one hand resting on the curve of her belly. Ben was driving, his short dark-blond hair neat, the kind of haircut that made him look older than I remembered.

Ben hopped out of the car to give us quick hugs, popping the trunk on his way, then sat back into the driver's seat so we could leave before security forced us on our way. Steph leaned over the passenger seat and waved, grinning widely.

"There you two are!" she called. "I was about to make Ben loop again. He gets road rage in circles."

Ben rolled his eyes. "LaGuardia is stressful."

Tory snorted. "O'Hare is no picnic either, and we do just fine navigating there."

"You little world traveler," he responded while looking in the rearview mirror.

Steph twisted around in her seat as we loaded our bags. "So good to see you both."

"You are glowing," I said, climbing in.

"I showered right before we left," she whispered conspiratorially. "Ben thinks it was for him. It was absolutely for you ladies."

Ben made a dramatic offended noise. Tory laughed.

"You look so cute!" Tory squealed, shutting the door just before Ben pulled out.

"I feel like a whale," Steph said with a half laugh.

Ben rubbed her belly at a red light and grinned. "You look beautiful, babe."

"He is just trying to get out of rubbing my feet tonight," she said, teasing him.

It was so good to see Ben so happy, at such an important stage in his life. He found a good marriage even though we weren't brought up to see that in our earlier years.

We picked up some sparkling water and wine at a corner store near Mom and Keith's, then pulled into their Tudor house a few minutes later. The wind chimes clinked as we walked up the front path.

Mom stood near the entrance; her dark-blond hair was shorter and had sightings of grey. She wore long earrings and a loose white top. Freckles scattered across her nose, the same way Ben's always had been.

She threw her arms around us the second we stepped inside. "My babies! Come in, come in. Keith's grilling salmon, and I'm making black beans. We just watched The Food Evolution documentary. We're eating for longevity now."

"How on point," Tory said with a smirk.

We exchanged a look, already laughing before we made it down the hallway.

I tossed my bag into the guest room and checked my phone again.

Still nothing.

Dinner was easy. Comforting. It felt good to be wrapped in family, in normalcy, even if tomorrow's plan kept tugging at the back of my brain.

Steph told us about the baby's nursery, her plans to stay home for several months, and how perfectly they'd timed everything with a summer due date. She was a first-grade teacher, endlessly calm and competent. She was everything you'd want your brother to marry.

Ben had definitely sown his wild oats before her. A string of girls that made us question his judgment, until Steph, the girl-next-door beauty. Organized. Kind to everyone. She balanced him in all the best ways.

After dinner, as we cleared dishes and Keith scratched his bald head, debating whether butter counted as dairy, Mom started stacking plates beside me at the sink.

"Are things still set for the wedding with that fancy boy?" Her tone was light, but her eyes were focused on the dishes in her hands.

"Yes, Mom, Tripp and I are engaged," I said, trying to sound confident.

"I don't want you to make the same mistakes I made."

"Mom, Tripp isn't Dad."

"They have a lot of similarities. Work, money, and their mothers all seem to take priority."

Was my mom right? I hated to admit she was ever right. Especially with her track record of multiple marriages.

I started to put leftovers in the fridge.

"He has his life together. He is responsible, smart, and considerate. Today, he wanted to meet me before I left for work just to say goodbye."

I knew it sounded weak.

"Honey, I just want to make sure you are happy... your energy vibration seems low."

"My what?"

She dried her hands, watching me like she was deciding whether to say more. "You remind me of myself at your age," she said finally. "I thought having someone take care of things was doing the right thing. That it would make everything feel safe."

I didn't know what to say. She'd only met Tripp once, long enough to decide he was polished and apparently a mistake. As we were leaving the kitchen, she touched my arm and said softly, "I guess this is the path you've chosen. I just hope it's one that's really yours."

Normally, I would have been defensive and taken it as passive-aggressive mom commentary. But the words stayed with me longer than I wanted them to.

Did she see something in me I was ignoring?

I didn't ask. I wasn't sure I wanted the answer.

By nine, Steph and Ben headed home. Mom and Keith went to bed soon after.

Tory and I stayed up in the guest room, sprawled across the queen bed in mismatched pajamas, passing a sleeve of cookies back and forth.

We giggled. Shared inside jokes. Talked about boys like we were teenagers again.

"You have to get Tripp out of those sweater vests," Tory said, mocking him.

"I know, they are nerdy. Even his pajamas are kind of nerdy," I admitted.

"Does he have them all monogrammed?"

I started laughing, barely able to get the words out, and nodded.

And then my phone buzzed.

BRADLEY

Hey, you, sorry for the delay. It's been nonstop. Can't wait to see you tomorrow. Let me know when you get there, and I'll have my assistant, Suzie, bring you back.

I must've made a sound, because Tory sat up fast. "Was that him?"

I just nodded, grinning.

She leaned over my shoulder. "Let me see!"

I was still smiling when I added, "You know who else might be there?"

She raised a brow. "Don't say Brett, the cousin." She shrugged. "He was funny, not hot."

"Maybe he got hot," I added.

We collapsed into the pillows in breathless laughter, a flash of who we used to be—girls with inside jokes and no real worries.

When Tory finally drifted toward sleep, the room settled into that soft, late-night quiet, and the truth pressed against me. Tomorrow I'd see Bradley, and some part of me already knew: nothing after that would feel the same.

14

DON'T LOOK BACK IN ANGER
HEATHER

By morning, my head was foggy, my heart a little too awake. I rolled over and reached for my phone, bracing myself before I even unlocked the screen.

A blurry photo from Nico and Marcus at a bar lit up my notifications.

NICO

Miss you. Don't forget who loves you most.

Still no word from Tripp, which was unusual. I'd texted him yesterday evening to let him know I'd arrived and added the work dinner to my calendar. He'd mentioned grabbing drinks with some old Yale friends last night.

The old me might've read into that, but this morning his silence sat differently. I decided to take it as a sign—maybe he was giving me space to be with my family. Mom, Tory, and I had planned brunch and a little shopping anyway, and I didn't want to let my overthinking steal the day.

We started the morning in a café in downtown Scarsdale, the front doors propped open to let in the warm air and the low hum of the street outside. Sunlight drifted across the wooden tables, catching on the ring of condensation beneath our iced coffees. Mom kept reaching for our hands as we talked, resting her fingers on my wrist, brushing Tory's knuckles when she laughed, like she was trying to hold on to every moment.

After brunch, we wandered past a bookstore and slipped into a boutique that smelled faintly of citrus and clean linen. The windows were open there too, the curtains lifting gently with each passing breeze. We moved through little shops, and I found myself doing what I always did—running my fingertips along fabrics, grazing their textures, imagining them reconstructed into tops, shawls, maybe even a headband.

Early in the afternoon, Mom drove us to the Scarsdale station. She pulled over at the curb, then turned toward us fully, elbows on the steering wheel.

"Heather," she said softly. "Sweetheart, look at me for a second."

I met her eyes, already feeling that flutter start up.

"It's okay to enjoy tonight," she said. "You're not married yet. Your life is still shifting. Sometimes weekends like this open a door you didn't know was there."

Tory gave me a look like she agreed with Mom.

Mom squeezed my hands, bracelets sliding softly down her wrist. "Just... pay attention to how things feel. Don't shut something out just because it surprises you."

Nerves tightened my throat.

She kissed our cheeks. "Go. Have fun. Let yourselves be young."

We hugged her goodbye, and she waved as she drove away, her ring catching the light, and neither of us said much after that. It felt like we were saving our words, like the night ahead already knew it would ask more of us than we were ready to give. I wondered if she looked up the concert. She knew about Bradley from the vacation, but did she know it was him?

"I'm fine," I said to Tory, though the lie sat heavy on my tongue.

Everything in me was buzzing, but not the good kind. The kind that made it hard to tell the difference between excitement and fear.

The train ride into the city passed in a quiet blur. When we stepped off at Grand Central, the familiar rush of voices and echoing footsteps swallowed us immediately. Tory grabbed my arm as we wove through the crowds, both of us pulled forward by the weight of the night ahead.

Outside, the heat hit us in a soft wave. We flagged down a cab, sliding into the back seat as the driver merged into Midtown traffic. Towers of glass and steel rose around us, bright and overwhelming, and for a second, I forgot how to breathe.

Eventually, we were rolling our suitcases through the W's lobby, the cool blast of air conditioning brushing our skin after the heat outside. The elevator doors slid shut around us, mirrors on all sides, and for a moment, it all felt suddenly, breath-catchingly real. Bradley was somewhere in this city. Tonight wasn't theoretical anymore.

When we reached our room, I dropped my bag by the door and walked straight to the window. Times Square flashed below in sharp bursts of neon, taxis weaving through traffic like they were in a hurry to outrun the day.

After a minute, I peeled myself away from the glass and started unpacking. We didn't talk much—just the quiet clink of makeup compacts, the low thrum of the curling iron heating up, Tory humming a tune I couldn't place. Everything felt suspended, like we were getting ready for something I couldn't admit out loud.

I sat at the small desk, brushing through my hair, my mind spinning faster than I could keep up with.

Tory glanced at me in the mirror, her own curls bouncing as she twisted the iron. "Give me that," she said, reaching out for my brush. "You're going to give yourself a split-end panic attack."

I handed it over, forcing a smile.

"I'm fine."

She nudged my knee with hers. "We're back to this again?" she asked, gathering a section of my hair and wrapping it around the iron. "Heather, you're not running off to Vegas with him. You're saying hi. He wrote a song about you."

"We don't know that."

Tory gave me a look—one of those long, pointed sister stares that said more than words.

I sighed. "He didn't reach out. Not in fifteen years."

"Maybe he was just young and dumb." She lifted a brow in the mirror. "But he found a way now—through a song. It's literally the most romantic thing ever," Tory squealed, unable to contain herself.

I didn't answer. My stomach felt like it was doing slow-motion cartwheels, the kind that made it hard to sit still.

"And let's be honest," she added, gently tugging a section of my hair straight. "You were heartbroken way longer than you admit. You just buried it."

I fiddled with my phone, avoiding her eyes. "I should call Tripp. I haven't really heard from him."

Tory rolled her eyes but kept curling. "Ugh. Text him.

But honestly? That's all the more reason you get to go tonight without any guilt."

She said it lightly, but the words settled somewhere deeper and snagged at the pit of my stomach.

HEATHER

Hope you're having a good weekend.
Miss you.

I stared at the screen. Did I mean that? I wasn't sure at the moment. Maybe it was just muscle memory, something I thought I should say. Something I used to say without thinking.

"There," I muttered, tossing my phone down onto the desk like it burned.

Tory leaned over with a can of hairspray and gave one final mist.

Then she stepped back, cocked her head, and gave a knowing smile.

"Alright. Hair's perfect. Now onto makeup."

She contoured and blended and flicked my lashes with mascara until I barely recognized myself in the mirror. I looked... like someone brave. Someone who wasn't scared to walk through a door she'd closed more than a decade ago.

I slipped into my outfit—dark denim and a black silk top; one of my own pieces. It was elegant but unfussy. A reminder that I still knew who I was, even if I didn't know what was about to happen.

We headed downstairs, and the doorman hailed us a cab. As we pulled away from the curb, I tried to breathe, but it felt like my lungs had shrunk two sizes.

Terminal 5 was already buzzing. The line wrapped around the block—guys in backwards caps and faded tour tees, girls in cutoff shorts or loose sundresses, groups passing around tallboys as they compared old setlists. It sounded like half the people in line had seen him play somewhere else first.

I almost turned to Tory and said we should leave. The crowd, the noise, the intensity of it all—it made something in my chest twist. Before I could get the words out, a petite woman with bright red hair and a headset stepped directly into our path.

"Hi—Heather?"

I blinked. "Yes?"

"I'm Suzie," she said, brisk and expressionless. "And I'm guessing this is your sister?"

"It is," Tory said, instantly straightening like she'd been called to the principal's office.

"Come with me."

We followed her as she cut through the crowd, moving us past the line and around the corner to a side door I never would've noticed. She flashed her lanyard to a security guard, who stepped aside to let us in.

Inside was a narrow, concrete hallway—exposed pipes overhead, the distant thump of the opener's sound check rattling through the floor. Suzie led us up a metal stairwell that opened into a roped-off balcony section overlooking the entire venue.

Cushioned benches lined the back wall, low sconces cast a warm amber glow, and from up here the whole place looked enormous—three levels of railings stacked like an old warehouse, people already crowding in with plastic cups in hand.

"This is your spot for the night," Suzie said. "If you need anything, here's my card. I'll come grab you during the last song."

She placed a matte business card in my hand, then she vanished like a stagehand between acts.

I looked at the card.

Suzie Schaffer
Tour Manager

Suzie with a Z. I wondered if she'd changed it for work or if her parents had simply spelled it that way.

Tory handed me a water bottle. "You good?"

I shook my head. "Nope."

The lights dimmed.

A ripple moved through the room—quiet at first, then swelling, like the inhale before a wave breaks. People rose to their feet, bodies leaning forward, the air tightening with expectation.

And then—there he was.

Bradley.

Guitar in hand. Head angled down, brown curls falling over his forehead. He stepped into the spotlight, and the roar that followed hit so hard it felt like it pressed against my ribs.

He looked the same. And completely different. Broader in the shoulders. More sure of himself. But when he lifted his head and that sideways grin appeared—the one I'd memorized without ever meaning to—something inside me dropped straight through the floor.

Fifteen years vanished in an instant.

It was still him.

And somehow, impossibly, it was still me.

The band launched into the first song, and the room exploded. Tory cheered. I just stood there, stunned, watching the way his fingers moved, how his whole body leaned into the music.

It was like watching someone pour their soul into the air, one chord at a time.

The lights shifted as the band slipped offstage. The bass still hummed in the air, but the crowd began to stir—a collective exhale after the rush of the first set.

Tory leaned in. "I'm going to run to the ladies' room and grab a drink. Want one?"

"I'm okay," I said, though I wasn't totally sure what I needed.

She gave me a look. "I'll get you one anyway."

I managed a nod, but my chest felt tight. Not panicked exactly, more like I was holding my breath and didn't remember when I started.

I picked up my phone without thinking. Just something to do with my hands.

One message. From Mom.

MOM

You girls go wild tonight. Love you Heatherbug.

I stared at the screen, then shook my head and placed the phone face down in my lap.

Tory returned a few minutes later, sliding into her seat with a water in one hand, and a beer in the other.

She held the beer out to me. "You need to take the edge off."

I took it without a word, the cold glass damp against my palm. I didn't really want it, but I lifted it anyway, letting the foam kiss my lips before taking a slow sip.

Bradley moved through the songs like he was built for it, completely in the pocket—his fingers flying over the strings like they were a part of him. The way he tipped his head back into the spotlight, the way his voice cracked at just the right moment, it felt like he was pulling pieces of me forward I hadn't let myself feel in years.

I sat frozen, afraid to blink in case I missed something.

Then Bradley stepped up to the mic. "Hey guys," he said, breathless from the last song. "Thanks for coming tonight."

The crowd screamed.

"This next one... this one's for someone I thought I'd lost. Turns out... I found her."

Tory grabbed my arm like she was anchoring me in place.

The first chord hit.

> *Met you barefoot in the sand,*
> *Salt on your skin and a pencil in your hand.*
> *We were two kids on borrowed time,*
> *Sunburned hearts and homemade lines...*

I froze.

Tory's eyes widened. "Heather. That's you."

> *You danced like you'd done it forever,*
> *Pulled me in like a tide,*
> *Said your name just once,*
> *But it never left my mind.*

I felt like I'd been dropped straight back into that night on the beach. His chin against my skin. His voice in my ear. His hand on the small of my back.

I forgot the crowd. Forgot Tory. Forgot the last fifteen years.

Now it's dreams and could-have-beens,
But I still hear that night again.

When the final chorus hit, the crowd went wild. But I was silent. Just listening. Every line peeled something open inside me.

The last note faded like the echo of a memory.

The room thundered with applause.

Then, like a scene change, Suzie reappeared at the edge of our section.

"Let's go," she said, calm and focused. "We've got about three minutes before the crush hits."

Tory squeezed my hand. "Don't trip."

We followed Suzie past a set of velvet ropes and into a service hallway that ran behind the stage. The music was muffled back here—thick and distant, like the walls were swallowing it whole. It felt instantly quieter, heavier, like we'd stepped into the city's underbelly.

Flight cases were stacked in uneven towers, marked with neon tape and scribbled set-list notes. Techs moved quickly, talking into radios clipped to their shirts. Someone jogged past carrying a bundle of cables, the scent of sweat and metal trailing after him. Everything vibrated faintly, the floor, the railing, even the air, leftover adrenaline rippling through the space.

Suzie led us around a sharp corner and pushed aside a heavy black curtain. Behind it was a small backstage lounge, nothing fancy, just a black leather couch, a mini fridge humming in the corner, a towel crumpled on the floor beside a half-open case of water bottles. The overhead lights buzzed softly, throwing long shadows across the concrete.

For a moment, it didn't feel like New York.

It felt like the inside of a heartbeat.

"He'll be about ten minutes," Suzie said. "Needs to cool off. You're good here."

Then she was gone.

Tory and I stood in the quiet whir of everything about to happen. I sat down slowly, feeling the vinyl couch groan beneath me.

The screams outside were fading. The music had ended. But the moment—the real moment—was just beginning.

15

BACKSTAGE GLOW

BRADLEY

My ears were still ringing.

Not just from the crowd—though they were loud enough to shake the floor—but from the kind of adrenaline that doesn't let go right away. The post-show comedown. The high and the hollow at the same time.

Terminal 5. New York City. Sold out.

If you told the little kid sitting in my dad's garage with a too-big guitar that he'd play a room like this someday, he never would've believed it. Those summers were the only time my dad felt part of me—music, jokes, chords, promises.

And then he left. Just gone.

After that, Uncle Gary stepped in. Not a musician. Not a dreamer. A lawyer. Level-headed. Predictable. Good man. He treated me like his own, made sure we were okay, and tried like hell to steer me away from anything that looked like my father's choices.

College. A solid career. A sensible life. Find a nice girl. Build something real.

He wanted that for all of us—Tommy, Brett, Jared, my

sister Jamie. He wanted safety. Security. A life with fewer bruises.

But I wanted this.

Music was everything to me. It pulsed through my veins, igniting a fire that couldn't be extinguished. The thrill of performing, the energy of the crowd, the rush of creating songs with my bandmates—it was what I lived for.

The lights faded, and the crowd roared one last time. A sound like nothing else on earth. It shook straight through my ribs. I stepped offstage into the narrow concrete hallway, sweat cooling on my face. Someone shoved a towel into my hand, another pressed a water bottle against my palm.

"Jesus, man." Brett was waiting near a tower of road cases marked in neon tape. "You torched that place."

Jared cracked a beer, foam hissing over his knuckles. "They were losing it up there. New York loves you."

I let out a breath that barely felt like mine. "It didn't feel real."

"It was fuckin' rad," Brett said.

We started walking, the three of us moving through the backstage corridor. The walls buzzed with leftover bass, thick cables coiled everywhere, stagehands brushing past us with clipped radios and urgency.

A girl with a laminate pass reached out and touched my arm as we passed, breathless, thanking me for the show before security gently steered her back. Another called my name like she knew me.

I nodded once and kept moving. The high was still in my veins, refusing to settle.

"You're on a different level tonight," Jared said. "This tour's gonna blow up."

"Let him breathe," Brett muttered.

But I wasn't thinking about the tour.

Or the next show.

Or the label.

My mind was racing—spinning—because I knew what was waiting for me. *Heather.* Here. Tonight. Anticipation coiled in my stomach, tight and electrifying. What would it feel like to see her again after all these years? Would the connection we had still be there, or had time changed everything?

I was thinking about how strange it felt to stand in the middle of the thing you fought for—and still feel like you needed someone to see it. To say they understood why you crossed the line anyway.

Then Suzie's voice buzzed in my earpiece.

"She's in the lounge. Just her and the sister. Privacy's set."

I stopped walking.

Jared swore under his breath. "No way. She came?"

I didn't answer.

Couldn't.

I peeled off my damp shirt and grabbed a clean one from the wardrobe rack. My hands shook—not from nerves, but from everything converging at once. The crowd. The climb. Gary's hopes. My dad's absence. And now—her.

Heather. Here. Tonight.

I thought of the years apart, the weight of the words left unspoken, the memories that came to me in dreams. What would it feel like to see her again? Would the connection still be there, or had it faded, like the applause? My heart raced with uncertainty.

"Alright," I said quietly. "Let's go."

As I walked toward the lounge, my heart raced with a mix of excitement and uncertainty—everything I had fought for had led me to this moment with Heather.

16

___

WHEN THE MUSIC STOPS
HEATHER

There he was. His forest-green eyes found me first.

Everything in the room seemed to pause. The buzzing lights. The muffled noise of the crowd outside. Even Tory beside me. It all slipped into the background the second I saw him standing in the doorway, looking like he'd stepped out of a memory I'd replayed way too many times.

Bradley didn't move. I didn't either.

I pushed halfway out of my seat before I knew I was doing it, my heartbeat knocking hard against its confines. My hands were suddenly useless in my lap, like they didn't know what to do with this moment. The backstage mirrors behind him threw bits of light around the room, catching on cables and gear cases, making the whole space feel slightly unreal, like I'd walked straight into a moment I hadn't actually prepared for.

I looked him over, searching for the boy I'd fallen for in Punta Cana. His shoulders were broader, curls a little shorter, jaw more defined. Familiar and not at all at the same time. But his eyes... those were exactly the same. The same green I used to memorize in the sun. And now they were on me, rooted and stunned, like he couldn't decide if he should breathe or speak or walk toward me.

I wasn't sure what to do either.

I'd imagined this moment too many times—on airplanes, in grocery-store lines, in all the quiet spots where my mind wandered. I'd pictured what I'd say, how I'd feel, how he might look at me.

None of those versions came close. Not to this. To him, standing here now, older and somehow softer and stronger at the same time, and me realizing I'd never actually planned for what it would do to me when it finally happened.

Tory stood too, trying to look subtle.

"Is there somewhere I could get a snack or a drink?" she asked, like she hadn't timed it perfectly to slip out and give us space.

The faint thump of drums from the stage seemed to snap Bradley back into motion.

"Yeah—yes," he said, like he forgot to speak. "I'll have Suzie come get you."

He pulled out his phone, the blue glow washing over his face, and sent a quick text. A knock came a few seconds later.

"Come in," he called.

Suzie stepped inside, steady and unbothered as ever, tablet in hand. Her tiny frame and red hair, a little nose ring catching the light. The hallway noise spilled in for a moment—crew voices, rolling cases, the leftover roar of the crowd—before she shut the door again and sealed us back into this strange pocket of quiet.

"Snack and drink request?" she asked.

Tory grinned. "That would be for me. Any chance I can meet the drummer?"

Suzie lifted one brow, a tiny unimpressed arch. "The rest of the band is in the green room. Follow me."

Tory poked her head back in as she left. "Have fun, you two."

When the door clicked shut behind her, the room fell into a different kind of silence—warm, charged, almost vibrating. I swallowed, suddenly aware of how close he was. I could feel it in my chest, in the back of my throat.

"I can't believe you're here," Bradley said. His voice had dropped, rough around the edges.

"I can't believe you're famous," I said, staying with his gaze.

His mouth tilted into a small smile. "How did you find me?"

"I was at my friend Nico's salon," I said. "Music was playing, and one of your songs came on. I knew the voice—your voice. Tory found you on Instagram."

He nodded slowly. "I told Suzie to flag any Heathers. Yours stood out. HeatherBdesigns."

A small laugh pushed out of me. "I'm glad she flagged it."

"I'm not surprised you ended up in fashion," he said, a little softer. "It always made sense. You had that sketchbook with you the whole vacation."

The way he said it—quiet, certain, like he remembered the exact version of me—made something twist and warm low in my stomach.

"You too," I said just as softly. "You made it happen."

We smiled at the same time. The whole room felt suspended, like we were standing inside something delicate and strangely familiar.

It was almost too much.

His phone buzzed, sharp in the quiet, pulling us both back. He hit ignore and slipped it into his pocket.

"So," he said, his voice shifting, lighter now, "where are you living these days?"

"Chicago," I said, trying to match his tone.

His brows lifted. "Chicago?"

I nodded, tucking a piece of hair behind my ear. The backstage light suddenly felt too bright, or maybe it was just the heat under my skin.

"I went a few years after college," I said, finding the words as I went. "I got an internship there—lots of steaming and sorting—and then the internship turned into something more. Something real. I wasn't expecting to fall in love with the city, but I did. So... I stayed. Tory is there, too."

His expression softened, warm in a way that made my chest ache.

"That makes sense," he said. "You were always meant to figure out where you belonged."

"I don't know about that."

"I do," he said quietly.

I had to look away again.

"Where are you living?" Even though I knew from Tory's stalking session.

"LA. It's not for me though." He ran a hand through his hair and relaxed his shoulders.

"No?"

"It's too busy."

My purse buzzed, sharp, unwelcome.

I glanced and saw Tripp's name light up. My stomach did a little dip. I let it go to voicemail. A pinch of guilt shot through me, fast and thin. I pushed it down and slid the phone deeper into my bag.

"Everything okay?" Bradley asked gently.

"Yeah," I said, taking a breath. "Everything's great."

He hesitated, studying me. He walked a little closer. I could hear my heart beating.

"Can I hug you?" he asked, voice low.

My breath caught. "Yes. Yes, you can."

He closed the space between us slowly, almost like he was letting the moment settle before stepping into it. And then his arms were around me.

The warmth of him hit first—real and familiar in a way I didn't understand but felt instantly. My chest pressed lightly against his, and something deep inside me loosened, like my body recognized him before I could even process what was happening.

His shirt smelled like citrus and clean wood and sweat, this warm, worn-in scent that pulled up something old and soft inside me. My cheek rested against the cotton at his chest, and for a heartbeat, everything else faded—the leftover noise from the stage, the lights, the years. It all fell away.

His hand slid to the small of my back, slow and sure, and the feeling of it there spread through me in a warm, quiet rush. My whole body felt tuned in, almost listening, as if I were syncing to the steady rise and fall of his breathing.

I didn't want to move. I didn't want the moment to end.

I just let myself go into it, let myself feel him, let myself exist in the one place I hadn't allowed myself to imagine too closely—held by him again.

It felt like something inside me was remembering how to breathe.

When we finally pulled back, I could still feel the heat of his hands like they'd left an imprint. His eyes looked a little dazed, a little undone, like he was still in it too.

"Wow," he said quietly. "That felt... really good."

My breath caught, soft and helpless. "Yeah," I said, smiling without meaning to. "It really did."

He hesitated, his eyes dipping to my mouth for the quickest second before he looked away again.

"I'd like to take you to dinner," he said.

"It's almost midnight," I said with a laugh.

"Then pancakes? We can go somewhere quiet. Somewhere private."

The flutter low in my stomach was impossible to hide. *He remembered my favorite food.*

"I'd have to bring Tory."

"She's invited," he said immediately. "Where are you staying?"

"The W in Times Square."

"I'm at the Mandarin Oriental," he said. "We're practically neighbors."

"Looks like fate has excellent hotel taste," I murmured, suddenly aware I sounded like my mom.

His grin was slow, confident, and dangerous.

"Jared and Brett are here too," he said. "They'll want to see you."

"It's like a vacation reunion," I said jokingly.

We stood there looking at each other too long until a knock came in, transferring us back to reality again.

"Come in," Bradley called.

Suzie reappeared, tablet still in hand. "Your car is waiting. Room for everyone."

"What about Tory?" I asked.

Suzie didn't blink. "I said everyone."

I leaned toward Bradley. "Is she always like this?"

"All the time," he whispered back. "She tortures Jared."

"Oh, I can see that."

Footsteps echoed. Tory strode in first.

"Did you two rekindle?"

"Tory," I groaned.

"What? I'm just checking. We have years of backlog."

Brett and Jared came into the room behind Tory.

Brett was still slender, all easy muscle and blond hair, styled to make him look mature. He smiled, composed, and reached his hand out to mine. "Good to see you, Heather."

I met his eyes and smiled, shaking his hand. "Likewise."

Jared didn't even try to pretend he was calm. He barreled straight into me, arms wrapping around my shoulders and lifting me off the ground. "Heather!"

"Hey—!" I laughed.

He set me back down, grinning, his big frame crowding my space. He'd filled out—broad, solid, the kind of build that made him look like he could've been a linebacker. His blond hair was a mess, and his eyes were still those soft, droopy ones he'd always had, like a basset hound's—sweet and a little sad and impossible not to love.

"Alright," Suzie announced, already halfway down the hall. "Let's go."

We followed her, the backstage corridor buzzing with leftover adrenaline. The crew's voices, the rolling cases, the distant rumble of the crowd bleeding into the walls—it all felt suspended, like the world hadn't quite decided what came next.

When we stepped outside into the New York night—electric, bright, loud—it felt like the city exhaled around us.

A sleek black car waited at the curb, headlights cutting through the glow of streetlights and neon signs.

We climbed in. Doors shut. Breath mingled. Something unspoken tightened the air.

And then we were moving into the night, into whatever this was going to become.

17

MIDNIGHT IN MANHATTAN

BRADLEY

The SUV door shut behind me, sealing the humid night out and dropping us into a pocket of cool, dim silence from the noise of the city. My pulse was still trying to come down from the stage, from seeing Heather, but the second I slid into the middle row and felt her beside me, close enough that her knee brushed mine, I knew that wasn't happening anytime soon.

What I felt then wasn't new. It was something imprinted rising to the surface—the same pull I hadn't fully shaken since the summer we were young enough to believe endings were optional. Losing her hadn't just been about missing a girl. It was about losing the version of myself who believed in things without calculating the damage first. Every city I'd lived in since, every song I'd written, had been shaped by that absence, whether I admitted it or not. Seeing her again tonight didn't just stir the memory. It reopened the question I'd been avoiding for fifteen years: what if the life I built only made sense because I didn't find the one I actually wanted?

Tory, Brett, and Jared were in the back, already halfway into a joke about something from the green room. Suzie took the passenger seat next to the driver, tapping quick notes into her phone with the efficiency of someone who's always three steps ahead.

"Mandarin Oriental, no other stops," she told the driver, and the SUV started moving.

Heather shifted slightly, and the soft press of her leg against mine lit up something in my chest I wasn't ready to deal with. I kept my eyes forward, pretending the city streaking by outside wasn't the most surreal backdrop to the one moment I'd been imagining for fifteen years.

I told myself this was just nostalgia. The past only felt loud because I hadn't visited it in a long time. But that lie collapsed the second I knew she was in the crowd, the second the last song left my mouth. The life I'd built suddenly felt temporary when placed beside the memory of her. I was afraid of what would happen if I didn't put those feelings somewhere before I saw her face again.

Tory leaned forward between the seats. "Is the dessert actually worth it?"

Jared nodded enthusiastically. "The chocolate cake is ridiculous."

"Of course that's what you'd prioritize," Brett muttered.

Their voices blurred in and out, background noise to something sharper—the way Heather's breathing changed every time we hit a bump, or how she kept her hands folded tightly in her lap, like she was trying to keep them still.

The SUV turned onto Columbus Circle. Lights washed across her face—amber, white, then a rush of red from a passing taxi. She looked different in every color: more mature, more beautiful than I remembered—if that was possible—and grounded.

Her hair was smoother than it had been on the island, the frizz long gone, left behind in the tropics. The nape of her neck was long and pale, a few loose strands brushing her skin, and the memory of what it felt like to kiss her there rose so suddenly it almost made me erupt in a boner. I had to look away, heart thudding, afraid of how visible my reaction might be, of how little control I seemed to have over what seeing her did to me.

I swallowed, adjusting my grip on my jeans. I wanted to tell her that seeing her again felt like standing in the doorway of a life I wasn't sure I was brave enough to choose. That part of me had spent years building walls so I wouldn't have to face the fact that I never stopped loving her. That tonight terrified me more than any crowd ever had. But the words stayed where they were, heavy and dangerous and real.

She finally spoke. "That song tonight... the one at the end. Was it new?"

I cleared my throat. "New-ish."

"And the lyrics... they felt—"

My mouth tipped despite me. "They came from somewhere." I lowered my eyes to meet hers. "Some things don't leave you."

Her eyes flicked from mine to my cheeks. "Like that dimple."

I couldn't help but let out a low laugh.

I knew exactly what she meant. I had written that song after hearing she'd be in New York. After realizing that distance doesn't erase certain truths. I had written it because I needed somewhere safe to put the *hope* I didn't trust myself to carry when I was standing this close to her. Because I was already wondering what would happen if this night became more than memory.

Her knee brushed mine again, and I didn't move. I couldn't. I stayed exactly where I was, because pulling away felt impossible and leaning closer felt reckless.

Behind us, Brett had leaned forward, fully invested as Tory told him about the PR firm she'd just started working with, nodding along, clearly interested. At some point, he cut in, completely serious, to ask what shampoo she used because her hair looked unreal. Tory laughed, told him the name, and Jared immediately said he should start using it too, which sent Brett into a playful argument about how Jared gets his hair cut at Super Cuts and his shampoo is L'Oréal for kids. Their voices overlapped, bright and easy, a little too loud, the kind of energy that came from being buzzed and ready for the night to really begin.

The rest of the conversation behind us dissolved into background noise.

What I was thinking about scared me. Not just if we might kiss. Not just the comfort of something familiar. I wanted the chance to find out if the future I walked away from was still possible, and whether choosing her now would finally make sense of all the years I spent pretending I didn't need that answer.

Suzie glanced back. "Two minutes out."

My stomach tightened. Two minutes until we stepped into a hotel suite together. Two minutes until I'd find out if the look in her eyes tonight meant anything... or if I'd made the whole thing up.

The car slowed in front of the Mandarin Oriental, headlights sweeping across the marble entrance. Valets moved toward us in crisp uniforms.

My heart kicked once, hard.

This was happening.

She was here.

I finally turned to her. Really looked. The same question I'd been carrying for years was sitting in her eyes too—not as a coincidence, but as something unfinished and waiting.

The car rolled to a stop.

Time to find out.

18

EVERYWHERE WITH ME

HEATHER

The car slowed in front of a curved glass awning, soft yellow light washing over the sidewalk, giving the moment a theatrical presence. The Mandarin Oriental rose above us; it was sleek, dark, reflective, like the kind of place the rich and famous stay.

Tory exhaled a low whistle. "Okay... so this is definitely not the Holiday Inn."

Bradley didn't say anything. He just moved first, opening the door and offering his hand to help me out, like this was normal. Like being pulled into his orbit was something I should be used to. I was fully aware of how the warmth of his hand felt in mine. The driver took over and helped the rest of the car out.

Inside, the lobby was warm and glowing, all soft lighting, polished stone, and tall arrangements of orchids. The whole place smelled faintly like bergamot and something richer underneath—cedar, maybe.

We took a private elevator up, Suzie flashing a key card at the panel. My stomach fluttered with every floor we climbed, each ding making my heartbeat feel louder.

Tory, Brett, and Jared were already in their own world, laughing like no time had passed since that vacation, like they'd never really stopped knowing each other. Suzie didn't seem amused by any of it. I was busy keeping track of my limbs, making sure I didn't pass out, acutely aware of how close I was to Bradley—close enough that I could have reached out and hooked my finger around his pinky.

When the doors opened, a suite stretched out in front of us, all glass and skyline, the entire city glittering beyond the windows. Floor-to-ceiling views of Columbus Circle and Central Park; everything glowing gold and silver and endless.

It didn't feel like a hotel room.

It felt like a whole other world.

Velvet couches in deep charcoal. A curved bar lined with small bottles of top-shelf liquor. A dining table set with empty champagne flutes. Soft jazz humming from hidden speakers. Every surface gleamed: chrome, marble, glass.

A hotel staffer rolled in a cart with dessert trays, tiny pastries that looked like jewelry, bowls of berries, and dark chocolate squares. And covered trays I suspected contained pancakes, maple syrup sitting next to them. The air smelled warm, sweet, alive.

People filtered in. Bandmates first, three guys that Bradley introduced to Tory and me —Greg, Pete, Alex— each giving Bradley the kind of greeting that said they truly loved him. Then a few others drifted in, glossy-haired girls, guys with long hair, some who reeked of weed—the kind of scene that made you feel like an outsider even when you tried not to.

One of the girls beamed when she saw Bradley.

"Brad! Great show."

She kissed him—one cheek, then the other. A double tap.

Something hot and sharp twisted low in my stomach.

Brad. I wonder if that's what people called him or just... her.

Tory caught the shift in my expression immediately. She leaned close, whispering, "You're fine. She's probably dated half the band."

Bradley looked over his shoulder at me like he felt it—like he felt *me*—and something in his eyes softened.

We ended up near the windows, just slightly away from everyone else, perched at the edge of a velvet chaise. The skyline beyond the glass flickered like it was breathing.

"Well," he said quietly as he settled beside me, his knee brushing mine again. "I know I said we would go someplace private, quiet, but this will have to do. It's just easier, and I don't want to lose this time with you. Tell me what you've been up to for the past fifteen years."

Even that tiny touch sent a spark jolting straight through me, sharp and tingly, like my body recognized him.

"Fifteen years is... a long time," I said, tucking a stray piece of hair behind my ear.

He smiled—soft, patient—like he'd already lived through every year of that distance too.

"I want to hear it all."

For a second, I almost asked *Why didn't you call?*

But the question was too heavy, too sharp for the moment sitting between us, so I held it.

Instead, I said, "Work's kept me really busy." His eyes were glued to mine. "I'm hoping to build my own line. And I have this opportunity with Bloomingdale's, which is... huge. I don't know. I feel like I'm rambling."

"You aren't," he said, leaning in just a little. "I always knew you were talented."

His eyes didn't move from mine. "I remember watching you draw and thinking, 'She's going to do something real with that pencil of hers.'" He smirked, his left dimple deepening. His confidence in me hit somewhere tender. I crossed my right leg over my left thigh, trying to collect myself.

"What about you?" I asked, motioning lightly around the room. "Besides becoming... all of this?"

He let out a breathy laugh, running a hand through his curls. "A lot of writing. A lot of messing up. A lot of trying again." He shrugged. "And Mario Kart. I'm actually unstoppable. Truly."

I laughed, the sound leaving me before I could stop it. Our eyes locking again. I had to look away before I got swallowed into those green lily pads once more.

The guilt hit. The ring I'd purposely left at the W.

The fiancé I hadn't mentioned. The tiny voice that whispered, *You should tell him.* But my mother's words drifted back: *Let the weekend show you something. You aren't married yet.*

Maybe it was reckless. Maybe it was wrong.

But sitting there beside him felt like slipping into a version of myself I thought I'd grown out of—but hadn't—and I didn't want to leave this moment.

He nudged my knee again, gentle, intentional.

"You seem happy," he said softly. "Like you're really doing what you're meant to be doing."

"Are you happy?" I asked, surprising myself with such a loaded question. "I mean, you really are doing it... your dream... this."

His mouth curved. "This?"

He lifted a brow. "You mean sleep-deprived, permanently jet-lagged, and pretending I know what I'm doing?"

"Bradley," I said, shaking my head. "You're playing sold-out shows. I'd say you know exactly what you're doing."

He looked down at his hands for a moment. "I know what I *want* to do. Writing helps. Touring... sometimes helps."

He paused. "But nights like this? You here. This feels... different."

My breath snagged. Heat rose up my throat.

One of his bandmates walked over with a joint, asking if either of us wanted a hit.

"No thanks... Greg, was it?"

"I'm Pete, the good-looking one; Greg is the loud one hitting on your sister."

Pete passed the joint to Bradley. He shook his head.

We talked in low voices after that—little pieces of our lives traded back and forth.

He told me about recording sessions at two a.m., about how he still gets stage nerves, about how his cousin Jared thinks he should live in Nashville, and his manager wants him in L.A.

I told him about fabric sourcing, about late nights sketching in my shared apartment, about how Tory eats half my groceries and steals my socks.

He laughed, leaning closer.

The air seemed to shift around us—slower, heavier, threaded with something new and old at the same time. The voices and music around us got a little louder.

Then he stood. Hesitated.

"I want to show you something," he said.

I met his eyes. "Okay."

When he reached for my hand, I didn't even think.

I let him.

His palm was solid, callused, a quiet shock of familiarity. My fingers curled into his like they remembered how.

He didn't let go.

He guided me out of the suite, past the soft thrum of voices and clinking glasses.

Down the hall.

Past the enormous abstract painting.

Past a line of golden sconces that washed the corridor in honey-colored light.

Toward a door left half-cracked.

The moment we stepped inside, the air changed.

Quieter.

Dimmer.

More intimate.

The bedroom was warm with amber light spilling from the bedside lamps. The duvet was smooth, turned down by a hotel staff. There was chocolate and a card addressed to Bradley on his pillow. His shoes were near the wall. A guitar case leaned open in the corner.

My heart was pounding in places I didn't know it could pound, vibrating my whole body.

Bradley knelt by his suitcase. Unzipped it. Reached inside carefully, like whatever he was touching meant something.

When he stood, he held a folded sheet of paper—edges worn soft with time.

My breath thinned.

He offered it to me.

Hands firm. Voice not.

"Open it."

My fingers shook as I unfolded the paper.

My drawing.

The one I'd sketched of him at the beach, sunburned

cheeks, wind-messed curls, the sky behind him like a watercolor wash. His eyes looking at something far away. That little smirk—teenage Bradley.

I hadn't seen it in fifteen years.

And he...

He still had it.

It was creased from travel, the pencil strokes a little faded, but it was unmistakably mine. Every line. Every smudge. Every corner I'd torn from a sketchbook.

"You kept this?" My voice cracked. I didn't mean for it to.

"Yeah."

His answer was quiet. Almost ashamed.

"It's been everywhere with me."

I looked up at him.

Really looked.

His jaw clenched. His eyes were warm, nervous, steady.

Not a rock star.

Not a stranger.

Just the boy I remembered and the man he grew into.

Something inside my chest folded in on itself, tender and sharp at the same time.

This was too much.

And not enough.

And everything.

"Bradley... " I whispered, because it was all I could manage.

He stepped closer—slow, careful, like any sudden move might break whatever thin line we were balancing on.

"Heather," he said, softer than I'd ever heard him.

And that was where the world stopped.

19

BETWEEN FLOORS

HEATHER

His gaze dropped to my lips, and mine did the same. The air was denser now. I could feel his breath, the heat radiating between us. I knew what we both wanted.

God, I wanted to kiss him. But I didn't. *I couldn't.*

"I need to get Tory and head back to our room." He blinked, like coming out of a trance. "Already?"

"Yes."

Panic pressed beneath my skin. I needed distance. I needed clarity. I needed air. I needed a reality check. I was engaged to Tripp.

And yet, I hadn't worn my ring tonight. I'd told myself it didn't match my outfit. But that wasn't why I left it behind. I left it because some part of me, deep down, wanted a moment like this. And now I had it. And I couldn't breathe.

I slipped out of the bedroom and into the suite's living space. The party was bumping—music, clinking glasses, a burst of laughter from across the room.

Tory was barefoot on a table, twirling, her curls flying wild around her face.

"Victoria Grace Brown," I said, trying to sound stern.

She beamed. "What? Come dance with me!"

Behind me, I felt him before I heard him. "Brown is your last name?" Bradley asked, his voice quieter now.

I nodded, barely turning.

"I didn't know that." He paused like he was thinking. "That's why I couldn't find you."

The words landed heavily. *He couldn't find me.*

I kept my eyes on Tory. I didn't trust myself to look at him.

"Sorry," I said, too fast. "We've got to go. I think Suzie will be thrilled to get you to bed on time."

"I don't have a bedtime," Bradley said with a low laugh. "Do you really have to go?" His voice had softened.

I nodded, trying to stay composed. "I think I do."

"I'll walk you both down," he said.

"I'll come too," Brett added behind him.

Tory hopped off the table and grabbed my arm. "Peak moment, right here," she sang out.

"Tory and I have to go," I said to Brett or the floor. I wasn't making eye contact with anyone.

"Brad, come have a drink with us," glossy girl said. My cheeks flushed. I didn't want him to have a drink with her, but I wasn't supposed to have an ounce of jealousy.

I had to get out of here before I did something more stupid than I already had done. What was I doing in a suite with band members about to blow up my life with a rockstar? Why did he have to become famous and make that song? I have Tripp and a life back home. A curated, well-planned life.

The four of us stepped into the private elevator.

Tory and Brett were laughing at something. I could feel

Bradley's eyes on me. I stared at the numbers as we dropped floor by floor, willing myself to hold it together.

Tory and Brett roared into another round of laughter. I swear they were getting drunker with each floor.

When we made it to the ground floor, the doors slid open. Tory and Brett stepped out first, still laughing.

I started to follow, Bradley's voice once again interjected.

"Wait a second, Heather."

I turned toward him; he grabbed my hand, pulled me back in, and hit the button again. The doors slid shut. Suddenly, it was just us.

The air snapped. Thicker. Louder. My pulse thundered in my ears.

"Please tell me I'll see you tomorrow," he said, his voice low.

I didn't answer. I couldn't form words.

He stepped closer. My back hit the mirrored wall of the elevator, then slid to the corner, where the cool glass curved into metal. I didn't move.

He looked at me like he already knew what I wanted.

And then he leaned down and kissed me.

Soft, at first. Searching. Like he was asking if I'd changed.

I hadn't one bit. I kissed him back.

His hands slid to my waist, pulling me closer. My fingers curled around his shirt, fisting into the fabric like I needed something to hold onto.

The elevator began to move.

He pulled back just long enough to hit the top floor button, keeping us inside.

Then his mouth was on mine again. Rougher. Hungrier.

His body pressed into mine, pushing me deeper into the

corner. My head tilted back, hitting the mirror behind me. I barely noticed.

His hands roamed. My skin burned. I felt his teeth graze my lower lip, then his mouth moved down the side of my neck, just below my ear, just enough to undo me.

I gasped. My legs gave slightly. I forgot who I was. Where I was.

I forgot why this was wrong.

All I knew was him. His mouth, his scent, the way he was touching me, as if no time had passed at all.

We were breathing hard, moving as if we might never stop.

Electricity pulsed through me—sharp and hot—shooting down my body.

I was wet. Aching for him. I could feel him against me. Hard. Big. There was no mistaking what he wanted. No mistaking what I needed.

And then—the elevator dinged. The doors didn't open. He hit the stop button. He'd kept us in. We both let out a breath, grasping for air and oxygen before we both went back for more.

His lips on me again, slower this time, his hand gently brushing the side of my face.

And that was the moment I broke. I pulled back. Just enough. Just barely.

He looked at me, eyes searching.

"I shouldn't have done that," I whispered.

"Why?" he asked, his voice still unsteady. "I've wanted to kiss you again for fifteen years."

I swallowed hard. The words hit me like a punch in the chest.

"Then you should have tried harder and called me."

"The piece of paper with your information got ruined in

the storm," he said. "I don't know how, but it smeared. I searched for you. I tried every combination of Mookie and several numbers. I just couldn't crack the code. I looked on Facebook, everywhere. You were just... gone."

His eyes were pleading. And kind. And honest. And it wrecked me because it changed everything. Because it meant this wasn't just in my head.

I pressed my fingers to my lips. They were still swollen. Still tingling.

And suddenly I felt faint. I stepped away, needing air, needing space. His eyes held mine.

"It's too late."

He stared at me, confused.

"I'm engaged."

20

FIFTEEN YEARS GONE

BRADLEY

I stood there stunned, my back pressed to the cool metal of the elevator wall.

Engaged.

The word kept looping in my brain like a bad chorus I couldn't rewrite.

She was fucking engaged.

I hadn't expected that. Hell, I didn't even expect to see her again. But when I did—when she was suddenly standing there in front of me after all these years—something in me shifted. The ground rearranged itself. And then, just as quickly, it cracked open again.

She thinks that I let her go. I hated myself for hurting her. I knew I could have tried harder to find her.

I didn't notice the paper had been ruined until it was too late. Her number, that screen name she'd scribbled down, both soaked straight through in the pocket of my jeans after we got caught in the rain. By the time I checked, they were gone—just smeared ink and a crumpled piece of nothing.

I'd played that moment over in my head more times than I could count. What if I had looked sooner? What if I'd slipped a note under her door? What if I had just asked for her last name?

But we didn't. I didn't. We were kids. We were careless.

The hotel wouldn't give me anything, not even her last name. I was just some teenage kid begging the front desk for a miracle. And I never got one.

So I did the only thing I could think of. I wrote songs. I played them everywhere. I told myself that if I ever had a shot at finding her again, it'd be through music. That maybe, just maybe, she'd hear me.

And she did. When it was too late. Too fucking late.

I pulled out my phone and checked her Instagram again. Still nothing personal. Just her work—clean, sharp designs, beautiful lines. There wasn't a trace of him. No ring photos. No couple shots. Just her.

So why did she come tonight? To toy with me? To see me one last time? For closure?

My head was spinning. And all I wanted was to be back with her. Back before the truth broke the moment wide open.

Now that I'd found her, I was going to lose her all over again.

I had walked into tonight with something already waiting inside me. I thought maybe seeing her would settle me, that the ache I'd carried for years would finally have somewhere to go. I imagined us talking, maybe laughing, maybe realizing that whatever we'd been back then hadn't actually ended—it had just been paused by bad weather and immature mistakes. And maybe we needed this time to grow into the people we would become. I didn't expect miracles. I just wanted the chance to see if the story I'd been holding onto was still alive.

Brett found me a few minutes later in the hallway.

"What's with the face?" He asked.

"She's engaged," I muttered.

He paused. "Well, shit... she's not married yet."

"It was a line, Brett. And I crossed it. I kissed her—and she kissed me back."

"Then maybe it wasn't a line for her," he said, shrugging. "She obviously still feels something."

Brett always knew my feelings for Heather. He was the only one who never made fun of me back then—for losing her number, for never letting it go. He remembered her screen name, too. Mookie something. We used to laugh about how ridiculous it was.

I texted Suzie.

BRADLEY

Let's wrap it. I'm done for the night.

By the time I got to the suite, people were starting to clear out. Bandmates. Groupies. Someone passed me a drink. I handed it off. Gave a few high fives. One of the girls asked if she should stay the night.

"I'm good," I told her. Maybe a little too quickly.

Jared and Brett were crashing on the couch.

Suzie stood in the doorway, like a tired schoolteacher.

"Lights out in ten," she said.

"Maybe you should stay the night to make sure we behave," Jared joked.

"Dream on," Suzie shot back.

I smiled faintly and disappeared into my room.

I checked my phone again. Nothing from Heather.

Stripping down to my briefs, I climbed into bed. Killed the lights. Let the dark settle around me.

But my mind wouldn't stop. Her lips. That kiss. Her fingers in my hair. I could've had her right there in that elevator. Now I know it would've been wrong. She is someone else's fiancée.

I turned onto my side, stared out at the blurred lights of the city skyline.

I guess I'll have a whole new set of lyrics after this. A heartbreak I'll try to turn into a hit. The same girl I almost had.

Another ending I didn't want.

Fuck. I thought kissing her would bring her back to me. I didn't realize it might be the thing that finally let her go.

21

AFTER THE APPLAUSE
HEATHER

My heart was pounding, my hands slick with sweat. My mind wouldn't stop racing. I just kissed Bradley.

And not some tame, polite kiss. It was an intense, breathless, toe-curling kind of kiss, the kind that almost made me forget I was in an elevator. The kind that made me want to rip his clothes off right then and there.

He was dangerous to be around. Addicting. Everything I used to love about him has just grown up and become sharper around the edges. Masculine. Confident. Those hands... I couldn't stop thinking about what I wanted him to do with them.

This was so wrong. Completely wrong. I was engaged to Tripp. I was behaving like a terrible fiancée.

The kind of person who does careless acts and regrets them later. The kind of person I've never been. I've never cheated in my life, not on a boyfriend, not even on a quiz.

I stumbled out of the revolving door, the warm night air hitting my skin like a slap. I needed space. Air. Distance.

Outside, I spotted Tory and Brett near the curb, cracking up hysterically and sharing a cigarette.

"Heather!" Tory called out, waving her arm dramatically. "Here, try this Parliament Light—it's amazing."

"I need to get back to the room," I said quickly, brushing past the haze of smoke. "I'll walk."

"Wait—I'm coming with you." Tory passed the cigarette to Brett and called out to the doorman. "Thanks, Carlo!"

"Anytime," he said with a grin. "You ladies need a cab?"

"Yes," Tory said. "We don't know where we are, Heather."

"We'll find our way," I replied without slowing down.

Brett followed Tory. "Can I get your number?" he asked, casually.

"Absolutely!" she said, taking his phone and typing in her digits. "Talk soon."

I had no idea what was happening between them, but I didn't have the capacity to care. I just needed to get back to our room. To breathe. To think.

We crossed the street, city lights flickering above us like an old movie reel. The streets were nearly empty at this hour, ghost-like after the earlier rush.

"Heather, wait!" Tory called after me.

I stopped at the corner of the street. Realizing Tory was right, I had no idea how to get back to our hotel.

She caught up to me out of breath. "Heather, are you okay?"

I honestly didn't know. I was a cheater, and I had just ruined my future. I started to pant at the thought of my behavior. I could feel sweat on the back of my neck and palms.

"Heather, look at me."

I made eye contact with Tory.

"Focus on my breath, okay?" She inhaled slowly, and I

followed, inhaling and exhaling with her. "Okay, good." She spotted a cab. "Hold on." She shot her little arm up, and the cab pulled aside.

"Let's get you in the cab."

She had me go first and slid in after.

"To the W, please, and can you roll down the windows?"

The cab driver looked back, probably to make sure I wasn't going to vomit in his car.

He rolled them down and stepped on it. Tory held my hand, and we rode in silence. Thankfully, it was a short cab ride away.

Tory swiped her card, and we stepped out to our hotel. I followed in silence. When we made it up to our room, I went into the bathroom and splashed water on my face as if it would wash away the sin I just committed.

Tory knocked lightly and then opened the door. "What happened?"

I took a towel to dry my face and looked in the mirror, about to cry. "Something that shouldn't have."

"Oh," she said, eyes lighting up far too much for my comfort.

I turned to her, my voice sharper than I meant. "Did you bring me here hoping I'd leave Tripp? Because if you don't like him, fine. But setting me up to cheat? That's low."

Her smile dropped. Her big brown eyes went wide.

"Heather—no. I never meant for anything to happen. I just... I don't know. It felt like fate, maybe."

Tears welled in her eyes, and instantly, I regretted the accusation. I felt the sting of my own guilt rising to meet hers.

"I kissed him," I admitted, voice cracking. "It was me. Not you. I'm so sorry." A tear rolled down my cheek.

I pulled her into a hug. We both cried. Then, somehow,

we started laughing, probably because we were exhausted and overwhelmed and couldn't figure out what else to do.

"Maybe we should get out of the bathroom," she sniffed, wiping her face.

We held hands like we used to when we were kids, afraid of the dark.

We changed into pajamas, the quiet settling between us.

"If it was just a kiss," Tory said gently, "maybe it's not worth beating yourself up over. It's not like you slept with him."

"I wanted to," I whispered. "I took my ring off. Put it in the safe."

She studied me, her tone soft. "Maybe you just needed to get it out of your system."

"Maybe." I loved her for trying to justify my actions. But I knew better; it didn't feel like a release. *It felt like an awakening.*

Once I got into bed, I grabbed my phone to text Tripp. The thought of his name made me feel sick. I typed anyway.

HEATHER

Sorry, I missed your call. I'll call you in the morning. xo

I felt like a fraud.

Tory was asleep seconds after her head hit the pillow. I wasn't so lucky. I tossed and turned, restless and hollow. I checked my phone. No text from Bradley. Nothing from Tripp. I even checked Bradley's Instagram like some love-sick teenager.

Who was I?

I was a girl who gotten one taste and couldn't stop craving more.

All these years, I'd wondered what it would be like with

him. What he felt like. What we could have been. There were so many conversations we never finished. So many we never even started.

I wanted to see him again, I wanted to see where he lived. I wanted to see what he did on his time off. I wanted more. I wanted those lips...

And yet, I belonged to someone else.

I must have fallen asleep late into the night or early morning, cause it came too soon. Our flight was that afternoon. Tory was still asleep when I got up and checked my phone again, still nothing from either of them.

There was a text from Dad, though.

DAD

Landed back in Zurich. Call me when you can. Love you.

He was always somewhere else, time zones away, well-meaning and distant in equal measure. It had been that way for years.

I washed my face and tried to look awake. I could hear Tory moving around.

"I'm starving. Let's get breakfast and go shopping," she said.

"I'm in for that," I said, even though a part of me wanted to slip over to Bradley's hotel and finish that kiss. Food and shopping might get me out of this funk.

We checked out of the hotel and left our bags with the doorman. The sun had returned in full force, making the city feel completely different from the night before. Everything looked brighter, cleaner, more real.

The doorman hailed us a cab, and we slid in as it pulled away from the curb, heading uptown.

"Is it okay if I ask how you're feeling today?" Tory asked, redoing her bun in the window reflection.

"I feel... conflicted," I said quietly. "Like a cheating asshole."

My voice softened. "And... alive."

She scooted closer and linked her fingers with mine. "You don't have to pick a lane or beat yourself up for feeling something."

I leaned my head onto her shoulder. "I left my ring on purpose. I knew what I was doing."

"It's okay. You're human." Her thumb brushed over my knuckles. "And honestly? I think anyone would be curious if a song was written about them."

I let out a laugh. "Are we doomed, though? Mom's three marriages, and Dad... well, he's Dad."

"We're not doomed," she said firmly. "They seem happy now. And maybe this is your chance to figure things out before you walk down the wrong aisle."

I squeezed her hand tighter.

"I hate to admit this, but it was one of the best nights of my life. Like walking into a dream I dreamt so many times, getting to live it, feel it... it was exhilarating," I said.

"You lit up last night. The same way you did on that island." Her voice softened. "It makes me believe in all the crystals, rabbit rabbits, and energy vibrations Mom talks about."

I laughed—really laughed this time. "Oh, Tory. You've always been the optimistic one. All five feet of you. The absolute best."

I nudged her. "Now talk about *your* love life. Enough about my problems. Any updates from Joel or Brett?"

Tory's smile tilted. "Joel knows Suzie. Says she's a total bitch at first, but great once you get past the wall. He also asked me out again. Tuesday night."

"And Brett?"

"He's funny. A friend."

"Fair. Joel is in the lead."

She nudged me. "I think you will like him. He is easy to talk to."

I smiled, and it warmed my heart to see Tory opening up to possibilities with someone new.

Next thing we knew, we were at our destination. I handed our driver some cash, and we stepped out and grabbed pastries and coffees from a small shop in Soho.

22

ONE MORE NIGHT

HEATHER

We walked down the street with our coffees; the city felt brighter than it should have for the way my stomach was twisting.

"Are you okay?" Tory asked gently. "You look... somewhere backstage."

I pulled in a breath. "I am going to call Tripp. Just to check in."

"A call to Tripp right before we go shopping? Is that really the best idea?"

I gave Tory a look, but she already had her compact open and was applying blush, not paying attention.

My thumb hovered over his name, and guilt started to creep back in. Fear.

Reluctantly, I pressed call.

It rang once, then went straight to voicemail.

Relief washed over me so fast it made my cheeks heat.

I wasn't ready to hear his voice. Not yet.

"Okay, now that's over with," Tory said, squeezing my hand. "Let's go have fun and get our minds off boys."

"That sounds perfect."

The neighborhood wrapped around us, a quiet side street lined with boutiques. Tory pointed at a storefront with pale blue trim.

"Here. *Marin & Co.* You'll like it."

I laughed. "You've never been here."

"I know your taste," she said, looping her arm through mine. "Better than you do."

The bell above the door chimed as we stepped inside. It smelled faintly of vanilla and fresh cotton. Racks of slip dresses and linen trousers glowed under soft lighting. A wall of handbags in muted tones ran like an ombré waterfall behind the counter.

The sales associate, tall, willowy, hair in a loose ponytail, smiled at us.

"Let me know if you need sizes."

Tory was already elbow-deep in a display of blouses. "Heather," she said, thrusting a dress at me, "you're trying this."

It was a navy silk midi with thin straps and a low back. Under normal circumstances, I would've chosen something far more practical. Today, practicality felt like a language I couldn't speak.

In the dressing room, the mirror was wide and slightly worn at the edges. I slipped the dress on slowly, smoothing the fabric along my hips. It fell beautifully, the kind of dress that made you stand taller without realizing it.

The girl in the reflection looked like someone I wanted to know.

Someone I wasn't sure I'd been in a long time.

My phone buzzed again.

I glanced at the screen. Tripp's name lit up. I swallowed hard and hit answer.

"Hi Tripp." *I hope my voice sounded normal.*

"Heather, how is New York?"

"It's good... great. We had a nice dinner last night." The lie slipped easily off my tongue. "Breakfast and shopping this morning."

"That's nice, glad you are having a good time."

"How are things? How is that case coming along?"

"It is taking up a lot of my time up here. I will be pretty swamped for a few weeks. Mother would love to set up some time with you next week to go over wedding details."

"Sure. I will call her when I get back."

"I am going to head out for lunch with Clint soon. Call me tonight when you get back. I can send my driver to get you from the airport if you would like?"

"That is so sweet. Tory and I will be fine in a cab. But thank you." *Guilt, guilt, guilt.*

"Don't forget about dinner Thursday, and wear something classy, maybe the pearls I got you for your birthday? Save your creative art pieces for a night out with your friends."

Creative art pieces... he meant one of my pieces.

Tory poked her head in between the curtain and gave me a look with her big doe eyes. I turned to pay attention to the call and closed the curtain on her.

"Be safe, Heather."

"Miss you." It felt like the right thing to say.

We hung up.

Everything felt different.

I stepped out of the dressing room.

Tory's eyes widened. "Oh my God. You look like trouble."

I snorted. "I don't know where I'd even wear this."

"Tonight?" she said, like it was obvious.

I blinked. "We fly out this afternoon."

"About that..." Tory tried to hide a smile, but failed. "Ben wants to grab dinner, and he's interested in coming to the concert tonight. Steph's hanging in with her sisters. So... "

She wiggled her brows. "What do you say? One more night? We can take the morning flight home. It'll be fine."

I looked back at the mirror.

At the woman in the navy dress who wasn't glowing at the thought of going home to her future husband, but was glowing at the memory of a boy on a beach who'd kept her drawing for fifteen years.

"Alright, one more night." I heard myself saying before my head could think straight. The thought of seeing Bradley for one more night made my heart pump faster.

Tory squealed softly. "Yes! I'll text Ben. You call the hotel. And your airline. And maybe... Bradley?"

My stomach flipped. "What! No, I can't call him, not with how I left things last night."

She could tell I didn't believe my own words. She just nodded, a quiet moment of sisterly understanding.

We paid, stepped back out onto the cobblestones, and the afternoon sun hit us in a warm rush. People walked by with iced coffees, shopping bags, and dogs tangled around their ankles.

The city moved around us, unaware that something inside me had shifted—the tiniest click of a clock turning, the smallest breath of possibility.

I wasn't sure what direction my life was pulling me toward now.

But it didn't feel like the one I'd planned.

And at this moment, that didn't terrify me.

It felt like... waking up.

23

IF FATE ALLOWS
BRADLEY

I had the morning to sleep in and wallow. Pale light crept through the edge of the curtains, and somewhere in the suite the faint clatter of dishes drifted in with the smell of butter and coffee. My phone said 10:42. My body felt like it had been wrung out and hung up to dry.

I dragged myself into the shower, let the water run too hot, then wandered back into the living area in a wrinkled tee and borrowed sweatpants.

The dining table looked like a catering mistake. Trays of pancakes, sausage, bacon, pastries, eggs, juices, coffees—enough food for a wedding brunch.

"Jared, I don't think you ordered enough," I said, reaching for the coffee.

He was already seated, hair wild, hoodie half zipped, demolishing a plate of eggs.

"You never know," he said around a bite.

The door opened with the soft click of a key card, and Suzie walked in, black blazer, tablet under one arm, sunglasses on her head like she'd slept in none of the same world we had.

"Oh, you're up," she said, already moving. "Soundcheck is at five. Car's coming at 4:30."

I leaned back in the chair, the caffeine finally starting to register, my brain lagging behind the morning.

"What about us, Pretty Little Ginger?" Jared asked, grinning like he lived for trouble.

Suzie stopped. Looked at him.

"What did I tell you about calling me that?"

"I forget... "

"Forget again, and you're off the groupie list."

Jared sat up straighter. "I am not a groupie."

"You follow Bradley around like one."

He puffed his chest. "I'm in real estate, sweetheart."

"How many houses have you sold?"

"Two," he said proudly. "That's not the point."

I watched them go at it, half awake, half smiling, the normalcy of it all doing something quiet and steadying to my nerves.

I'll show you one day, baby." Jared said with a half-wit smile.

"You know what? Ginger was better. And don't ever call me baby again. Bradley, a word?" she said, tilting her head toward my room.

I followed her down the short hall, the carpet soft under my feet, the low drone of traffic filtering in through the glass. My room smelled faintly like hotel soap and yesterday's cologne.

"What's up?" I asked, closing the door behind us.

She folded her arms, studying me in that way that meant she already knew the answer to whatever she was about to ask. "What happened last night? With this long-lost Heather?"

"It's not going to work out," I said, keeping my voice

even, though just hearing her name still sent something sharp through me.

Suzie's brow lifted. "If you really want her, fight for her."

"She's engaged."

The word sat between us, ugly and final.

Suzie exhaled through her nose. "You're telling me there were no feelings left? She just showed up as a friend and kissed you like a friend?"

My stomach tightened. "How did you know about that?"

She gave me a look. "Bradley. I know everything that goes on in this band."

"I don't want to cross any lines."

"Didn't you already?"

I ran a hand through my hair. "She wasn't wearing a ring."

Suzie's eyes sharpened. "Exactly. She didn't wear it for a reason. Don't be an idiot."

"I don't like messy," I said. "I'm not a homewrecker."

"They're not married. If you walk away now, you're going to regret it, and then I'll have to suffer through another album of sad songs."

I let out a breath, the corner of my mouth lifting despite myself. "You really should be nicer to Jared."

She pointed at me. "Shut it. Go take a walk. Clear your head. Maybe you'll run into her. But be back by 3:30."

I grabbed my sunglasses and a hat, not ready to deal with fans or my own reflection just yet.

Out in the living space, Jared looked up from his phone, one sock half on, hair still doing whatever it wanted.

"I just heard from my mom and dad," he said. "They told me to tell you, 'break a leg.'"

"Tell them I miss them," I said, and I meant it.

Suzie swept past us in the hall, already moving at full speed, blazer on, phone in hand.

"I'm out, boys. Three-thirty. No funny business."

"So four-thirty," Jared said with a grin.

"Jared," I warned, but I was smiling. "I'm going to take a walk," I told my cousins.

"Oh yeah? Where to?" Brett asked, trying very hard to sound like he didn't care.

"Just around."

He tilted his head. "Let's head to SoHo."

I frowned. "Why would we go there?"

"Maybe the right people," he said, eyes lighting up. "I know someone who might know someone you want to run into."

I shook my head. "You're ridiculous."

"Let's go. Jared, you in?" Brett called toward the bathroom.

"Nah," Jared said, already pacing with his phone. "I've got to make a work call. Client's got a leak and a showing tomorrow. I'll meet you guys later."

"See ya," Brett said, bending to tie his shoes.

"Alright. Peace."

We rode the elevator down in silence, the doors opening to the swirl of Columbus Circle. Taxis honked. Heat shimmered off the pavement.

"You sure you know where they are?" I asked once we were in the back of a cab, the vinyl seat radiating heat under my palms.

"Yep." Brett tapped his fingers against the cracked cushion, drumming some invisible beat. "They're shopping in SoHo. We'll cross paths. Totally natural."

I snorted. "Nothing says subtle like stalking my teenage crush through lower Manhattan."

He gave me a sideways look. "Look, if you're not going to reach out and you actually have a chance to see her again, you're stuck with me orchestrating fate."

"Orchestrating fate," I repeated. "Sounds super casual."

He grinned. "Trust me."

I leaned back, watching the city change block by block. Midtown's glass and noise softened into tighter blocks and low-rise buildings. The cab's meter clicked upward as we crawled past cyclists, vendors, tourists dragging shopping bags.

My pulse wouldn't settle.

"What's the plan here, Brett?" I finally asked. "Does Heather even know we're coming?"

"Nope," he said, popping the *p* like it was the most obvious thing in the world. "We're just grabbing coffee. If we run into her, great. If not, you get caffeine. Win-win."

I shook my head, staring out the window as the cab rolled through a yellow light. My pulse had already started doing its own thing.

The truth was, I didn't know what I'd do if I saw her again.

Or what I'd do if I didn't.

Brett leaned forward, peering through the windshield. "Here's good," he told the driver. "Prince and Mercer, please."

The cab nudged to the curb and rolled to a stop.

I paid before Brett could argue, pushing a couple of twenties through the divider slot. My palms felt warm—too warm. The kind of warm that meant adrenaline was doing laps in my bloodstream.

We stepped out onto the sidewalk.

Prince Street was amped with Sunday energy—café tables crowded with iced coffees and half-eaten pastries, dogs on their proud walks, the metallic click of someone unlocking a bike. Sunlight spilled across the cobblestones, sharp and bright.

I was about to ask Brett where he thought she might be when he nodded across the street. And there she was. A red sundress that hit mid-thigh, swaying as she moved. Freckles warmed by the light. Hair darker at the roots now, pulled back in a loose braid with a few strands falling around her face.

She looked like something I'd made up.

Except she was real. And getting closer.

We slowed, giving them space to cross.

Tory spotted us first. "Well, well," she said with a grin. "Funny running into you boys."

Heather stopped just shy of the curb. Her eyes found mine, held, and didn't look away. For a second, her breath caught, and I could see it in the way her chest lifted, the tiny hitch.

"Hi," I said, quieter than I intended.

"Hi," she murmured.

There was a beat—one long, suspended moment—before she added, "We're... staying another night."

That made something inside me jolt. "You are?"

She nodded once. "We are."

I took the words in and, without a beat, asked, "Do you want to come to the show tonight?"

Her lips parted, like she wasn't expecting the question—or maybe she was.

She didn't answer right away.

She didn't have to.

I felt it anyway—the pull, the possibility, the way everything between us seemed to pause. She glanced at Tory with a small smile, and without meaning to, I smiled too.

"Yes! We'd love to come," Tory jumped in.

And for the first time since last night, hope didn't feel like something I needed to protect myself from.

It felt real.

"Shoot, I need to run to CVS—nail polish remover," Tory said, holding up her fingers. "Heather, I'll meet you back at the room?"

"I need Band-Aids," Brett added, already peeling off with her.

Heather watched them go, then looked back at me, lips curved.

"They are the worst little liars."

"I have to admit, Brett told me we were going to 'run into you' on purpose."

"Oh, smooth," she said, smiling.

"That's what I said. How did we do?"

"Pretty obvious."

She shifted her weight on the curb, the sunlight catching in the loose strands of her hair, her fingers brushing the strap of her bag like she didn't quite know what to do with her hands. Watching her do that—the same small habits from years ago—made something tighten low in my chest.

"Can we talk?" I asked.

She glanced down first, then back up at me, her mouth pressing into a small, uncertain line.

"Sure. Look... I'm sorry I didn't wear my ring. Or tell you about my engagement."

I hate to admit that I was a little disheartened that she launched right into the engagement. But it needed to be addressed.

She had it on now, a massive rock that didn't seem like her. She struck me as someone who'd prefer something vintage, delicate, something with a story.

But maybe I didn't know her anymore.

We started walking, falling into the kind of casual small talk that fills the space when you're trying not to say the important things too soon.

"Did you sleep okay?"

"What did you do this morning?"

We found a tiny café for coffee, with a chalkboard menu and narrow tables tucked against the brick wall. We ordered two Americanos and split a chocolate chip cookie she'd been eyeing like it was calling her name.

We took a table outside. SoHo moved around us—footsteps, voices, the clink of cups—the sun catching across her shoulders and the line of her collarbone, pulling my attention to every place I shouldn't be looking.

I was halfway through telling her something Brett said that morning when I noticed a girl and two guys lingering near the edge of the patio, whispering, pretending not to stare. I tugged the brim of my hat lower.

I wanted the world to wait its turn.

I wanted this time with her.

But eventually they walked over.

"Bradley Hart?" the girl asked, already grinning.

"Guilty."

The guy in the Grateful Dead tee nodded hard. "We're huge fans. Been following the tour."

His friend in the Patagonia shirt added, "Great show last night."

"Thanks," I said.

The girl lifted her phone. "Could we get a picture?"

"Sure."

I stood, but before I could reach for the phone, Heather said, "I'll take it for you."

Her voice was soft and genuine.

"Thank you so much!" the girl squealed.

"Alright, get close," Heather said, lifting the phone. "Okay, one more."

I should've been looking at the camera. But my eyes stayed on Heather—on the small crease near her cheekbone when she smiled, on the way her braid caressed her shoulder as she steadied the phone. She made even this feel easy.

"This one looks great," she said, handing it back.

They thanked us and drifted away.

I sat again. "Sorry."

"For what?" she asked, lashes lowering, eyes soft. "For having people who adore you? You're too humble." She broke off another piece of the cookie and ate it slowly.

"So, Heather Brown... " I said, watching her tongue sweep a bit of chocolate off her lip—slow, unthinking, almost enough to make me lean across the table.

"Yes, Bradley Hart?" she teased.

"Why didn't you tell me you were engaged?"

Her smile slipped. "Bringing out the big guns. But fair."

I waited. She knew I wasn't letting it go.

"You already know why," she said quietly. Her eyes darkened, open in a way that made me want to reach for her. I had to form words, so I didn't brush her cheek.

"Who's the lucky bastard?"

"His name is Tripp Kensington. Chicago. Law firm."

"Tripp," I repeated. "That's... a name. He sounds fancy."

"Hey. Be nice."

"I'm kidding. Mostly. I just didn't picture you with a guy who dry-cleans his socks."

She laughed under her breath. "Oh yeah? And who did you picture me with?"

Me. God, me.

But instead, I just smiled at her—slow.

She caught it. Her breath stilled for half a second.

"You must have girls falling all over you," she said. "You've got that whole sexy rock-star thing."

Then she reached up and brushed a curl off my forehead, her fingers drifting down my cheek until her hand rested on my jaw. Her touch lingered. Too long. Long enough to undo something inside me.

Before I could think, I turned my head and kissed her hand.

Her breath hitched.

"I'm sorry," I murmured.

"I don't think you are," she said in a hush.

She was right.

"The only thing I'm sorry about is that we didn't find each other sooner."

She looked down, holding onto that like it hit her deep in her soul.

"I think," she said softly, "we have a lot of lost time."

"Then tell me everything," I said. "Everything I missed."

"I want to know things about you, too," she said, eyes brightening.

"I'll tell you anything."

My phone buzzed. Suzie.

I gave Heather an apologetic look before answering. "Hey, Suze."

"Okay, don't hate me," she said, already stressed. "We're trying to squeeze in some press this afternoon. Any chance you can come back a little earlier?"

"No can do," I said immediately, meeting Heather's eyes.

Suzie let out a breath. "Alright. I'll push it back. Just get here by 3:30. I'll make it work."

"You always do," I told her, then hung up.

Heather's phone buzzed too. "It's a text from Tory, coming up with more bogus reasons why they aren't back here. Those two think they're so stealth," she said with a hint of amusement in her face.

We finished our coffees, but more people were starting to look over. Time to move before the bubble pops.

"Want to walk?" I asked.

"Sure. Actually... would you want to stop by The Drawing Center?"

"I'd be down for that."

We walked side by side—closer than friends should. Our hands brushed once... twice... and I shoved mine into my pockets before I grabbed her hand and didn't let go.

"I can't wait for you to see this place," she said, already slipping into her art mode. "It's been here since the '70s. It's kind of iconic."

I watched her talk about line work, texture, and emotion.

Watched the way she came alive as she spoke.

And the truth settled in: I was falling for her. Again. Still. Maybe more than before.

All I could think was whether she'd left that ring behind because she was unhappy.

Whether maybe... just maybe... there was still something here.

24

FADED LINES
HEATHER

The Drawing Center looked small from the outside, just a clean white façade tucked along a quiet stretch off Wooster. But the moment we stepped in, the noise of SoHo dropped away.

Cool air.

Soft footsteps.

White walls and high ceilings.

A hush that felt like stepping underwater.

"I love it in here," I whispered.

Bradley nudged the door closed behind us. He smirked, flashing those green eyes that made my pulse trip a little faster.

We walked into the first gallery—minimalist strokes of black ink on large sheets of paper. Thin lines arcing, intersecting, pulling apart again.

"It's about tension," I said quietly, leaning in to read the placard.

Bradley stepped beside me, close enough that his shoulder brushed mine and sent a ripple up my neck. "Looks like attraction to me," he murmured.

That word hit low in my stomach.

I stepped forward to hide it, pretending to study the next piece—an architectural pencil drawing, precise and controlled. He followed, the air between us tightening with every step.

He leaned close, his breath skimming my ear. "You look all studious," he whispered. "Makes me think of when you used to draw on that trip. You always bit your pencil when you were concentrating. Drove me crazy."

Heat shot through me. I closed my eyes for a second, fighting the image of biting the curve of his neck instead. "I can't believe that's what you remember."

"I remember a lot more than that," he said, lips curving slightly.

I inhaled and slipped into the next gallery before my knees forgot how to work.

This room was longer, narrower, with freestanding white wall panels creating soft turns. We paused at a large charcoal portrait of a girl—messy hair, sharp eyes, a mouth built for secrets.

"She reminds me of someone," Bradley whispered.

My pulse dipped. "Who?"

He didn't answer. Just looked at me like the drawing had said something he couldn't.

I swallowed and stepped around the floating wall panel. The space behind it was quieter, tucked slightly out of sight. He followed carefully.

I stopped too abruptly, and he bumped gently into my back.

"Sorry," he said, steadying me with one hand on my waist.

His touch sank straight through me. Vibrant. Intoxicating. Too much.

I turned, planning to step away, but he moved at the same moment. Suddenly, we were face-to-face. Close enough to feel his breath graze my mouth.

Neither of us moved.

It was something dense enough to taste.

His hand stayed at my waist.

My fingers lifted on their own, brushing the side of his shirt, skimming up until they found his chain.

The same one he'd worn as a kid.

The one from his dad.

My fingers curled around it.

"Heather," he breathed in a slow whisper, like he was afraid of how my name sounded in his mouth.

I should've stepped back. I should've remembered the ring on my finger. I should've remembered Tripp.

But Bradley wasn't looking at me with simple want. It was yearning and memory and something softer underneath that scared me more than anything.

I looked at his lips.

He looked at mine.

We were a fraction apart.

He tipped his forehead toward mine—just barely—his nose brushing mine in the faintest, most reckless touch.

I felt him exhale.

I felt myself lean.

"Bradley," I murmured, touching his jaw.

His hand slid from my waist to the back of my hip, a slight tug, and he pulled me closer.

"We shouldn't," I sighed.

"I know," he said, but he didn't move.

Neither did I.

For one suspended second, we hovered on the edge of something that felt like falling—his lips close enough to warm mine without touching, close enough that one inch would erase every reason I had to stop.

I wanted him.

Desperately.

And he wanted me.

It was the same pull from that night in the ocean years ago—undeniable, dangerous, and somehow soothing all at once.

A soft cough echoed somewhere in the gallery.

We broke apart instantly. The spell snapped.

His hand dropped. I stepped back, pretending to examine a drawing I couldn't see through the blur in my eyes.

Bradley cleared his throat. "We should, uh... keep going."

"Yeah," I said, though it barely came out.

We walked into the next gallery with a careful few inches of space between us.

But my body still burned with the ghost of where he'd touched me.

And the ache of the kiss we almost had.

25

EXHIBIT ALMOST

BRADLEY

My dick didn't get the message that she was taken. My pulse was still hammering as if she'd actually kissed me—like I'd actually backed her against that wall panel and let every year of wanting her finally break loose. I could visualize whispering her name as she cried into my ear. *I'm fucked.*

She moved slightly away, but the heat didn't.

Christ, I could still feel her fingertips on my jaw. The ache. The almost.

One step. One more second. That was all it would've taken to ruin both of us in that gallery.

We walked the last few feet through the room, trying to pretend nothing had happened, but my body was still in that moment—pressed to her, leaning in, tasting the anticipation on her lips.

She paused in front of a crooked little ink drawing, black swirls and tangled lines. It looked like something a toddler would make with a Sharpie.

I needed the break. Something stupid. Something that was not her mouth.

"Well," I said, stepping beside her, "here it is. Finally. A piece of art I truly understand."

She blinked at me, then at the drawing.

A little giggle came out of her, her shoulders loosening.

"You're cute," she said, still smiling. "It's abstract."

"It's a big scribble," I said. "I could've drawn this hungover."

"You did draw like this hungover," she teased. "Remember your drawing of me?" She smiled with the corners of her eyes.

"That was the best stick figure known to man. Maybe they should give me a wall here."

She cracked up, shaking her head, and I swear I felt something in my chest unclench just watching her.

We stepped into the last alcove, a dimly lit space with a single light installation glowing against the wall. Just a warm amber rectangle, shifting like a sunset in slow motion. The light washed over her face, her collarbone, before spilling across her shoulders.

She stopped to look at the art on the wall.

I stopped to look at her.

That glow made it impossible not to stare at her—her silhouette softened, her skin lit like something I wasn't allowed to touch. It painted her in warmth and shadow and every inch of the tension that had followed us from room to room.

She was the most beautiful thing in this place. Untouchable and completely off limits. *Fuck, fuck, fuck.*

Almost, I thought. Almost had her. Almost lost my mind.

She turned and caught me staring. Her cheeks warmed, and she gave me the smallest, most reckless grin. *Fuck, fuck, fuck.*

"We have pretty much seen it all. Shall we head out?" she whispered.

"Okay, lead the way," I said, though part of me wanted to stay in that light forever.

We stepped onto the streets of SoHo, the noise swallowing us instantly: horns, voices, the rumble of traffic. But even with the chaos around us, the echo of that almost-kiss beat through me like a second heartbeat. I needed to do something with my hands so I didn't grab her waist and hold her close to me.

"You hungry?" I asked.

She nodded. "I could eat."

We grabbed slices from a corner pizza place, the kind with paper plates that fold under the cheese. She took a bite, eyes fluttering shut like the pizza was the best thing to ever happen to her.

"I forgot how good New York pizza is," she said, licking a bit of sauce from her bottom lip.

Everything from the museum slammed back into me. Every instinct I shouldn't have.

Every part of her I wanted to taste.

Don't stare at her mouth. Don't think about her pressed against you.

Don't think about the warmth of her this close to your lips.

Her phone started to buzz.

She glanced at the screen, and her whole face changed. Shoulders tensed. Smile dimmed. Her eyes flickered with something that looked like guilt.

She hesitated, thumb hovering over Decline.

Then it rang again. I could see his name on the screen, the fancy boy. *Lucky SOB.*

She looked at me, sorry written all over her face. "I should take this."

"Go," I said, even though everything in me hated it.

She stepped away, not far, but far enough for her voice to drop lower, softer, meant for someone else.

"Yes...

No, I'm just out...

I'll call you later...

Tripp, yes, tell your mother I will call her tomorrow. Please. Okay. Bye. You too."

She walked back over.

"Sorry about that." She looked flustered.

"No need, you okay?" I didn't like seeing her hurt and confused.

She hesitated, like she wasn't sure she should say it out loud.

"I don't know." She paused. "I just... I feel—"

Her cheeks flushed, and her eyes glossed with a shine she hated showing anyone.

"Hey," I said softly, stepping closer. "It's alright."

She shook her head, trying to blink it away, but the crack in her voice came anyway. "I didn't expect today to feel like this."

Without thinking—without giving myself time to reconsider, I pulled her into me. And she didn't tense, or freeze, or pretend she didn't need it.

She melted.

Her hands slid to my sides, her forehead resting against my chest, her chest rising and falling unevenly like she'd been holding everything in too long.

I closed my eyes, letting the moment settle into my bones. Holding her felt like a homecoming, too right, too much like everything I used to want and everything I wasn't supposed to want now.

Her heart was racing against mine.

Mine wasn't doing much better.

My phone buzzed in my back pocket. Once. Twice. Three times.

I didn't want to let her go. But responsibility had the worst timing. I pulled back just enough to grab my phone.

Suzie.

SUZIE

WHERE ARE YOU

Press waiting

MOVE NOW

I can't stall forever

Send your location. The driver is on his way.

I exhaled slowly. "I have to get back."

I sent the driver my location.

"My driver can take you back to your hotel."

"That's okay, Tory texted me she is on her way."

"You're sure?" I stepped closer, not ready to let go of this moment.

"I'm sure," she said gently. "Really." I didn't want to leave her.

I tossed our plates and wiped my hands before turning fully toward her.

"Heather."

She looked up, eyes still soft, still charged, still holding the echo of what almost happened in the museum.

"Please see me tonight after the show."

Her pulse stuttered, and her lips parted.

"I—" she started, then stopped.

A black SUV slowed toward the curb, my driver spotting me. Hazard lights blinked as he pulled in.

I stepped back before I grabbed her again like an idiot. "Just think about it."

She nodded with a little smile.

I walked backward a few steps, watching her watch me. The city swirled around her, but she was standing perfectly still, caught between two worlds.

I hopped in before I did something stupid, like run back and kiss her in the middle of SoHo.

I turned toward the window, watching her shrink in the side mirror—standing alone on Wooster Street, sunlight catching the edges of her hair.

I didn't look away until she disappeared behind a cluster of people crossing the sidewalk.

And the whole drive back, one thought wouldn't leave me:

If she walks through that door tonight... does that mean I have a chance?

26

LIKE A PRAYER
HEATHER

It was becoming painfully clear: I couldn't be around Bradley without wanting him.

It wasn't just the way he looked at me—like he already knew what I was thinking before I thought it. It was how my body responded, traitorous and electric, like no time had passed at all. Like the girl I used to be was still right there under my skin, waiting for him to pull in her direction.

I used to make quiet deals with God. Silly little bargains I never said out loud.

If he calls me, I'll give up chocolate for a month.

If I could run into him, I'll be nice to Ben for the rest of my life.

As the years went on, I convinced myself I'd made all of it up—what we had, what he meant, what I felt that it was just a vacation thing. A summer thing.

That he wasn't real.

But then he'd written a song, and here we were; all it took was a smile at me over SoHo traffic, and it was like the last fifteen years never happened.

Like none of it ever left us.

My phone buzzed.

TORY

Almost there. Stay put. I need those jeans.

I sent her my location and paced a little on Wooster Street, still trying to steady my breathing. The city buzzed around me—delivery bikes weaving by, people arguing over the last outdoor table, a mom on a stroll with her baby listening to a sound machine. My whole chest felt like it was still in that gallery with him.

Tory popped out of a cab half a block away, waving like she was in a parade. She hiked her purse up her shoulder and headed toward me with the kind of purpose she reserved for iced coffee and gossip.

"How was your afternoon?" she asked, eyes narrowing with practiced suspicion.

"I think we have a problem."

"Hmmm." She bumped her shoulder into mine. "How am I not surprised?"

"Let's go get these life-changing pants." It was easier than saying *I almost kissed Bradley Hart in a museum, and I think my heart is about to exit my body.*

"They really make my booty look good," Tory said. "I need them for my date with Joel."

"Joel? Officially, Joel?"

"We'll see. He might be the one. Or my barista might be the one. Or the doorman I talked to yesterday. Hard to say."

I huffed out a laugh. "How was Brett?"

"Oh, Brett is adorable. Sweet as hell. And absolutely not my type. Also—he's dating the cutest guy."

I blinked. "He is?"

"Yep. Only Bradley knew. Well... and now you." She

tossed her hair. "Honestly, I knew. He dresses better than me, and that's usually a giveaway."

I laughed again, tension easing just a bit. "I'm happy for him. And glad you two rekindled your friendship."

"Sure, sure," she said, waving that off. "Now, back to the real headline. Bradley Hart. Don't skimp on details."

My phone buzzed again. I was half hoping it was Bradley. It wasn't.

MOM

Steph is having back-to-back contractions. We're headed to the hospital to meet Ben.

My heart thudded. She wasn't due for two more months. This was too early.

Too fast.

"Tory." My voice cracked. "Mom just texted. Steph's in the hospital."

Tory's eyes widened. "Oh my gosh. Okay. We need to get there."

"We need a cab or something," I said, fumbling with my phone. "We have to head to the suburbs."

Another text lit my screen.

BRADLEY

I'm sorry I had to leave like that. Are you with Tory?

My throat tightened. I typed quickly.

HEATHER

Yes. With Tory. We have to head to the burbs. My sister-in-law is in labor, two months early.

Seconds later:

This wasn't the time for pride or politeness. This was an emergency.

His reply came instantly.

I stared at the screen for a second too long, heart twisting at the way he was coming to my rescue.

Within fifteen minutes, a sleek black SUV pulled up to the curb, the window rolling down.

"Hello, Heather," the driver said with a polite nod. "Bradley sent me."

"Hi," I breathed. "Thank you for coming."

Tory slid in beside me, already scrolling for updates from Mom.

I gave the driver the hospital information, and we pulled away from the curb—SoHo blurring behind us, the city folding into the distance as we headed toward whatever came next.

I tried to focus on my sister-in-law, the urgency, the things that actually mattered.

But the truth pressed against my ribs, steady and undeniable:

I hadn't even left Manhattan yet, and I was missing the

wrong man. *Get a hold of yourself.*

27

SWEET NIECE OF MINE
HEATHER

The hospital waiting room had that constant quiet that made everything feel suspended—bright lights, stiff chairs, a vending machine buzzing like it had been working overtime for years. Tory and I walked in and immediately spotted Mom near a row of seats.

Her short, damp hair was pulled into a tiny bun with loose pieces falling around her face. She kept brushing them back without noticing. The moment she saw us, she let out an exhale.

"Oh, girls." She came toward us quickly and wrapped her arms around both of us. "They just took her back. Ben said they needed to do the C-section right away."

My stomach tightened. "That means the baby is coming now?"

She nodded her head. "Yes, it is early. But I read the horoscope this morning, and today's supposed to be a strong day for new beginnings." She nodded, trying to anchor herself to the idea. "Keep your thoughts positive and clear."

My pulse did a little skip at the thought of mom's words.

Keith stood a little behind her, quiet and steady the way

he always was, especially when Mom's nerves were running high. He gave us a small nod.

We sat, though Mom never stayed seated long. She'd sit for a few seconds, then stand again, rubbing her hands along her arms or looking toward the hallway like she expected someone to appear at any second. She answered her phone when Steph's parents called; they were flying out tonight.

Tory leaned closer to her and squeezed her hand. "She's going to be okay; I just know and believe it."

Mom smiled and squeezed Tory back. In my mind, I kept repeating, *please keep Steph and the baby safe.*

The room settled back into its strange stillness. The kind where time felt both frozen and too fast at once. Every time someone walked through the hallway doors, our heads snapped up. Every time it wasn't Ben, our shoulders lowered again.

The doors finally opened, and this time it was Ben. His expression said everything before he even spoke.

We were on our feet instantly.

"She's here," he said, his voice cracking. "She's here, and she's okay. And Steph's okay too."

Mom let out a choked sound, covering her mouth as tears filled her eyes.

Ben took a shaky breath. "She came out breathing. They're taking her to the NICU since she's early, but they said she's strong."

I felt the air rush out of me. "What's her name?"

"Sofie," he said, a quiet, emotional smile forming. "With an F."

Tory wiped a tear from her cheek. "That's adorable," she said.

Ben nodded. "They said we can go in one at a time."

Mom went first.

Keith followed.

Then Tory.

When a nurse waved me in, I followed her through a dim hallway and into the NICU.

It was calmer than the rest of the hospital—soft lights, nurses speaking just above a whisper, machines humming in a steady rhythm. The nurse guided me toward one of the isolettes.

Sofie lay inside, tiny and tucked beneath a knitted hat, her breaths small but even. Wires curved gently around her arms and chest, monitors blinking beside her. She didn't look fragile. She looked focused. Like she was already doing exactly what she needed to do.

"She's beautiful," I whispered.

Ben nodded, blinking back tears. "I still can't believe she's here."

"You are going to be an amazing dad," I said quietly.

We stayed like that for a few seconds, just taking in the miracle sitting between us.

A nurse gave me a gentle nod, and I stepped back to let Ben spend time with his new daughter.

The hallway felt calmer than when we'd arrived, as if the whole building had let out the breath it was holding.

My phone buzzed.

BRADLEY

On set break. I can't stop thinking about you. Is everything okay?

I felt myself smile for the first time that day.

HEATHER

She's here. Sofie. Early but strong.

> **BRADLEY**
>
> Thank God.
>
> I think my next song is going to be for baby Sofie.

Now he is writing songs for my brand-new niece. *Could he be any cuter?* I had to stop thinking of him this way.

I should be calling Tripp to tell him the news.

Keith broke me out of my inner debate. "I'll drive you girls back to the city," he said gently.

We said goodbye to Mom, gave Ben a firm hug, and then Keith led us toward the sliding doors.

The drive through the city was soft and slow, headlights and street lamps streaking past the windows.

I sent Tripp a photo of Sofie with the caption "a little surprise came early".

As the skyline finally came into view, Keith broke the silence. "I'm glad you girls decided to stay. What perfect timing. That Sofie sure is sweet."

"I'm glad Tory convinced us to stay an extra day," I said softly. "It was meant to be."

"Gosh, she was so tiny. Little Sofie." Tory's voice drifted from the back seat. "Seeing Ben as a dad is pretty surreal."

When we pulled up to our hotel, Keith parked at the front and twisted in his seat to face us.

"Girls, we need to come visit soon. We miss you both."

He got out and hugged us tightly before slipping back into his car.

"It was great to see you and mom. Thank you for the ride," I said.

"Thanks for driving us. We were so lucky to be here for this big family moment," Tory added.

We waved as he pulled away, then headed inside. The

lobby was quiet, and the air smelled faintly of flowers and polish. We made our way to the elevator, both of us exhausted.

I checked my phone to see if Tripp texted back, but there were just a few photos from Mom of Sofie.

"She's taking this grandma role very seriously," I said with a smile.

"I'm sure she's already planning to fill that baby's room with stones and crystals," Tory teased.

We laughed as the elevator doors slid open.

"I'm beat," Tory said, yawning.

I wasn't tired. I was running on the day's events. I knew we had an early flight, but I didn't think I could sleep knowing Bradley would be only a few miles away. I had to see him. *One last time.* My heart was being reckless. I started to think about Mom and the horoscope. *Did that apply to everyone today? New beginnings? Was I thinking crazy?*

"I might go see Bradley," I said, softer than I intended.

"Heather," she said, giving me a look. "You should if your gut is telling you to. You don't have to sleep with him, but something is calling you to see him."

I was afraid I wanted to do more than just see him. I was instantly filled with guilt. It was twisting inside. Yet, I wanted to play with fire. *What is wrong with me?*

I started to organize my stuff so tomorrow would be an easy exit. I didn't change into my pjs yet, in the hope that Bradley would reach out.

Just as I was about to call it, my new favorite seven-letter word popped up.

BRADLEY

I just finished up here. We are heading back to the hotel. Can I see you again?

> HEATHER
>
> Yes, please.

The pull to him was getting stronger, and I let my heart win over my guilt. It was wrong. But I didn't want to spend another fifteen years wondering about the boy who made a song about me.

> BRADLEY
>
> Want me to come pick you up?

> HEATHER
>
> I can meet you at your hotel if that's easier.

> BRADLEY
>
> I will come get you. It is late, I don't want you wandering the streets alone.

> HEATHER
>
> I wouldn't be wandering, silly Bradley.

> BRADLEY
>
> I will see you soon, silly Heather.

I shook my head with a grin, guilt slipping away and excitement taking its place.

Tory was nearly asleep when I came out of the bathroom. I whispered where I would be so she wouldn't be worried if she woke up and I was gone.

I slipped out quietly, the hall echoing with my soft footsteps, the elevator ride down dragging like a lifetime. The lobby was nearly empty, just the doorman nodding politely.

Outside, the temperature felt perfect. The black, sleek Cadillac pulled up, and the window rolled down.

"Hey, pretty lady. Need a ride?"

Was this my "*Mr. Big and Carrie*" moment?

I didn't even hesitate. "Abso-fuckin-lutely."

I hopped in and slid into the seat beside Bradley, my pulse doing this ridiculous little skip.

"How are you?" he asked, his voice warm, sincere in a way that I didn't know I needed.

"I'm relieved everything's okay with Sofie and my sister-in-law," I said, then added in a hushed voice, "And... I'm glad you reached out."

"God, me too." And with that, he hooked a finger around mine.

The car ride was quiet after that, our fingers laced, the silence thick with all the things we weren't saying. The pull between us only grew stronger as the city lights blurred by. When the driver slowed to a stop, Bradley climbed out and came around to help me from the car, his hand warm around mine.

The lobby passed in a haze. We headed straight for the elevators, drawn to each other like gravity had shifted.

Inside, he pressed the button for his floor. The small space wrapped around us, heightening everything. His eyes gripped mine, and I couldn't look away.

"How was the show?" I asked, searching for a moment of normalcy, though my voice wavered.

"The show was good. The crowd went wild over a new song. 'Petals After Rain'."

"Petals After Rain," I repeated softly, the words tasting fragile on my tongue.

He nodded, still watching me.

"Yeah. They wanted more, so we ended with a cover— 'Loving Cup.' The whole place was vibrating." A slow smile touched his mouth. "And then I texted Suzie to get me to you as fast as possible."

I blinked. "You did?"

He stepped closer, our shoulders nearly brushing.

"I didn't want the night to end without seeing you again."

Heat crept up my neck. "I'm really glad you did," I said close to his ear.

He glanced at my mouth, and something low inside me tightened.

The elevator hummed upward, every floor clicking by like a countdown. I moved closer to him and touched his hand lightly; he turned face to face, and his lips grazed mine —light, deliberate—sending a spark straight through me.

The space between us dissolved. I hooked a finger through the belt loop of his jeans, tugging him the slightest bit closer. His hand slid to the back of my neck, warm and sure, drawing me into him.

Our lips met, and everything else fell away.

The kiss was fire—aching, reckless, the kind of release that felt years overdue. His mouth traced down my jaw, finding the spot beneath my ear that made my breath stutter. My body faltered before I could catch it, and I clutched at his shirt, steadying myself against the rush of heat tearing through me.

The elevator dinged. Neither of us reacted.

He grabbed my hand—urgent, almost desperate—and pulled me down the hall. He fumbled the key card once, muttered "fuck", then got the door open.

Inside, the room glowed with soft lamplight, shadows flickering across the walls. He turned to me slowly, like he was afraid one wrong move would snap whatever fragile restraint he had left.

"Heather," he murmured, brushing a strand of hair behind my ear, his fingers lingering on my cheekbone.

I rose onto my toes and kissed him again, unable to stop myself. This one was messier, fueled by days—years—of tension. My hands flattened against his chest, feeling the hard, steady thud of his heartbeat under my palms. His grip tightened on my hips, pulling me flush against him, and a sound slipped from me that I couldn't swallow back.

His mouth left mine only long enough to trail heat along my throat.

"God... " My voice fractured on the word.

"Heather." His voice was rough, strained, like the syllables were scraped out of him. He pressed his forehead to mine. "I want you so bad. I've wanted you since we were kids. But we shouldn't... "

My voice trembled. "I want this too. I don't know if I can... stop."

He let out a groan—sharp, pained—his thumb brushing my lower lip like he was memorizing it.

"We have to try," he said close to me, though the words sounded like punishment.

Every nerve in my body screamed at the space he put between us. My lips still throbbed from the kiss, my pulse racing, the ache settling low and insistent. I nodded because I had to, not because I wanted to.

He searched my face, his jaw tight, then the corner of his mouth lifted in a crooked way that only made it worse—gentler now, but still burning.

"We'll... figure out something to keep our minds off it."

The tension shifted, softer but no less potent, like a string pulled taut between us. A silent promise. A warning. A guarantee.

This wasn't over.

Not even close.

And the not-having was its own exquisite kind of torture.

28

LET'S PLAY TWO

BRADLEY

I was burning up. Every nerve lit with need. If I didn't pull back, I was going to tear Heather's clothes off and lose myself against the soft curve of her neck, down to her breasts. My head was clouded, drunk on her.

She was fighting it too. I could see it in her eyes, the way she tried to hold herself. She was someone's fiancée.

"Maybe we should play a game," Heather blurted, her voice tight.

"A game?" I asked, dazed.

"Like twenty questions," she said, shifting a little, as if distance could save us. "Something to distract us."

Heather started backing up, working hard to give us space, but the magnetic pull between us wouldn't loosen. I followed her, step for step, a wolfish prowl overtaking my train of thought.

I grinned. "Or maybe truth or dare. I dare you to show me—" She took another step back, and I followed.

Her smirk was quick and sharp. "We'd better stick with twenty questions." Another step, another followed.

We locked eyes again. She bit her lip, and my body

reacted before my brain could catch up. I pulled her toward me like a reflex I couldn't control.

Her hands framed my face. Her lips crashed against mine. Heat shot through me, my body aching for more.

"Shit," I muttered, pulling back before I lost it completely, groaning a little at the separation. "Let's get back to the game."

"Yes, the game," she whispered breathlessly. "You go first."

"What's your sexual fantasy?" I teased, grinning.

"Bradley... " she warned. "I think you already know." She bit down on her lip as she sat in the corner of the couch, eyeing the other corner, hoping I would sit.

"Do I? Spare no detail," I said, appeasing her and choosing the other corner but stretching my arm on the back in hopes my openness would draw her back in, at least just to touch her and keep me grounded for as long as I could have her.

She shook her head, eyes wide. "That wouldn't solve anything."

"Alright, alright," I chuckled. "Something easy. What's your favorite food?"

"Pancakes." Her grin was quick, playful.

"Ah, that's right, I knew that."

She paused, sitting up a little straighter as her gaze locked onto mine.

"How did you become famous?"

I wasn't expecting this question. "It wasn't overnight. I worked for my Uncle Gary for several years during the day, and I did gigs at bars, clubs, weddings—anywhere really." She looked at me intently, like she was catching every word.

"One night when we did a gig at a bar in Nashville, the right person happened to be sitting in the audience.

He came up to me after the show. Slid me his card. He was a producer." Her eyes continued to take my words in. "The next day, I put my two-week notice in, and things began to snowball over time. I guess right time, right place... fate."

Her lips curled, "I'm not surprised all this happened." Her tone shifted, soft and serious. "You have an unforgettable voice."

"I never doubted you either, Heather." The moment felt suspended between us.

Before it could settle too heavily, I lifted an eyebrow.

"Do you sleep naked?" I asked.

"Bradley! The answer is no, I love pajamas."

"I bet if you slept next to me, you wouldn't need them." I gave her another eyebrow and a smirk. "I would keep you warm and cozy."

"I'll keep this game on track. What's your favorite animal?" she asked with her hands folded.

"Sea lions," I said immediately. "They're basically the dogs of the ocean."

She laughed, light and sweet.

"Yours? I am going to assume it's in the cat family."

"How did you know?" she said, laughing.

"You couldn't stop talking about those cats in Punta Canta. Plus, you mentioned Mookie multiple times. Total cat person."

"I am. A thousand percent," she admitted. "I still think about all those stray cats," she said with a frown and her eyes big and glossy.

"I'm a dog guy. I've always wanted a golden retriever. I would already have one if Suzie didn't tell me I'd be an awful human for leaving a dog home while on tour."

Heather's smile faded a little. "I'd love a cat again someday," she whispered. "But Tripp... he's allergic." Her face grew serious.

"Well, son of a gun," I murmured.

We stared at each other, silence stretching. She crawled closer until she was right against me, so close it almost hurt.

"What's your biggest regret?" she asked.

"Losing your number. Not finding you sooner."

Her lips trembled, a tear slipped from her, "I guess writing a song to reach me was pretty clever."

I brushed her tears away, pulled her into my lap, and held her tight. I inhale her scent. Her hair smelled faintly of peaches, of her, of every memory that had haunted me since we were teens.

We held each other, and when our eyes met again, she asked softly, "Where do you see yourself in five years?"

I didn't hesitate. "With you and a dog named Gus, and a cat named Mookie Jr in the country."

Tears slid down her cheeks now, and my throat ached.

"What about you, Heather?" I said, wanting the answer to be with me and our fictional pets.

"I don't know anymore." She exhaled, frustrated but not breaking. "I convinced myself that kind of feeling only happens once. That I'd already had it."

The space between us tightened.

"But you're standing here, and it feels the same as it was." She shook her head slightly. "And I don't know what to do with that."

She dragged her hands down her face, then let them fall. For a second, I thought she was going to retreat again.

"I want those animals."

The air stilled.

"I want you, Bradley. I have always wanted you."

I kissed her lips. She kissed me back, urgently and

desperately. We collided again. I was hard and starving for her. My mouth moved down her neck to her collarbone, and she let out a soft whimper that nearly undid me.

"Fuck, I want you," I breathed.

"Me too," she said, breaking the kiss just long enough to meet my eyes. "Me too." Then she pulled back, pressing her forehead against mine. "But we have to get back to the game."

I groaned. "The game?"

"Whose turn is it?" she asked between kisses.

"Who the hell knows?" I muttered, kissing her again.

She curled against my chest. Her eyes fluttered close, her breath evening out. I held her, restless and hard as a rock, torn between heaven and hell.

We drifted in and out of sleep, curled together, kissing, pausing, starting again. By the time the sun crept up, a different kind of dawn was rising with it.

29

THE SONG WE NEVER FINISHED
HEATHER

I woke to the sound of fingers moving over guitar strings. Bradley sat on the edge of the couch, the guitar resting across his knee; morning light cut across his shoulders, highlighting the contours of his defined arms. His attention was focused on the strings, an unfinished melody taking shape beneath his hands.

I rolled onto my side, propping myself up on my elbow, taking in the way his brow furrowed in concentration. "Is this something new?"

"It's a song that was always there, but the lyrics are just forming."

I watched his hands glide over the strings, each movement settling into a melody that felt like it was meant just for us. "Remember that song you made up for me when we were young?"

His fingers never stopped, a nostalgic smile creeping onto his lips. "I remember it every damn day."

"That was the day you made me show you my sketches." I felt a rush of warmth at the memory, my heart fluttering at how far we'd come.

He glanced at me, his gaze warm, the corners of his mouth lifting slightly. "I always knew you'd have your own fashion line."

I let out a small laugh, feeling a blush creep up my cheeks. "I'm not there yet, but I am putting a lot of eggs into this opportunity with Bloomingdale's."

His mouth curved slowly, confidence radiating from him. "Every girl in Manhattan, Chicago, and L.A. is going to be wearing Heather B Designs."

My lungs tightened around the moment, a mix of excitement and fear. "This might sound silly, but you made me believe in myself back then," I said, my voice softening. "Even when I didn't."

He set the guitar aside and moved closer, our knees brushing together, sending a thrill through me. "You did that for me, too. I told you only one percent of musicians make it, and you looked me dead in the eye and said, 'You'll be that one percent.' I never forgot those words."

I looked at him, feeling the weight of unspoken truths. "When I lost your number," he said softly, his expression serious, "I was more determined than ever. Making it was the only way I could prove it—to myself... and to you. That I was who you said I was. That I'd find you."

The room went still, our breaths mingling in the space between us. I reached for his hand, and he laced his fingers through mine, his touch safe and reassuring. Then he leaned in and kissed me, a sweet, lingering connection that ignited a fire inside me.

My phone buzzed, pulling me back to reality. I glanced at the screen and winced—Tripp. I couldn't answer. Lying next to Bradley's, enveloped in his music and laughter, felt like both my lowest point and my peak. The contrast made me dizzy, *reckless.*

I checked the screen again—missed calls from Tory and Alena. A wave of anxiety washed over me. Then I saw the time, and my stomach dropped. "Oh shit. I missed my flight."

Bradley pushed himself up. "Oh no. Is there something I can do?"

"I don't think so... unless you can magically get me a flight home immediately."

His eyes widened, as if he actually could. I called Tory, bracing for her remarks. "Hey, I'm so sorry—"

"Don't worry, I bumped our flights to tonight," Tory interrupted. "I took the day off, so I'm good. Honestly, I had a feeling things would run late. It's raining in Chicago, so if you need to blame the delay on the weather, go for it."

Relief flooded through me, and I let out a sigh. "You're always one step ahead."

"I'm out shopping. Bags are with the doorman at the hotel if you need anything. Just let me know when you're up."

"Scratch that. You're three steps ahead."

"Accurate."

"Give me thirty minutes. We'll meet for breakfast?"

"Take your time, I am trying on so many gorgeous shoes." The thought of her in five-inch stilettos made me smile. I knew she was in her happy place.

"What time's our flight?"

"Six-forty tonight."

"Perfect. Love you, see you soon."

"You too. Say hi to Bradley for me." I shook my head as we hung up.

I called back Alena. She told me she'd moved my three o'clock to tomorrow afternoon and asked if I had measurements for another client. She said to enjoy my trip, that I never took time off.

"Thanks, Alena. You're a godsend." Skipping work was something I rarely did, yet here I was, wanting to stay in this bubble with Bradley for as long as possible.

"Everything okay?" Bradley asked, his fingers twisting into my hair, now a frizzy mess from sleep. His curls looked effortlessly tame in comparison, and I couldn't help but admire how relaxed he seemed.

"Yes. Tory saved me. She moved our flights again. Thank God for Southwest and no change fees."

He gave me those wide, green puppy-dog eyes that made my heart race. "So... does that mean I get to see you longer?"

I laughed, the warmth in my chest blooming. "I need a change of clothes and a toothbrush. And a hairbrush. My fro is out of control."

"I like your fro," he teased, that dimple flashing in his cheek.

"What do you use in your hair?" I asked, genuinely curious.

"Shampoo. And sometimes leave-in conditioner. You can borrow some. Take a shower here."

"I don't have anything to wear."

His grin widened, an infectious spark igniting between us. "How about this: I'll grab you some pancakes and clothes. You shower, and I'll be back shortly. Then we can take a walk."

"When's your flight?"

"I'm taking our tour bus. We'll leave later. I'm going to stay at my mom's for a couple of days. I've got shows in Cincinnati this weekend."

"That's sweet. You must be looking forward to it."

"Yeah. It'll be nice to have some time at home."

"Where after that?"

"Alpharetta for two nights. We end the tour in Chicago."

I bit my lip, torn between wanting to see him again and the weight of my fiancé.

"Maybe I can see you when I'm there?" His eyes looked hopeful.

"I'd like that," I said softly, my heart racing. "But... I need to figure out my life."

"The fiancé," he said quietly, his expression serious.

I nodded. "I'm going to be honest with him. I don't know what it means yet for my future."

"Heather... slow down. First, go shower. I'll help if you need," he said, giving me that wicked grin that made my heart flutter.

I swatted his chest, laughing.

"Okay," he said. "You do your thing. I'll be back shortly. What size clothes do you wear?"

"You don't have to buy me an outfit—"

"I want to," he said, grinning again. "Something you'll remember me by."

"Good thing, because I was going to forget about you. I wear size 26 pants and medium tops. Are you sure I can't give you my credit card?"

He shook his head. "I got this, Miss Brown. I'll also grab you a toothbrush. Anything else?"

"I think I'm good."

I texted Tory to ask her to come by the hotel when she was done shopping, then sent a quick message to Tripp.

HEATHER

Hey, my flight got delayed. Landing late tonight. I'll call you tonight. XO

TRIPP

> I am going to be working late. If I don't answer, I will call on my way to work. Safe travels. Two words. Seven letters.

I was going to be sick. I had to confess to Tripp.

Bradley leaned in before leaving. "Wait. One more thing." He brushed my messy curls aside and pressed a kiss to the hollow of my collarbone. Soft and deliberate. My knees went weak. Fire bloomed low in my belly. And then he was gone.

"Bye, beautiful," he called, as if he'd said it a hundred times.

In the shower, hot water spilling over my skin, I lingered on his shampoo and conditioner, memorizing their scent. Trying to memorize him. The truth was undeniable: the last three days with Bradley felt more alive than the last three years with Tripp.

By the time I stepped out, wrapped in a towel, Tory was nearly at the door. I heard the knock and let her in.

"Well, well," she said, eyebrows raised.

"He's grabbing clothes for me," I explained, my heart racing at the thought of him.

"I was just borrowing his shower."

"Obviously the night got away from you. Do share."

"We didn't sleep together, if that's what you're implying. But I wanted to. I'm the worst fiancée."

"Maybe it's just proof Tripp isn't the one."

"I'm going to tell him everything. I owe him that."

"If you want out, then yes, this is your exit."

I swallowed, feeling the weight of my choices. "When I'm with Bradley... it feels like the world melts away."

"Like you're living in a song?" Tory teased.

"Yes. Unreal, but so real at the same time. His life is chaos, city to city."

"Things to think about. Even so, Heather, I'm glad you found each other." One corner of her mouth lifted, but her eyes stayed serious.

"Me too. Thanks for the push."

"It wasn't me. It was the song that found you. I just booked the trip."

The door opened, and there he was—my rock star. Bags in hand: a shopping bag in one, food in the other.

"Those smell amazing," Tory said, reaching for the food.

He handed me the shopping bag. Inside was a perfectly soft, worn-in black AC/DC T-shirt, dark denim in my size, and—my cheeks burned—a lace bra and panties.

"Everything down to the underwear," he said with a shrug and a smirk.

"You dirty dog." Tory laughed.

I shot him a look, biting back a smile. "I'll be back. Don't eat all the pancakes."

After breakfast, we headed out for a walk. Tory created another excuse about checking out a few more shops. I was grateful for her trying to give us space; she was a true shopaholic, so I guess it was killing two birds with one stone.

Bradley and I walked close but didn't hold hands. Although his fingers swept mine several times, I held onto his pinky for just a moment. But with people around us, the guilt came on stronger.

"Can we talk?" he asked, his voice composed.

"Yeah, I guess we need to."

"This whole thing—us—it feels intense, doesn't it?" Bradley asked, his brow furrowing slightly as he searched my eyes for an answer.

"Intense and confusing," I admitted. "I didn't expect to feel this way, especially so soon."

"Maybe it's too soon for this conversation. But I have to know if what I'm feeling for you is real. Do you feel it too?" I could see the vulnerability in his gaze.

I did, with my whole heart, but I was engaged to another man. The weight of that truth pressed heavily on my chest.

I took a deep breath. "I've spent so long trying to do what's expected of me, following this path. But being here, with you... I feel alive. Like I can be this version of myself, like that girl back on the island."

"I feel that too," he said, leaning closer, his eyes searching mine again as if trying to uncover my deepest fears.

"But there's Tripp. There's a life I've built back in Chicago."

"I know. I don't want to wreck something for you if it honestly makes you happy."

"A part of me is really scared," I admitted, my voice trembling slightly. "This was just a weekend... just like Punta Cana. It could all go away. I was really hurt by you for a long time."

"I know, Heather. I should have tried harder. I really had no way of knowing what to do. The internet wasn't what it is today."

He turned toward me, guiding me off to the side of the path as we navigated through the crowd. His fingers brushed against my arm, and I felt anchored in his presence.

He moved his hands to my shoulders and looked me in the eye. "Maybe we needed those fifteen years to get where we wanted and to hold onto the words and the belief we gave one another."

"Maybe we did. But how do we know this will work?" I questioned, uncertainty hanging heavily between us.

The sun dipped lower, casting a warm glow around us, amplifying the urgency of our conversation. "What if we just... stripped everything down? What if we stopped worrying about following a path and just let it happen?"

"That sounds terrifying," I said without a beat.

He tucked a piece of my hair behind my ear. "But it could be exciting too. I want to know you—the real you, free of expectations."

He smiled, a glimmer of hope lighting up his eyes.

"I want that too. But it's not easy... It could get messy. Your life is chaotic, and that makes me nervous. At the same time, you make me want to fight for my dreams and live in this world with you."

"You are part of my dreams," he said with emotion. "If we found each other after all this time and we still feel that same thing we once felt, I'm certain we have a chance." The vulnerability in his eyes was disarming.

"I want to kiss you," I said, my voice barely above a whisper, filled with longing.

He didn't wait for permission and leaned down to meet me, capturing my lips in a kiss that was tender and smooth, igniting every nerve in my body. It screamed, *yes, Bradley*.

He reached for my hand again, fingers interlacing. "Whatever happens, I want you to know that I'm here for you. No matter how far apart we are."

Tears prickled at the back of my eyes. "You make me feel seen, Bradley. I don't know what the future holds, but I know I don't want to lose you."

"You need to go home and figure things out," he said softly, sincerity in his voice. "I will be waiting for you if you choose me."

As we stood there, just two souls connecting in a moment that felt both fleeting and infinite, I knew that whatever happened next would tilt my life off its axis.

30

IT'S THE LITTLE THINGS
HEATHER

The plane touched down just after nine, Chicago warm and buzzing beneath the windows, that sticky June kind of night where headlights shine against pavement, and everything smells like summer.

By the time we reached the apartment, I was dead on my feet. I kicked off my sneakers by the door, luggage abandoned exactly where it dropped. My body wanted sleep, but my mind was still somewhere between New York and him.

I texted Tripp first, because that's what engaged women do.

HEATHER

Home. Just walked in.

His reply came minutes later — fast, efficient, transactional.

TRIPP

Great. Dinner tomorrow at Gibsons? 7.

Guilt crawled under my skin. I typed back before I could stop myself. Relentless.

HEATHER

Sure. See you then, xo.

Just as I was going to toss my phone, it lit up again.

BRADLEY

I miss you.

Torture.

Seeing that only solidified what I'd been trying not to admit—this wasn't fantasy, or nostalgia, or some fever-dream. It was real. Too real.

I shouldn't have feelings for him. I should ignore him, be loyal, be *good*.

I should be home, in Chicago, leaving New York and everything that happened there behind.

My eyes drifted to the unopened bridal magazine on my nightstand.

To the ring on my finger—beautiful, heavy, not me.

I slid it off. Slowly.

My finger felt startlingly bare. Startlingly *right*.

And as if my heart controlled my hands instead of my head:

HEATHER

I miss you too.

The admission tasted like sin and relief all at once.

Then—like someone who'd trained for this, like someone I didn't want to be—I deleted the messages.

Even though I wanted to reread them a thousand times.

Sleep didn't come gently.

It fluttered in and out like a nervous heartbeat, and every time I drifted off, his face surfaced again—the way he said my name, the hush between our words, the almosts we didn't dare cross. I woke before sunrise, sheets twisted around my legs, mouth dry from wanting something I shouldn't.

My phone lay beneath the pillow like a secret.

I showered, pulled my hair into a loose knot, and tried to step back into my real life—or the life I was supposed to want. Chicago's air in June was warm, forgiving. Birds were loud. Taxis hissed over wet pavement. Everything looked normal enough to pretend I was too.

On the train ride to the studio, I stared out the window at office buildings and couples walking dogs, and I forced myself to do the responsible thing first.

I called Tripp.

It rang once.

Twice.

Then straight to voicemail.

His recorded voice—polished, composed, untouchable—filled my ear.

You've reached Tripp Kensington. Leave your name and—

I hung up before he could finish. No breath left for formalities.

A second later, his automated text buzzed through like a machine.

TRIPP

Can I call you later?

I typed a reply that felt equally hollow.

HEATHER

Okay. Talk later.

My thumb hovered—Should I say "I missed you"? Should I ask how he is? Should I force something real between us? But I let it go. Let the message send as is. Clean. Minimal. Safe.

By noon, my inbox owned me again. Sketches, client notes, fabric orders, fittings. It felt good—grounding, structured—like slipping into a life that had clear rules, unlike the one my heart was trying to rewrite.

But every time my phone buzzed, I hoped it was him.

Bradley.

Not my fiancé.

That thought alone made my stomach churn, but not enough to stop how badly I wanted to feel his presence again.

The day blurred, pencil between my fingers, muslin draped over the dress form like a question I was still answering. I spent hours sketching variations of one neckline—softer curve, deeper plunge, maybe a barely-there strap that only existed to tease the eye. My desk was a graveyard of rejected lines and half-ideas, but the work kept my hands busy when my mind refused to be.

Alena popped her head in near four, holding a stack of invoices.

"You want me to send these to accounting?"

"Yeah," I said without looking up. "And can you check if the pearl trim shipment arrived?"

"On it." She disappeared again, leaving behind citrus perfume and the very faint sense that the world outside my sketch pad still existed.

I kept working.

Slide, curve, shadow.

Erase. Redraw.

Pretend my pulse wasn't waiting for a vibration that hadn't come.

At some point, sunlight shifted across the studio wall—

golden, then dimmer, then thinning into early evening without my permission. When I finally looked at the clock, it was 6:32.

I still had one pattern to finalize before I could shut down, but my phone lit beside me, screen bright in the quiet.

A photo filled my screen—black cover, white serif font, unmistakable.

COCO CHANEL: AN ILLUSTRATED BIOGRAPHY

BRADLEY

Saw this at my mom's bookstore. Thought you might like it.

I was smiling until I felt the bite of graphite against my lip—pencil caught between my teeth like some teenage tell.
He saw something and thought of me.
Simple. Devastating.

HEATHER

Aren't you thoughtful? I love it.

BRADLEY

I hear she is some fashion icon.

HEATHER

You heard right. She is THE icon.

BRADLEY

Call me when you can.

I wanted to call him right then and there. To hear his voice.

HEATHER

I will.

I didn't delete the messages this time.

I let them sit there—glowing on my screen like something living, breathing, dangerous.

I set my phone down and bit the eraser end of my pencil without realizing, a stupid smile tugging at my lips. Then I forced myself back to work—seams, necklines, stitch lines— but everything blurred. I couldn't drown out the memory of his voice or the way he said my name. Couldn't drown out the picture of that book, his hands holding it. Me, in his thoughts.

After another glance at the clock, I exhaled sharply.

6:42 p.m.

If I didn't leave now, I'd be late.

Garments could wait.

Bradley definitely needed to wait.

But Tripp could not.

Gibsons was crowded and loud, full of steak, smoke, and laughter that felt like it belonged to someone else's life.

Tripp was already seated—phone in hand, thumb tapping like he might bill the minutes.

He stood when he saw me and brushed a kiss against my cheek, polite, practiced.

Dinner moved like a meeting agenda.

Partners. Billable hours. The case he dominated last week.

Market shifts. Martini preference debates.

Not one question about my sketches.

Or my workload.

Or me. Unless it was wedding related.

Maybe I was looking for flaws, waiting for the universe to hand me a sign.

Or maybe the absence of curiosity was the sign.

I ate my steak quietly, nodding when appropriate, feeling like a spectator in my own relationship.

When the check came, he pressed another kiss to my cheek—dry, clean, nothing like the ones I couldn't forget.

Two fingers raised to the waiter. Final. Finished.

We stood, walked out together.

Outside, under the awning, the Chicago evening, streetlights smearing warm bronze across pavement like paint.

His car pulled up, and he turned to me, "Do you want a ride home?"

"It's the opposite direction, but thank you."

We kissed goodbye, brief and neat, like we were closing a file.

He smiled. I smiled back.

And yet—all I could see were green eyes under stage lights.

A voice whispering, *call me when you can.*

A Chanel book chosen just for me.

I was meant to marry Tripp.

Wasn't I?

We had the blueprint.

Safety. Status. A plan.

So why did it all feel like fabric cut on the wrong grain?

As I watched the taillights fade, something inside me tugged in the opposite direction—toward Ohio, toward music, toward wildfire.

Toward Bradley.

31

INHERITED SILENCE
BRADLEY

Mom wouldn't let me pay for the Coco Chanel book, even though I tried twice at the counter. She just eyed me over her glasses, lips pursed like she was chewing on a question.

A book like this, she wanted to ask, *and for whom?*

But she only smiled, tucked it into a brown paper bag, and said, "You can pay by taking your mother to dinner."

Fair trade.

We closed up the shop together, lights dimming in rows, her keys jingling in that same rhythm I grew up hearing. I'd only be in town a couple of days—long enough to breathe, to reset, to remember who I was outside spotlights and hotel rooms. And long enough to sit across from the person who raised me into something better than the man before me.

Dinner was simple. Pasta, wine, the comfort of routine.

"How's the store?" I asked.

She shrugged, like always. "It's getting by."

I knew the truth. She never cashed the checks I mailed, so I paid the landlord directly and told him to lower the official rent so she wouldn't notice. She thought the universe was cutting her a break; I let her believe it.

Her fork paused mid-air.

"I really want to know why you're buying fashion books."

My lips curled. "Thought I'd explore haute couture. A man can evolve."

"Bradley Hart," she said, not fooled for a second. "No one suddenly takes an interest in fashion without a woman involved. Please tell me there's someone."

I stared into my wine. "A friend. She came to the New York show. It's... complicated."

She didn't press; that was her talent, really. She only nodded, eyes soft.

"As long as you're happy. My sweet boy."

She'd been calling me that since I was five, and every time it landed somewhere inside me, I wasn't sure I'd earned it.

"I think you're biased," I joked.

"Maybe. But I'm proud. You turned out wonderful."

A laugh scraped out of me. "Why? Because Dad didn't?"

Her smile thinned.

"I don't like the man, but even he had charm. He disappointed us, yes. But don't live your life afraid you'll become him. You are not him."

She said it so firmly that I almost believed it.

Later, after we returned home and she fell asleep halfway through *Back to the Future*, I pulled a blanket over her and slipped into the garage. Dad's things still lived there, dust-coated but patient.

A bin of cassettes. Old guitar strings. A photo album.

I shouldn't have opened it, but I did.

There we were, him holding me on the couch, tiny fingers wrapped around the neck of a guitar twice my size. Me smiling like he was the whole world. Him smiling like maybe, for a second, he belonged in it.

I sat on the cold cement floor, album open across my knees.

Mom raised us alone. She built a life out of scraps she didn't ask for. She loved soft, and it cost her. Heather had that softness too—the kind people take advantage of. The kind I was afraid I'd break if it was ever mine to hold.

He never got famous. That was the tragedy. He had the kind of voice that made people lean forward, like he was singing directly into their ribs. Behind a guitar, he was electric. But once the strings were silent, the best of him went with them.

I heard stories that after shows, women would hover. And he let them. Not because he was in love with them, but because he was in love with being wanted.

Drugs came after. Or maybe before. It blurred. What I remembered was my mom pretending not to notice the lipstick on his shirt that wasn't hers. The way he'd promise he was done and mean it for about a week.

I used to think staying away was the safest thing I could do for someone like Heather.

But I didn't want to stay away.

I was walking straight toward her. But now I'd found her too late.

I closed the album gently and returned it to the bin, as if putting it back could keep history from repeating.

I turned off the garage light and stood in the doorway,

the house behind me glowing warm with my mother's touch: love, lived-in, and earned the hard way.

I would never be him. I just didn't know yet if I deserved to be better.

32

THE CHAIN
HEATHER

The morning light pressed gray against the blinds, but my phone was brighter, buzzing with notifications before I'd even sat up. Emails crowded my inbox: deadlines, fabric shipments, and fittings. Each one stamped urgent like the world would collapse without me. I scrolled for a moment, then flicked over to Nico's texts.

HEATHER

> Sorry for missing all your texts. It's been a crazy week catching up with work. I'm definitely in for tomorrow.

The dots appeared almost instantly.

NICO

> Just glad you're okay. But don't think you're getting off that easy. I want to hear all about this little love reunion with the rocker boy.

I groaned, pressing the phone to my forehead. Of course, Tory must've told him.

HEATHER

You two are impossible. And nosy.

NICO

Always. Now come by the salon tomorrow
before we go out. Blowouts on me.

HEATHER

You don't have to do that.

NICO

I know. But you'll thank me when heads
turn. Don't be late.

Despite everything—the heaviness from the week, the emails already clawing at me—a smile slipped across my lips. My chest loosened in that familiar way it always did when Nico reminded me I wasn't alone in this city. Nico had always been my tether. No matter how messy I got, he reminded me who I was. Who I had been before men complicated everything.

By nine, the atelier was already a hive of motion. Dani, my seamstress extraordinaire, rattled off a list of hems and alterations while I tried to balance a phone call with a supplier, a courier drop, and the espresso that was rapidly cooling on my desk. Fabric bolts leaned like drunken soldiers against the wall; sketches fanned across the table, half-finished, each one demanding more of me. The air smelled like starch, steam, and ambition. My reflection in the mirror behind my desk looked tired—hair in a loose knot, smudged liner, eyes that hadn't slept enough—but present.

People thought fashion design was runway lights and inspiration. The truth was blood under fingernails, endless revisions, and clients who changed their minds faster than I could thread a needle.

But it was mine. And I wasn't letting go.

Around noon, a subject line stopped me cold.

Bloomingdale's – Follow Up Request

I opened it fast, breath caught in my throat.

We'd love to set a follow-up meeting for next Wednesday at 4 pm.

For a long beat, I just stared. *Bloomingdale's.*

I imagined my designs stepping past these walls into glossy windows and beneath fluorescent lights, strangers brushing hands across fabric I'd once sketched at midnight. I pictured my father, walking past a display, pausing, pride softening his face as he said, *My daughter made that.* I thought about telling Bradley—the way his eyes would light up, the way he looked at me like every dream I had was already real.

I typed back with shaking hands, thanking them for the opportunity, and of course, it was a big fat *Yes.*

When the reply whooshed into cyberspace, I leaned back, grinning at the ceiling. For the first time in weeks, hope rushed through me like champagne bubbles.

But as the afternoon dragged, the shimmer dulled, replaced with the murmur of dread. Another dinner with Tripp and his clients waited.

I thought back to when we first met. How he'd opened doors with that quiet, measured charm, how his confidence had felt like shelter after years of drifting. He was always polished, always in control, ordering wine without glancing at the list, pulling out my chair with perfect timing. I admired that certainty in him. Maybe even mistook it for love. Yes, he admired himself.

Back then, I needed someone to anchor me. Something

that looked like security. I wanted to feel chosen, wanted, worth showing off. And Tripp, in his seamless, put-together way, made me believe I was. He knew how to make life look tidy. Manageable. Like nothing could fall apart if we followed the rules and kept everything shiny.

Yes, he liked people admiring him. But I told myself it was part of the package. He was settled, dependable, and poised.

For a while, it worked. The chemistry was fine. The sex was good enough. I convinced myself this was love. Clean. Predictable. The kind you could frame and hang.

Until Bradley.

Bradley had turned everything upside down. With him, there were no tidy lines. I wasn't composed. I was undone. He didn't make me fit into a picture; he made me forget pictures existed. For the first time in years, I felt roused.

And now, as the afternoon ticked toward evening, I couldn't escape the truth. *I had settled.*

My phone buzzed. A photo filled the screen: Bradley's guitar, propped casually against a chair, sunlight sliding across the wood.

BRADLEY

Can't stop writing. You did this.

The air thinned. I pressed the phone to my chest, my pulse drumming against it. One photo, one line, and he was here again, a few states away, collapsing into the space between heartbeats.

I didn't reply. Couldn't. But I carried it with me, woven under my skin, humming like a song I couldn't forget. The guilt was following step by step.

By seven, I was stepping out of the Uber on a quiet, manicured stretch of Astor Street where ivy climbed the façades of old brownstones like they'd been rooted for centuries. Tripp's partner's place was the kind of address whispered with certain reverence, the sort that made you stand a little straighter when you rang the bell.

I wore the dress Tripp suggested: a fitted black sheath, modest neckline, nothing to seek attention. "Classic always plays well," he'd say. I wondered if he meant that if I wore this, then I was playing well. I studied myself in the window's reflection—dark hair smooth, lipstick perfect, everything composed on the outside while I felt split open underneath.

Amber light spilled from the tall windows, catching the gold hardware of the door as it opened before I even knocked. Inside, everything smelled of polished wood and expensive scotch. Voices floated from the parlor, low, confident males. And a few women who stood by their husbands, nodding along.

I found Tripp standing near a marble fireplace, posture perfect, a tumbler in hand. He caught my eye, gave the subtle approving nod I'd once lived for. "Heather." He moved smoothly as I approached, brushing my cheek with a kiss that landed like air. He had a drink set aside for me. He handed it over. "Thanks," I said. I took a sip. And the night continued, with my place beside Tripp as expected.

Dinner moved like an agenda. He spoke about the firm, about numbers and wins, about someone's promotion three seats down the table. He praised himself without sounding like he was—that was his skillset, elevating himself while convincing the room they were lucky to be invited to listen. I nodded at the right moments. Smiled when expected. Played my part. All the while, Bradley's guitar photo burned in my pocket.

The night ended the same way it always did: with polite

handshakes and promises to "circle back," the language of men who lived in boardrooms.

Outside, Tripp's black town car was waiting. Tripp opened the door for me, chivalry as performance, and asked, "Do you want to spend the night?"

"I have to work early, but I'll ride back to your place with you." It was out of the way and inconvenient, but I had to get the truth out.

The car pulled away from the curb, the city's lights smearing like watercolor across the window. My heartbeat thudded against the quiet, the words I'd held in all week.

Tripp loosened his tie, checked his watch. I watched the city slide past the window and felt the words rise.

"Tripp," I said softly.

He didn't look up from his phone. "Mm?"

I swallowed. My hands were cold; I tucked them beneath my thighs to stop them from shaking.

"There's something I have to tell you."

That got his attention. His phone lowered a fraction.

"I kissed someone," I said, before I lost my nerve. "In New York."

I expected stillness. Anger. Betrayal. Something real.

Instead, Tripp's head tilted back, and he let out a low laugh, sharp, amused, almost appreciative. He shook his head like I'd just told him a joke.

"Didn't think you had it in you, Heather."

His tone made my stomach drop. I stared at him, waiting for the real reaction, the delayed explosion. But his lips were curled with something cold behind them. Something amused and calculated.

"I... I thought you would be upset."

"Upset?" He laughed again. "If you think I haven't messed around myself, you are adorable. Or naïve."

The world seemed to tilt, the city a blur. You would think we were discussing travel logistics, not infidelity.

"This relationship is actually shaping up better than I expected," he said, adjusting his cuff. "We have the genetics for smart kids. You have a career that we can use as a tax write-off. You just go in when you need to."

My breath turned to ice. I felt like I was in a nightmare I couldn't wake up from. He wasn't reacting to a confession; he was negotiating terms.

"As long as you are discreet," he continued. "We can be adults about this. Don't get sloppy with it. No drama. A respectable marriage needs structure."

He paused, like he'd just solved something strategically brilliant.

"This could work for us, Heather."

Work. Like a contract. Like an investment he expected a return on.

My pulse hammered, disbelief turning into thick chalk in my mouth.

"That's what you think love is?" I whispered.

We pulled up to his place. He leaned over and kissed my cheeks. "I will see you Saturday for dinner. It's in the shared calendar."

Suddenly, I saw it all so clear now. Love wasn't the currency. Appearance was. And kissing someone else wasn't the fracture in our relationship, but the escape route.

33

RED IS NOT FOR APOLOGY

HEATHER

After I wrapped up work on Friday, I headed straight to Nico's chair at Salon Buzz. I hadn't spoken to Tripp all day, no text, no follow-up.

The second I told him everything—the car ride, Tripp's laugh, the way he talked about marriage like it was an investment portfolio—Nico froze mid-curl, staring at me in the mirror like I'd just confessed to murder.

"What. A. Little. Prick," he said slowly, eyebrows climbing like elevators.

A humorless breath left me. "Yep."

He spun my chair toward him, cape still around me like a shield.

"So, what are you going to do?"

The question was heavy, and I wasn't sure if I could answer out loud just yet. I knew Nico understood me better than I understood myself.

"I am going to get drunk with you and Tory tonight."

"That's my girl." He grinned, satisfied.

🎵

Dinner at Girl & The Goat was loud and energetic—cocktails too smooth, tiny plates disappearing too fast.

By midnight, we landed at The Hangge Uppe, pulsing floor, sticky lights, sweaty strangers. I moved like I'd been underwater for years and finally surfaced. Hips loose. Hair wild. No ring on my finger.

"Yes, Heather!" Nico shouted above the bass.

"Drop it like it's hot!" Tory screamed back, spinning me by the wrist.

We danced until the music melted into our bones, until I felt like a badass. I was gaining control of my life and the direction it was heading. It was a time to be alive.

Until movement stopped feeling performative and started feeling instinctive.

Hours later, Tory and I stumbled up the apartment steps, heels in hand, night buzzing through us.

And then, louder than I meant to, maybe louder than the city ever wanted:

"FUCK TRIPP KENSINGTON!"

Tory doubled over laughing, shushing me through hiccuped giggles.

I woke the next morning with a dull headache and the awareness that dinner was coming whether I wanted it or not.

Tory and I spent the afternoon stretched across the couch, cartons of takeout stacked on the coffee table, a movie playing that neither of us followed. When it was time to move, my body resisted, heavy with the sense of stepping back into something already decided.

When I stood in front of my closet, something was different. I wasn't muted. I wasn't small.

I chose red.

Red lips. Red dress. Hoop earrings he once called *trashy*.

Perfect breakup armor.

Shaw's glimmered with polished silver and careful lighting. Tripp stood as I approached, eyes skating down my neckline, like I'd violated a silent dress code.

"You're late," he said.

"I know."

No apology.

He kissed my cheek—polite, precise, hollow—and sat.

"We should order the fish special. I was thinking fish for the wedding, you know? Light, elegant—"

"Tripp," I said, voice steady, "there will be no fish at my wedding. I'm not going to marry you."

His laugh cut through me. "You're joking. You kiss someone else, I stay calm, and *you* break things off? Over a little lapse in judgement?" He leaned back, one arm draped along the banquette, posture relaxed. His gaze moved over me slowly, assessing.

"It isn't about the kiss," I said. "It's about what it showed me."

He tilted his head slightly. "You're reacting. That happens. Feelings spike. It doesn't mean you dismantle a life that works."

I gestured lightly between us—the table, the room, the quiet confidence of everything already arranged.

"This life was never built with me."

"You're really willing to give this up? The best opportunity of your life?"

He leaned back, incredulous. "You'd rather have *ordinary*?"

"Tripp." My voice didn't waver. "I'm not a business deal. I'm a woman who wants love, not side interests with other people."

He looked at me for a beat.

"Love isn't a strategy," he said. "It's what you build *after* everything else is in place."

"You don't include me in the planning. We never even talked about an engagement," I said. "You surprised me in front of all *your* friends and family."

His jaw tightened. "We were on the same page."

"You didn't ask," I said. "You didn't make sure my family could be there, other than my sister and best friend. You didn't even ask my parents or brother."

"Sure I did, and they weren't available on such short notice," he said, taking a sip of his drink and adjusting his pinky ring.

"You are missing the point. It's not just that incident. You started planning a wedding with your mother before I'd even seen a venue."

He straightened, smoothing his cuff. "I was handling things."

"You liked that I didn't push back," I said. "You liked that I went along with it. Just like how you thought I would give up the career I love once we had children."

"That's not control," he said. "That's efficiency."

"It's deciding my life without me."

He leaned forward now, voice lower. "You wanted steadiness. You wanted someone who could take the lead. I didn't change. You did."

The words landed cleanly. Precisely.

And something settled.

"You're right," I said. "I did change."

I met his eyes. He held the contact, waiting for the turn back toward him.

"I learned what it feels like to be asked instead of assigned," I said. "To be heard instead of managed. To matter in the room."

His mouth pressed into a thin line. "That doesn't last."

"Maybe not," I said. "But I won't talk myself out of wanting it."

He leaned back again, retreating into certainty. "You're trading stability for a feeling."

I picked up my glass and drained it.

"I hoped this could end kindly," I said, reaching for my finger and pulling the ring off and placing it on the table. It landed with a soft, unmistakable sound. "But we stopped having the same conversation a long time ago."

I stood.

He said my name once, clipped and controlled.

I didn't turn around.

I walked until the restaurant fell behind me, until the Red Line entrance came into view, my dress flashing beneath the streetlights as the city moved around me.

The night felt open.

I took myself home.

And I smiled the whole way.

34

THE SOUND OF HIS VOICE

HEATHER

By the time I reached my apartment, exhaustion pressed into my bones. I climbed the stairs, key biting into my palm, and stepped inside.

Tory was curled on the couch under a blanket, *Dirty Dancing* flickering on the TV.

"Hey," I said softly.

She muted the screen and turned. "You're back early. How did it go?"

I lifted my left hand—bare, where the ring had been.

Her eyes widened. "Wow. Just like that?"

"Just like that."

The words sounded clean. Honest.

"How do you feel?"

I leaned my shoulder against the wall, letting the cool paint steady me. The question waited, patient.

"Relieved," I said. "Free. Like a fool."

"You are not a fool." She patted the couch beside her. "Come, sit."

"I need to change. Be right in."

In the bathroom, I wiped the makeup from my face.

Mascara shadowed beneath my eyes, lipstick already fading. Evidence of a night that had mattered. The woman staring back at me looked unfamiliar in a way that felt earned—less polished, more honest. I'd stepped out of a life that had been quietly decided without me, and the truth of that stayed.

I pulled on pajamas, grabbed cold Chinese takeout from the fridge, and joined Tory on the couch. We ate straight from the cartons, knees pulled up, the TV more of a background than a distraction.

Tory glanced at me, then smirked. "So," she said, "are you going to at least give me the CliffsNotes?"

I shook my head once, a tired laugh slipping out.

"The short version?" I said. "He kept trying to tell me what to think about my own decision. Like I couldn't be trusted to break up with him without guidance."

Tory's mouth tightened. "Typical Tripp. Trying to lawyer you."

"Always," I said. "He and his mother—calculating every move I made, making sure it fit inside their box." I stared down at the carton in my lap. "Every time I stepped out of line, there was a consequence. Subtle. Strategic. Enough to remind me where the boundaries were."

Tory exhaled slowly. "You were walking on a leash."

"I didn't realize how tight it was," I said. "Not until I stopped agreeing."

She studied me for a beat. "Did you bring up Bradley?"

"No." I shook my head. "I didn't leave Tripp for Bradley. I left Tripp for me."

I paused, choosing the truth carefully.

"But Bradley's existence... it pushed something awake. A direction I hadn't seen with another man since I was a teen living off that week of lust."

Tory's expression softened. "That matters."

"It does," I said. "Not because it promises anything. But because it showed me what was possible when I was allowed to take up space."

She leaned back against the couch. "That's clarity."

I let that settle. It fit.

"Thanks for being here and helping me step in the right direction."

"Always." She leaned her head on my shoulder.

Later, in bed, I picked up my phone. My fingers hovered over Bradley's name for a moment before typing. The tension drained from my body, like something that had been holding me in place finally let go. I was free to text him without guilt.

HEATHER

Hi there. How did tonight go?

I lay awake waiting. Within minutes, my phone buzzed.

BRADLEY

Hey. It went great. The crowd is loving the new songs inspired by you. I'm wrapping up here. Any chance I can call you shortly?

A smile spread across my face.

HEATHER

Yes. Please.

I felt sixteen again, waiting for a call I'd only ever dreamed about.

When the phone finally rang, it was close to one a.m., but I didn't care.

"Hi," I said.

"Hey," he said, his voice low and warm. "God, it's so good to hear your voice."

"Yours too."

"I take it was a good show?" I asked.

"A great one. How was your night?"

I laughed softly. "Tory and I watched *Dirty Dancing.* Clearly... a great one too."

"That does sound nice."

I smiled, surprised by how easily it came.

"I saw a shooting star earlier," he said. "Made a wish."

"Cheesy," I teased. "What did you wish for?"

"That we could keep playing our game of twenty questions."

I laughed, curling deeper beneath the sheets. "It's late, but I think I'm up for one or two—if I can go first."

"Deal."

"What's your favorite movie?"

He groaned. "That's cruel. Tie between *Pulp Fiction* and *The Godfather.* You?"

"*Mrs. Doubtfire.*"

He laughed. "Could you be any cuter?"

Happiness exploded deep inside.

"Okay, your turn," I said.

"If you could go anywhere in the world, where would you go?"

"That's easy—Cincinnati."

The smooth baritone of his voice washed over me as he laughed, then his tone shifted. "Heather... when can I see you next?"

"I hope soon." My throat tightened. "I have to tell you something."

"Okay."

"I'm single," I whispered into the dark. "I broke off my engagement."

"Is this my fault?" he asked, carefully. "If it is, I'll back off. I'm not going to take something from you you're not ready to give."

"I should have never said yes in the first place."

"I'm sorry if I complicated things in your life."

"You didn't. You showed me what it feels like to be seen." I paused, letting the truth settle. "Around you, I didn't feel like I needed permission to exist."

He stayed quiet, giving me the space to finish.

"I didn't leave him for you," I said. "I left because being with you helped me trust my own voice."

"I'm glad you're okay," he said. "And I respect the hell out of how you got here."

"Well, Heather Brown," he added, lighter now, "I'm going to keep calling you—if that's okay with you."

"It's more than okay," I said, smiling.

"Get some sleep. I know what I'll be dreaming about tonight."

"Me too, Bradley Hart."

When the call ended, I set my phone on the nightstand. As it darkened, I felt a new chapter beginning.

I knew it was fast. But for the first time in a long while, the pace felt honest.

After years of pretending with the wrong man, I wasn't interested in hiding from myself—or from what came next.

35

SOUNDCHECK OF THE HEART
BRADLEY

After I got off the phone with Heather, the room felt too quiet, like something had shifted and hadn't settled yet.

She was single. She was available. She wasn't someone else's fiancée anymore.

She's really free.

The thought looped through my head, loud and electric, impossible to shut off. But beneath the adrenaline was something heavier, slower.

What if I ruin her?

The question came uninvited, familiar as muscle memory.

I lay back on the bed, staring at the ceiling. For a second, I let myself picture what it could look like—her in the front row, backstage passes, late nights that blurred into mornings. The version of me that had always existed on the road.

And then what?

The image slid, like it always did.

I was twelve, sitting on the front steps with my mom's old windbreaker pulled tight around my shoulders. The porch light buzzed overhead, the sound sharp against the quiet street. She'd said he'd be home by dinner. Then by nine. Then she stopped giving times at all.

I waited anyway.

Every pair of headlights lifted something hopeful in my chest before passing by. Inside, my mom sat at the kitchen table, pretending to balance a checkbook with money that was already gone. He'd taken it again. Promised he was close to something big. Promised he'd fix things.

He always promised.

Months could pass like that. No calls. No explanations. Just absence.

By the time he showed up again—thin, wired, apologetic —I was already mowing the lawn, making dinner, telling my mom we'd be fine. I became the man of the house before I understood what that meant. Music was the one thing I kept for myself. I poured everything I couldn't say into it, told myself I'd turn it into something solid. Something that stayed.

I wouldn't disappear. I couldn't.

But wanting Heather meant risking overlap. Touring. Distance. The same disappearing act, dressed up as ambition.

What if wanting her isn't enough?

Sometime after three, exhaustion finally won. I fell asleep with the question still running through me, unfinished.

My phone buzzing against the nightstand dragged me back to consciousness.

I squinted at the screen.

11:07 a.m.

Suzie.

I answered it sitting up, the room still heavy with sleep.

"It's after eleven," she said, clipped and caffeinated. "Sound check's at three. And your booking manager needs you—Europe wants six months. January start."

Six months.

Six months away.

I swung my legs over the side of the bed, pulse quickening.

"Paris. Berlin. London. Rome," she continued. "This is the kind of tour artists kill for."

Any other year, I would've said yes before she finished the sentence.

This is what you wanted.

This was the dream. Stadiums. Legacy. Momentum.

But the picture felt incomplete now, like something important had been cropped out.

How do I finally get Heather back just to leave again?

Suzie paused. It was brief, but it was there.

"That hesitation?" she said. "That's new."

"I'm thinking," I said.

"You're overthinking," she shot back. "This is your career, Brad. You don't stall momentum for a maybe."

She isn't a maybe.

But I didn't say that.

I dragged a hand over my face. "I'm not saying no."

"I need more than 'not no,'" she said. "Europe wants commitment."

The immensity of the decision clamped around me.

Music had always been the thing I ran toward. The thing that saved me. The thing that kept me from turning into my father. But now it was asking something back.

What does it cost to keep both?

"I'll call you later today," I said.

Suzie exhaled. "Get your head straight," she said. "This is what you've worked for."

The call ended. The room stayed quiet.

I sat there for a long moment, staring at the floor, the hum of the city filtering in through the window.

I want her. I want this life.

Heather meant grounding. Realness. Someone who saw the man before the stage.

The career meant movement. Distance. Everything I'd built to keep from standing still.

Can I choose love without shrinking?

I stood and headed for the shower, rehearsals, the stage —all the moving parts of the life I'd made.

But every step felt like the beginning of a question instead of an answer.

For the first time in my life, the dream I'd been chasing —stadiums, global tours, everything I thought I wanted— didn't feel complete on its own.

And that scared the hell out of me.

36

THE FINAL CUT
HEATHER

By Monday morning, freedom had a to-do list.

I spread sketches, swatches, and line sheets across my studio table, balancing coffee on a stack of lookbooks, trying to wrangle my nerves into something productive. The Bloomingdale's meeting replayed in my head like it was still unfolding—every question, every pause, every moment where I'd had to answer without flinching.

They wanted me back on Wednesday. Second round. Serious.

That word alone shifted the air in the room. Serious meant numbers. Serious meant timelines and production minimums, and people depending on me to get this right. It meant that if I said yes and stumbled, it wouldn't just be my pride on the line. It would be Dani's hours, Alana's faith, the quiet belief we'd all been building piece by piece.

I let that settle without pushing it away.

I ran my fingers over a swatch of washed cupro that draped like a secret meant to be worn by a goddess, soft but intentional. I'd paired it with a clean V-neck, understated in a way that felt almost rebellious. Last year, everyone was screaming athleisure: mesh, slogans. I wanted quiet pieces that slid into a woman's life and sharpened everything else around her. Clothes that didn't ask to be noticed but always were.

By mid-morning, Dani, the seamstress, stepped into the studio, already assessing the midi skirt on the dress form.

"A quarter inch lower here," she said, pinching the front waist. "And take half an inch off this seam. Let it move."

Exactly what I'd been thinking.

She laid pattern paper across the cutting table, pencil moving with calm certainty while Alena organized swatches and labeled garment bags. The room filled with the sounds of work—the scrape of graphite, the tear of paper, the low thrum of focus. This was where I trusted myself most. Where instinct and discipline met and something clean came out of it.

We worked like that for two days.

By Tuesday night, revised samples stood by the door in garment bags, lined up like quiet proof. I stood there longer than necessary, counting silhouettes, mentally walking through price points, asking myself hard questions without flinching. Could I produce this at scale without compromising the line? Would I still recognize it once it moved beyond these walls?

On Wednesday morning, the sky over downtown Chicago looked pearl-gray and expectant. Alena offered to come with me, and I was grateful for the company. Two sets of hands made the trip feel more manageable.

We rolled garment racks out to the curb. The Uber ride was quiet, the city sliding past in reflections of glass and steel. I didn't rehearse answers. I didn't need to. The work had already spoken for me.

The building behind Bloomingdale's gleamed.

Security checked my ID and printed a sticker with my name before directing us to the seventh floor. Upstairs, the corridor felt like a living mood board. Racks lined the walls, each tagged and labeled. Assistants moved past with iPads, murmuring about margins and sell-through. It smelled like coffee, paper, wool.

"Hi, Heather." A woman with a neat ponytail smiled. "I'm Maya. Come on in." Alena and I took turns shaking Maya's hand, then followed her into the conference room she'd indicated.

The room was glassed-in, overlooking Michigan Avenue. Bottled water, branded notepads, two rolling racks—one holding my samples, the other empty and waiting. On the wall, a trend board read: *Spring—Feminine Utility / Pastel Revival / Modern Minimalism.*

Elise entered with a leather folio and an energy that suggested decisions were her native language.

"We've been reviewing your line," she said. "There's something here. Elevated but wearable isn't easy to execute."

Maya lifted the slip dress from the rack. "We can see her in this. Saturday night, Gold Coast. Under three hundred."

Elise nodded. "We're thinking a capsule. Ten to twelve styles. Exclusive. Dresses under two seventy-five, tops under one fifty, outerwear under four fifty."

She looked directly at me. "If we launch in spring, we'd need a February to March delivery. Five to seven hundred units per style. Can you handle that?"

"Yes," I said. The answer came without hesitation.

As we moved through the rack, Elise paused at a cropped jacket. "This could skew trend-heavy if you're not careful."

I stepped closer, touched the sleeve. "That's why the cut stays clean," I said. "The fabric carries the interest. She won't get tired of it."

Elise studied me for a beat, then nodded. "Good."

She slid a packet across the table—line sheets, timelines, vendor terms highlighted in yellow. "Flagship distribution to start. Chicago, New York, San Francisco, LA. Plus online. If it performs, we scale."

She leaned back, eyes sharp. "We'd also like to feature you digitally. Campaign rollout. Social. Our customer wants to know who designs her clothes."

My chest tightened, but my voice held. "I'm open to that."

Elise smiled once, satisfied. "Review the agreement. Confirmation by Friday."

When we shook hands, it felt like more than a formality. It felt like a threshold.

The moment the elevator doors closed behind us, Alena grabbed my arm and beamed. "I knew it."

37

ON THE ROAD AGAIN

BRADLEY

We'd barely caught our breath from Dallas before we were back on the road again—next city, next stage, next crowd. Tour life moved on momentum alone. Forward, always forward. Somewhere between sound checks and meet-and-greets, Suzie kept circling back to Europe. I hadn't answered her yet.

It wasn't because I didn't know what the offer meant. I did. Six months. Major cities. The kind of tour that carved your name deeper into the industry.

What I hadn't done was talk to Heather.

On these buses, with bodies stacked into every corner and someone always listening, there was never room for a real conversation. Thought fractured here. Privacy didn't exist.

When we pulled into Nashville the night before the weekend run, I finally slipped away. Headphones rested around my neck as I walked along the riverfront, the city vibrating low and restless beside me. Tomorrow night I'd be onstage at Ascend Amphitheater, open air, the river right at our backs. It was the kind of venue you remembered.

I dialed Heather before I could overthink it.

She answered on the second ring.

"Hello," she said, bright but threaded with exhaustion.

"Hey, darlin'. Just wanted to hear your voice."

Her laugh came easily. "I love the sound of that."

"What are you wearing?" I asked, smiling into the dark.

She groaned. "A tailored suit. I'm still at work."

"Hot."

She laughed again, the sound loosening something in my chest. "I am actually overheating."

"What's keeping you there so late?"

"I have to tell you something. Something big."

I slowed my steps, the gravel under my boots crunching louder than before. I stopped walking altogether, the river stretching dark and patient beside me.

"Tell me."

"I got offered a capsule with Bloomingdale's," she said. "Exclusive. My own line."

The words settled in before I spoke. I could hear the adrenaline under them, the careful disbelief.

"That's incredible," I said. "I'm so damn proud of you."

She exhaled softly. "Thank you. I still can't wrap my head around it."

"It's going to be intense," she went on. "Some travel. Production. Deadlines. But I want to make room for us if we can."

I stopped walking.

"Well," I said, steadying myself, "I've got something too."

She hummed, waiting.

"My summer run ends in Chicago," I said. "I'll be there for a full week. Rehearsals, press, then downtime. I was hoping we could spend some of it together. No rushing."

She didn't answer right away. When she did, her voice carried affection.

"That sounds perfect. I'd love that."

The word *perfect* landed heavier than I expected.

My phone buzzed then. Suzie. Persistent as ever.

"I've got to go," I told Heather. "But I miss you. And I'm proud of you. More than you know."

"I miss you too," she said. "Goodnight, Bradley."

The call ended, leaving me alone with the river and the weight of everything I hadn't said.

I should've told her.

Europe wasn't just another tour. It was six months of airports and borrowed beds, of cities bleeding together if you stayed too long. It was momentum and legacy. It was also the thing that had pulled my father farther and farther from home, until absence became his language.

I remembered being a kid, watching my mother sit at the kitchen table long after dinner, the phone beside her untouched. Music had taken him first. Then the rest followed.

I wasn't him. I'd built my life trying to prove that.

Heather had just stepped into something she'd earned inch by inch. Tonight belonged to her. I couldn't bring myself to lay my uncertainty beside her joy, to introduce weight where there should be lift.

Because once I said Europe out loud, it became real.

And once it was real, I'd have to face what it might cost.

A week in Chicago felt like something offered rather than planned. Mornings together. Shared space. The unglamorous rhythm of daily life. The kind of closeness that showed you who someone really was.

Maybe that was what I needed first.

I wasn't holding back because the conversation didn't matter.

I was holding back because the answer would.

I stayed there a while longer, listening to the river cut steadily through the city, and let the question rest where it was.

Chicago would tell me what I needed to know.

38

AT LAST

HEATHER

It was finally the end of September, and the climate was slowly changing that feeling when you know autumn is coming. The air was crisp, and you needed an extra layer once the sun dipped behind the skyline. And it was finally time for Bradley's tour dates here in Chicago.

Tonight we had each other. Just us in real time.

He was taking me to dinner on Roscoe Street—candles, pasta, a table for two tucked beneath string lights and ivy. But my hands trembled with a different kind of anticipation, one no dinner could satisfy.

I stood in front of the mirror, tugging the silk straps of my black slip dress over my shoulders, smoothing the fabric where it skimmed my hips. Simple, but in that Chicago kind of way—understated, slinky, confident, daring when seen up close. I paired it with a soft gray shawl, delicate gold hoops, ankle-strap heels, and the Saint Laurent clutch I'd been saving for the right night.

This was the night.

Nico was perched on my couch, blow-dryer in hand,

fussing over my hair like he was preparing me for the Met Gala.

"Sweetheart, if Bradley Hart is coming to pick you up, we are not sending you out with wind hair," he announced.

I laughed, nerves prickling delicately across my skin.

"You're something else."

"I'm a visionary," he corrected, smoothing my blowout sleek and glossy over my shoulders. He dusted bronzer across my cheekbones, lengthened my lashes, then stepped back with the pride of a man presenting art.

"Chic. Modern. Deadly. He won't survive this look."

Tory breezed in moments later with wine in hand, stopping cold when she saw me.

"Oh, he's done for. Absolutely slaughtered."

Something inside me loosened at that. Excitement cut through the tight coil of apprehension that had lived in my stomach all day.

The buzzer sounded.

My heart kicked hard as I crossed the room. In the minutes before the knock, the world narrowed to sensation —heartbeat, perfume, silk against skin.

I opened the door.

Bradley stood there. Real. Close. So familiar it almost hurt.

His eyes swept over me slowly, reverently.

"You're stunning," he said, low and with a husk.

Emotion rushed through me—relief, disbelief, anticipation all at once. "Thank you."

His smile unraveled me in a single pull. Unsure of what would happen once we finally touched, I let a shy smile and a knowing glance in his direction share all my thoughts.

Introductions blurred. What stayed was the way his gaze kept finding mine, as if he were grounding himself there.

"Use protection," Nico called out like a menace.

When his fingers threaded through mine, solid and sure, it felt inevitable.

Downstairs, a black car waited beneath a streetlamp. He opened the door for me, his other palm brushing the small of my back. My skin tingled beneath my dress. The moment we slid inside, his restraint fractured.

He cupped my face between his palms. His eyes darkened as they traveled down the neckline of my dress, lingering with admiration.

His lips hovered just inches from mine. I could almost taste him. My mind went blank. My heart pounded. My breath turned audible.

"You're the most gorgeous woman I have ever laid eyes on," he said, his voice rough and low. "Please give me permission to kiss you."

"Please do," I breathed.

All restraint shattered.

His mouth met mine with a force that felt like breaking free.

He kissed me slowly and claimed, like time owed him something. The warmth of him, the familiar scent of him, the way he fit against me so perfectly, it made my head spin. My hand curled into his shirt without thinking, pulling him closer.

"We're supposed to go to dinner," I murmured, my breath already uneven.

"Dinner can wait," he said, his hand sliding higher along my thigh. "I've waited fifteen years for this."

Something in me gave way when he said it. My body had been pining long enough.

He broke the kiss only enough to lean forward and let the driver know about the change of plans.

His lips were back on me again. The outside world vanished. We clung to each other, hands wandering, words turning into confessions we'd never dared to say out loud. I didn't even realize the car had come to a stop.

"Welcome to The Thompson Hotel, Mr. Hart."

We pulled apart, breathless. I knew it was only for a moment. All I could think about was how fast we could make it upstairs.

♫♪

In the elevator, he pressed me back against the mirrored wall—then paused. Foreheads touching. Breathing the same air. The wanting was worse than the touching, like every second he didn't kiss me added another year onto our wait. I could feel the weight of our history hanging between us, begging to be acknowledged.

The tension surged, thick and unbearable.

"Maybe elevators are our thing," he breathed against my mouth. I laughed—breathless—then gasped as his hand slipped up my thigh beneath the hem of my dress.

"Nothing is getting in our way tonight," he whispered against my ear.

Then, without warning, his hand went higher, and he slid a finger inside me.

My body recognized him instantly, like it had been waiting all along. "Fuck," slipped out of my mouth without permission.

"Oh, Heather Brown," he murmured into my ear, his voice a sultry promise, "how I can't wait to do just that to you. And make you unravel over... " A kiss behind my ear. "And over." Another kiss sent shivers down my spine. His fingers moved teasingly where I craved him most, just enough pressure to drive me wild.

As he slid my underwear aside, his touch ignited every nerve ending, and just as the world around me began to fade into bliss, the bell chimed.

Too soon.

A shared sigh escaped our lips as we pulled away, his eyes glinting. "Don't worry, I'm just getting started." A slow, mischievous smile spread across his face as he took my hand and led me out of the capsule of lust.

The hallway felt endless. Carpet under my heels. His fingers locked in mine. Every hurried step tightening the coil.

Inside the room, the door clicked shut behind us—final as a vow.

For a beat, we just stood there, looking at each other. Taking it in. His eyes reading every thought I couldn't form.

Then he crossed the room, and his mouth was on mine again, starved and reckless, his hands moving slowly, deliberately, like he still refused to rush even now.

"Years," he growled against my lips. "Dreaming of all the things I'd do to you."

I couldn't speak. Words didn't form, just the silent begging in my eyes.

"More times than I can count," he murmured, sliding one strap of my dress down, painfully slow. "How it would feel to touch your breasts again."

Kisses traced the line of my shoulder. The other strap down. "How it would feel for you to wrap your hand around me when I needed you."

Still no words—just breath, thin and unsteady.

More kisses scorching along my collarbone. With

agonizing slowness, he unzipped my dress, letting it pool at my feet.

"I'd think about how it would feel to slip inside you from behind," he continued quietly, "and grab that beautiful ass."

I stayed mute except for a small, broken plea.

"What was that, Heather?"

"I... "

He knelt and tugged my panties down, moving slower than paint dries. I was soaked with need, the torture of his patience almost unbearable.

He kissed me between my legs, unhurried, starved, savoring every drop. His mouth moved over me with devastating precision.

"Bradley... I... I'm going to... " I let out a soft moan, my mind fogging at the edges.

He looked up at me with crinkles at the corners of his eyes, devilish dimples flashing like hazard signs.

Without warning, he scooped me up and laid me gently on the bed. This time, he didn't speak. He didn't need to.

Each touch closed the distance time had carved between us.

His eyes stayed on me as he pulled his shirt over his head and tossed it aside. The chain he'd worn when we were younger still rested against his chest, familiar enough to make something in my body quiver. I caught it with my fingers and pulled him back down, needing to taste him again, needing to know he was real.

My hands shook as I unzipped his pants. He stilled them with a quiet breath, helped me push the fabric down, and kicked it away. When there was nothing left between us but thin layers and heat, the air felt loaded and dense with everything we hadn't said.

He slid a finger inside me, slow, knowing, deliberate. My

body answered instantly, lifting, reaching, betraying me. His eyes never left my face.

"Tell me if you want me to keep going," he said.

"Yes," I breathed.

"God," he murmured, watching me. "Look at you. You are a goddess. You feel exactly how I imagined."

I reached for him, my hand closing around him through his briefs. The sound he made—low and rough—went straight through me. I pulled the fabric down, freeing him, and the sight of him made my stomach flip.

This wasn't anticipation anymore. This was commitment.

When he reached for the condom, tearing it open with his teeth, the confidence of it undid me completely.

"I'm not rushing this," he said quietly as he positioned himself. "I want all of this."

When he finally pressed into me, it was careful, deliberate, giving my body time, giving us time. I gasped, clutching his shoulders as he filled me inch by inch.

For a moment, neither of us moved. His forehead rested against mine; our breathing tangled.

The weight of him inside me felt binding. Real. Unavoidable. Something in my chest loosened, emotion surging so suddenly it stole my breath. This wasn't what I'd imagined in the quiet, lonely moments over the years. It was slower. Heavier. Familiar.

Bradley watched my face, searching. When I nodded—barely—relief flickered across his expression before he moved again.

He set a steady, unhurried rhythm. Every movement felt intentional, as if he were listening to my body, adjusting to my breath, staying right there with me. Fifteen years of restraint lived in that slowness—in the way he never disappeared into the act, never left me behind.

"Stay right here with me," he said against my ear. "I've got you." He reached between us and found me, strumming his fingers with the same control and precision he gave his guitar.

The world narrowed to his body, his voice, my name on his lips. All the wanting and waiting poured out at once, years of holding back unraveling with every measured movement.

When the tension finally snapped, I cried out his name, clinging to him as everything broke open inside me.

Only after he was sure I was spent did he slow, guiding me carefully as he shifted us, his touch never losing its gentleness. He kissed my ear as he turned me onto my stomach, easing back inside me with deliberate control, his hands warm and steady at my waist.

This time, he moved even slower at first, pulling back completely before filling me again, deeper each time, slower, more demanding. The sensation built too fast, too strong, until I was shaking, breathless, undone.

"Don't go anywhere," he said, his voice strained. "I want to feel every second of you."

"Yes," I cried.

"I need you to take me now."

That was all it took.

He pushed as deep as he could, finally letting go, his breath breaking as he said my name. The force of it pulled another wave through me until I was trembling, holding on as everything spilled loose at once.

He stayed there for a long moment, anchoring us both, before easing us down gently—careful, tender.

After, he pressed a kiss to my temple and slipped away

only long enough to take care of what needed to be done. When he returned, he gathered me against him, his arm firm around my waist, my back tucked into his chest.

"You make me feel like I've finally come home," he murmured into my hair.

I lay there listening to his heartbeat, knowing something had shifted, and that neither of us was pretending otherwise.

My body felt loose, unguarded, like I'd finally stopped holding myself together by force.

"I'm starving," I said, grinning.

He huffed a quiet laugh, his hand sliding along my side. "Sounds like a pancake emergency," he said. "And maybe whipped cream."

His eyebrows lifted just enough to make the promise unmistakable.

I shook my head, biting my lip before I could stop myself. "You're lethal."

"Mm," he murmured, pulling me closer. "You have no idea."

He kissed me again, our laughter slipping between kisses as he rolled us together, unhurried, like there was nowhere else we needed to be and nothing left to outrun.

39

UNCHAINED MELODY

BRADLEY

After we finished eating, I put on a pair of boxers and pushed the cart out of the bedroom and into the small living space, the room settling into that quiet, late-night stillness that only comes once everything else has been taken care of.

I brought my hollow-body guitar back in with me. There was a melody stuck in my chest, restless, asking to be let out.

"Is it okay if I play you something?" I asked.

She was sitting up against the headboard, pillows stacked behind her, wearing nothing but my t-shirt and a pair of black panties. The shirt barely skimmed the tops of her thighs. *Fuck she looked hot.* "You can always play for me," she said, laughing softly.

"You just bring it out in me," I said, biting the pick in my mouth.

I sat at the edge of the bed and started strumming, low and easy, letting the sound find its shape. I pulled my notebook from the nightstand and jotted a few lyrics, a couple of notes that felt unfinished but promising.

She glanced over. "Ah," she said, amused. "A musician at work. In the moment."

"Come here," I said.

She scooted closer, curiosity written all over her face, and I lifted the guitar, settling it carefully over her shoulders. She laughed quietly.

"I've never actually held a guitar before," she admitted. "It's lighter than I thought."

"It is," I said.

I sat behind her, close enough to feel her warmth, the hollow body hanging lower than her waist because of the way the strap sat on her shoulder. It looked oversized on her frame, but when she shifted, it settled, like it belonged there.

"Let's start simple," I said.

I reached around her and took her left hand in mine, gently placing her pointer, middle, and ring fingers on the fretboard.

"Press here. And here. And here." I nudged each fingertip into place. "That's a cowboy chord."

She tried to hold it.

"Ouch," she said, wincing as the steel bit into her skin. "That hurts."

I smiled against the side of her head. "You don't have any calluses built up yet."

"I guess I have some work to do," she teased.

I took her hand and brought the hurt finger to my mouth, sucking it gently while I held her gaze. She stilled, brown eyes darkening, breath catching just slightly.

"Better?"

She nodded, her eyes wide and her mouth slightly open.

"Let's get back to making music." I tried to be serious, but the corners of my lips lifted.

My right arm came around her next, slow and unhurried, until my hand covered hers. I slid the pick between her fingers, adjusting her grip, my thumb brushing the inside of her palm.

"Now watch this."

I guided her hand as we strummed. The sound spilled out full and rich, filling the room. Then I shifted her fingers.

"D to G," I said. "Hear that?"

The change was immediate.

She lit up. "Wow," she breathed. "We did that."

I smiled. "You can make it speak however you want."

She tried again, fingers clumsy at first—pressing too hard, then not enough. Each time she missed, I corrected her carefully.

Then, without really thinking about it, I placed my hands over hers and moved with her. I let a quiet tune slip out—something shaped by the moment, by her, sliding easily from chord to chord.

She glanced back at me, a glint in her eyes. "Your hands certainly know what to do."

I was sitting behind her, close enough that my knees pressed into her hips, my hands still guiding hers on the strings. When the last note faded, I leaned in without thinking and brushed a kiss against her cheek.

She stilled for half a second, then turned her hand, brushing my cheek. I shifted, just enough to catch her mouth with mine.

The kiss was slow, tender, soft, playing its own tune.

When we pulled apart, she rested her forehead briefly against my jaw.

"That's one good jam," she said softly.

I smiled, brushing my thumb along her fingers. "You're my jam." A little laugh came out of her, making me laugh with her.

I set the guitar aside carefully, as if the moment deserved the same attention the music did.

"Are we going to wake up and find out all of this was a dream?" she asked, looking up at me.

I grinned, but it didn't feel like a joke. "I hope not. It feels like we're just getting started."

She exhaled softly, her forehead resting against my chest. "We haven't left the bubble yet."

"No," I said, my hand sliding to her back, holding her there. "We're still safe up here."

She shifted in my arms, tilting her head back to look at me. "Now that the tour's done... what's next?"

I knew what I should've said. Europe sat there, loud and waiting. The responsible answer. The full answer.

Instead, I stayed where we were.

"I've got a little time off," I said. True enough. "A few weeks before anything else starts."

Her eyes brightened, just slightly. "Really?"

"Yeah." I brushed my thumb along her arm. "I was thinking... maybe you could come out to L.A., or I could come back here."

Her tulip lips curled up, making shape, soft and tentative, like she didn't want to spook it. "That sounds... nice."

"It does," I said. And it did. It felt easy to picture. Natural. Like it didn't require convincing.

She rested her head back against my chest again. "I like the idea of not rushing out of this."

"Me too," I said quietly.

Neither of us said anything after that. We didn't need to. The plans weren't plans—just possibilities we let sit between us, warm and unchallenged.

Still inside the bubble. Still safe.

40

BACK TO EARTH
HEATHER

We stood side by side at the sink, laughing at our reflections through toothpaste foam and toothbrushes, elbows bumping as we cleaned our pearly whites. Every time our eyes met in the mirror, something tightened low in my stomach. The absurdity of it. The intimacy. The fact that this was us—grown, years later, brushing our teeth together like it was the most natural thing in the world.

Every glance deepened the surreal feeling that we were here, now, lusting all over each other without apology. This wasn't memory or fantasy anymore. It was real and happening right in front of me.

After a who-could-brush-the-longest contest I hadn't known we were having, Bradley caved first, spitting into the sink. I followed after.

"I win," I said.

"I don't think so," he countered.

"I did outlast you."

He leaned down, close enough that I could feel his breath. "Then I think I need to do a taste test."

"Fair."

He kissed me, swirling his tongue into my mouth in a way that made my legs falter instantly. I lost my balance, laughing into him, and he caught me easily, hands firm at my hips like he'd known exactly how far to push.

"All right," he said against my mouth, pulling back just enough to look at me. "I've got to get a move on, or Suzie's going to be all over my ass."

He turned toward the shower and switched it on. "But, since you have been a little dirty girl, I think I should clean you up."

I huffed out a laugh, still breathless. "I thought we didn't have time."

He glanced back over his shoulder, eyes darkening, his lower lip caught briefly between his teeth.

"I think I can be efficient."

He caught my arm and spun me back, his eyes darkening. "Get in."

That look alone did it. I lifted his T-shirt over my head, exposing my breasts; his gaze dropped immediately.

"Oof," he muttered. "I'm already hard."

He slipped my panties down, and when I pushed his boxers off in return, he wasn't exaggerating. One look at him and I was soaked, my body responding faster than my brain could catch up.

We stepped in. The water cascaded around us. He pulled me in and kissed my collarbone, then down to my nipples, taking turns on them, making sure they had equal playtime. A breathy squeal slipped out of me without my permission.

He lowered to his knees, kissing my torso and then between my thighs. He pressed his mouth to me and moved his tongue in rhythm only he could find. The pleasure rose inside me like a crescendo, building till I called out his name again and again.

When I was finished, I pulled him up and wrapped my hand around him, moving the skin back and forth. I kept my eyes on his face, tracing every reaction until his head fell back.

"Jesus, Heather."

Hearing my name encouraged me, and my pace quickened as I mirrored his responses. When he climaxed, a surprising swell of pride bloomed in my chest.

I don't think Tripp and I ever did anything out of the ordinary. Sometimes he wanted to schedule sex—Saturdays only. Spontaneity was never really in the cards for him. Bradley didn't wait. He wanted me when he felt it, and being wanted without warning, without planning, unlocked something I hadn't realized was dimmed for so long.

We stayed under the spray longer than necessary, foreheads pressed together, and we both caught our breath as reality crept back in around the edges.

We toweled off and dressed quickly. As we moved, the air crackled with an energy that felt different, charged, a reminder of the intimacy we had just shared. The quiet that followed felt heavier now—laden with unspoken thoughts and desires.

We had to leave the top of The Thompson and come back down to earth.

Up there, twenty-four floors above the city, his life had felt contained. Manageable. Almost normal. But elevators don't let you stay suspended.

As the doors slid shut, his hand settled at my waist, rooting me. The descent felt longer than it should have, each floor ticking past like a reminder that whatever we'd just experienced couldn't stay untouched for long.

Right before the doors opened, he leaned in, his lips brushing against my ear. "Stay close," he warned quietly. "It's a mob."

I nodded, not fully understanding what that meant, but the heat of his body against mine sent shivers down my spine.

Then the doors opened.

Light exploded first. Cameras. Voices shouting his name from every direction. My heart slammed against my ribs as panic rushed in sharp and sudden.

"Bradley, over here!"

"Is this your girlfriend?"

"What's her name?"

I froze, instinct screaming to disappear. Bradley didn't hesitate. His body shifted instantly, shielding me, his hand locking tight around mine as he pulled me forward.

With Tripp, being seen had always felt staged— measured, managed, as if I were part of the presentation. This was different. No one wanted *me*. I was collateral, swept along in the wake of something incandescent and out of control.

"Let's make a run for it," Suzie said sharply.

Bradley glanced back at me. "Keep your head down. Don't answer anyone. Don't let go."

I didn't.

Inside the SUV, the door shut and the noise vanished so abruptly it left my ears ringing. I let out a rush of air, grateful it was over.

"You okay?" Bradley asked, already turned toward me.

"I think so," I said, still shaken. "That was... intense. New York wasn't like that."

Suzie spoke from the front seat without looking back.

"New York was different. He blew up mid-tour. Numbers doubled by August. Privacy's limited now."

Limited privacy.

The phrase landed heavier than I expected. I'd always lived behind the scenes, quiet and controlled. This was neither.

We pulled into the Aragon Ballroom. Bradley leaned in and kissed me, lingering just a beat too long, giving me more tongue than I was sure Suzie wanted to witness.

"I'll see you tonight," he said softly.

Suzie turned to the driver. "Get her home safe. Make sure she's inside."

The car pulled away, leaving me alone with the silence and the echo of what I'd just stepped into.

Bradley wasn't just talented.

He was famous.

And sitting there, still shaken, I wondered how big his world really was—and whether there was really room in it for someone like me.

41

THAT'S THE WAY

BRADLEY

I woke up a little past nine, my head already buzzing with thoughts about tonight's show. Soundcheck, set tweaks, interviews—the machine never really shut off; it just waited for me to catch up.

But Heather was still asleep beside me, and for a moment, none of it existed.

She lay on her side, hair fanned across the pillow in dark waves, lashes resting against her cheeks, lips slightly parted like she'd been smiling in her dreams. There was something rare about the quiet around her—like she brought it with her, a sanctuary in the chaos of my life.

I'd spent years surrounded by noise. Applause, crowds, voices shouting my name.

And still, this was the thing that shook me to my core.

In the other room, I ordered room service without thinking too hard about it—coffee, fruit, extra pancakes—because I already knew she'd want them.

When I came back, Heather's eyes were open, a sleepy smile tugging at her mouth.

"Hi," she said softly. "Sorry if I overslept."

"You didn't." I sat on the edge of the bed, brushing my thumb along her arm, feeling the softness of her skin beneath my fingers. "I was just... here."

She grinned at that, then frowned slightly. "I should probably go brush my teeth."

I leaned in and kissed her anyway. "You probably should," I teased.

"You turd." She laughed, playfully shoved me, and slipped out of the covers.

"Wait, I was kidding." I pulled her back down for one more kiss. My chain dangled over her, and she caught it gently.

"You had this when you were young," she said in a low, serious voice. "I remember it."

"My dad gave it to me. I should probably toss it since I haven't heard from him in a decade."

"Really? Not once?"

"Not once. And if he showed up now, I'd assume he wanted money."

Her hand brushed my cheek. "I'm sorry. That must hurt."

"I tried to bury it. Not let it get to me anymore."

Her brows knit, her voice soft. "You don't have to bury it all alone, you know."

Something in me uncoiled. And suddenly, more came out than I intended.

"Yesterday," I said quietly, "I know you were scared."

Heather's eyes lifted to mine.

"Outside the hotel. With the cameras." I swallowed. "You were quieter after the show."

She didn't deny it. Just nodded.

"I watched it happen," I continued. "And I'm terrified this part of my life is going to push you away."

"It would scare anyone," I said. "Especially someone who lives the way you do."

Her brow furrowed. "The way I do?"

"Small," I said gently. "Careful. Quiet... intentional." I paused. "My life is loud. It's not your dream life."

She let out a slow breath. "You are right." Silence stretched.

"But," she added, voice steady, "I like you in my small world." Her hand reaching for mine, "I'm not pretending it didn't affect me. This is outside my comfort zone."

I nodded. "Good. Don't pretend."

She looked down at our hands. "I like ordinary things," she admitted. "Brushing my teeth next to you. The fact that you remembered I love pancakes. The way you look at my sketches like they matter; the way you believe in me."

Something in my throat clenched.

"That's the part I want," I said. "The part where I don't lose you to my life."

She was quiet for a beat, then said, "I was scared. But I don't want you to give this up. Your life is big and loud." A small tug at her lips. "I'd obviously rather be tucked up in your hotel room."

I let out a soft laugh. "What happens when we want daylight?"

She thought for a second. "I don't know."

"I've got a lot of hats and sunglasses," I said.

Her smile widened. "We could get wigs."

I laughed and took her hand, pressing a kiss to her knuckles.

"I'll always keep you safe," I said quietly. "I just don't know what all of this will turn into yet."

"Neither do I," she said. "But I'm here."

The hotel phone rang, disrupting our moment.

I rolled my eyes, leaned over, and lay on my back, "Hello." It was Suzie.

"I'm on my way up. Are you alone?"

"I'm not."

"Well, are you decent?"

"Give me five minutes."

"You've got three."

I scrambled—I got up and changed, face splashed, hands washed. Right on time, she knocked.

"Suzie, what a surprise."

"Shut up, Bradley. You need to tell me about Europe. They don't have patience anymore."

I felt Heather freeze in the other room.

"Can we talk about it on the ride to the venue?"

"You've been sitting on this too long."

Her tone sliced through whatever peace we'd had this morning.

"I'll meet you in the lobby in twenty," I said flatly.

Her glare sharpened. Mine matched it.

"You have one hour. Got it?"

"Got it," I said, a little ruder than anticipated.

I shut the door—harder than I should have.

The sliding door from the bedroom to the suite opened behind me.

Heather stepped out.

"Europe?"

I sighed. "Yes. I've been meaning to tell you. I just didn't want to ruin our week."

"When?"

"January."

"For how long?"

"Six months."

"Oh."

Her expression stayed composed, but I could see a flicker of tension in her eyes.

"I didn't want to ruin this week. I should've told you sooner."

"I'm not upset if you go," she said quietly. "I'm upset that you kept it from me."

She was right.

"I don't want to be a small piece of your life," she continued. "A week here. A memory there."

Neither did I.

"I don't want that either," I said. "I want this to be... *real*."

She studied me for a long beat, then nodded once. "I'm here," she said. "For now. On purpose."

Relief hit hard.

"So am I," I said. "And I won't waste it."

🎶

The lights hit me like fire the second I stepped onstage. The roar was deafening, my name shouted, chanted, screamed. It never stopped feeling surreal, like my soul stepped outside my body every time I experienced this moment.

Somewhere out there, Heather was in the crowd. I couldn't see her—the lights were blinding me—but I felt her. Every lyric I sang, I knew she was catching it. Holding it.

Backstage after the set, a few girls who had been lingering near the band slipped through the chaos. One in a sequin top with a tiny nose ring stepped right into my space and dragged her palm slowly across my chest.

"You were so sexy tonight."

Her friend leaned in beside her. "We know a killer afterparty." She brushed my hair off my forehead like she already knew me.

There was a time when that kind of attention felt normal. Easy.

"I've got plans," I said.

That's when I saw Suzie's red hair cutting through the crowd, and behind her, Heather. Tory. Joel. Nico. Marcus.

I was pretty sure they had seen it, judging by the look on Heather's face and the way Tory's eyes went protective.

I walked straight to Heather and kissed her. I wanted to reassure her.

"Hell of a show," Joel said. "I know a quiet dive bar you won't get recognized at if you want to check it out."

"Perfect," I said.

♫

The bar was dark, sticky, low-ceilinged, neon lights reflecting off cracked booths. No one cared who I was, which was exactly what I needed.

Heather laughed with Tory, Nico, and Marcus. Cheeks flushed, hair falling into her eyes. I watched her like an idiot, like a man who knew—finally knew—what his heart had been trying to tell him:

She was my girl.

By the time we all piled back into the car, everyone was buzzing. Heather curled into me as if she'd always belonged there.

When we turned onto my hotel's street, we saw a wall of people, cameras ready to explode.

Before the driver slowed, Heather whispered, "Let's go to my place."

I gave the driver new instructions. He dropped off Tory

and Joel at Joel's place, then Marcus and Nico at Nico's. Finally, he pulled up to Heather's brownstone.

No cameras.

Relief washed through me.

"Thank you, sir," I said, handing the driver a hundred.

Heather led me inside, up the narrow staircase to 3B.

Her apartment was small, inviting, and cozy. A quilted purple duvet. Fashion sketches pinned to a cork board. A photo of her holding a cat.

"Mookie?" I asked.

She laughed softly. "Yes. That was my Mookie."

Another photo caught me—her in a white dress in Punta Cana, her smile like sunshine. Maybe that was the moment I really fell for her, years before either of us was ready.

She handed me a sweatshirt and a stack of blankets.

"Come on. I want to show you something."

We climbed to the rooftop. The night spread around us —Chicago glowing, stars cutting through the dark where they could.

I sank into an old lounge chair. She nestled in front of me, her back against my chest. I wrapped my arms around her, fitting her against me like she belonged there.

"You can see some stars from here," she whispered.

I didn't look up.

I looked at her.

Whatever was growing between us felt fragile and permanent in a way nothing else in my life ever had.

42

JUST THE TWO OF US
HEATHER

Bradley's Chicago run was over, and for the first time since he'd arrived, it felt like the city had loosened its grip on him. *On us.*

No sound checks, no rehearsals, no backstage groupies, no interruptions from Suzie, no early morning meetings for me. Tory would be away for work and then was planning to stay with Joel at his place; she was practically glowing at the thought of playing house, which only added to my excitement. It meant Bradley and I could finally be alone. I started my opportunity at Bloomingdale's next Monday, and for the first time since college, I had a whole week off. The relief of it felt decadent, like slipping into a hotel robe you didn't pay for and deciding to keep it.

We checked out of his hotel Monday morning and went back to my place. He carried a soft duffel and his guitar case up my stairs and dropped them in the living room like this was something we did all the time.

"Home sweet temporary home," he said, flashing that dimple that always made me feel like I was in on something.

The day stretched in the best possible way. We ordered

food, watched movies, *The Hangover* and *Wedding Crashers*, and argued about which one was better until he pelted me with a throw pillow and we dissolved into laughter. At some point, we ended up tangled together on the couch, his hand gripping my waist, my cheek pressed to his shoulder.

It was easy. Dangerous in how easy it was.

That night, when he fell asleep before I did, his arm heavy across my stomach, I lay there listening to the ordinary sounds of my apartment and thinking how quickly he'd slipped into them. *Like he fit.*

By Tuesday afternoon, I needed daylight. Movement. Proof that we could exist outside my four walls.

We walked the Lakefront Trail near North Avenue Beach. Bradley wore a baseball cap and dark sunglasses. I wore my bravest face. For forty-five minutes, we passed as normal—two people sharing a pretzel, discussing how Chicago could easily be one of the prettiest cities till winter hit.

He laughed when a bubble machine on a stroller sent a string of iridescent orbs toward us, batting one away with the same gentle focus he used when he brushed hair from my face.

For a moment, I forgot about Bradley's other life.

Then the first flash went off.

Bright and sharp, like someone snapping a camera inside my head.

Voices followed—his name, loud and familiar—and the air shifted. Phones lifted. People stared.

"Don't let go," he murmured calmly, already taking my hand.

We walked, brisk and purposeful, like we'd practiced this. Inside the car, my chest trembled when I realized I'd been holding my breath.

"You okay?" he asked.

"It's just... a lot," I said honestly. I wasn't sure if I could get used to this.

"I know." His thumb traced slow circles on the back of my hand. "I'm sorry."

"Can I ask you something? One thing?" I asked.

"Anything."

"Do you ever wish you had a normal life?"

"Only if I risk losing you," he said quietly.

That night, my phone buzzed with a text from Nico. A screenshot from a tabloid of us and another next to it, Bradley wedged between a few girls in sparkles, tube tops, and pleather, all leaning in like they belonged there.

NICO

You are way hotter than those desperate tramps. PS, aren't you glad I just did your roots?? You're welcome.

I groaned. Bradley leaned over my shoulder and kissed the top of my head.

"I hate this," I said quietly.

"I know, darlin'." His forehead leaned into mine. "You can't buy into these tabloids. They are garbage."

"I don't like being part of a gossip magazine." That was the only part I could admit.

The photo burned at the edge of my vision. One girl's hand was too close to his chest. Another's smile felt too confident. My jaw tightened before I could stop it.

"Look at me." He stepped back slightly so we could see eye to eye. "*You* are my girl."

His girl.

He pulled me back into him.

"Nico is right. You are a hottie, and your hair does look good."

That night, he insisted on cooking. "I told you about my famous nachos," he said, like he was defending a title.

He took over my kitchen with surprising seriousness, singing along with Zeppelin while he chopped peppers and layered chips with care. When he slid the pan into my too-small oven, he crouched to inspect it like a proud parent.

"You're very serious about this," I said.

"I got to feed my girl," he said gravely. And I couldn't help but hear him call me that, making all the feelings from earlier today disappear. I was his. He was choosing me. Isn't that what I had wanted... to be chosen?

We ate standing at the counter, fingers messy, laughing when the cheese stretched too far. At some point, he said, "Okay. Questions," like it was a sacred ritual.

"I love our questions."

"Favorite snack."

"French fries," I said, immediately.

"Wrong. It's these nachos. But I will allow fries as a side."

"Guilty pleasure TV," I volleyed.

He squinted. "Murder mysteries. Yours?"

"Gossip Girl."

He laughed. "I wasn't expecting that, but it might be every girl's favorite show."

"Favorite word?"

He tipped his head, considering. "You."

"That's cheating."

"Then 'home.' But only because it includes 'you.'"

I pretended to be annoyed and then kissed him till we ended up on the kitchen floor, the tile cool against my knees, his laugh warm against my mouth. We didn't make it to the couch. The oven door fogged with steam, and I learned exactly how delicious it is when someone who can command a stage of twenty thousand lowers his voice just for you.

The following night, we decided to be social. We met Tory, Joel, Marcus, and Nico out for a meal. A tucked-away restaurant. A back entrance. A corner banquette that felt almost private. For a while, it worked—stories, shared plates, his hand resting at my waist like it belonged there.

When we exited the restaurant, there were several cameramen ready to hijack our privacy. By the time we reached the car, my hands were shaking.

"I'm sorry," he said.

"You didn't do this," I said under my breath. "I am afraid of being turned into a storyline," I said before I could soften it. "A headline. I don't want to be the messy girl who dated the musician and got eaten alive by the comments section."

"I can't promise what the world will do," he said. "But I can promise how I'll protect you in it. And how I'll be here with you through it."

I tucked myself into him and believed him more than I believed the weather app or my horoscope or anything that pretended to tell the future.

Back at my apartment, he rubbed my feet from the opposite side of the couch until the tension drained out of me, leaving something quieter behind.

"We need to talk about Europe," I said eventually. "Six months. What does that look like for us?"

He didn't rush. "Distance," he said honestly. "Phone calls, FaceTime. I could fly you to me anytime you want."

"I have this opportunity at Bloomingdale's," I said. "That's me finally planting my feet; I can't just jet off whenever."

He nodded. "I understand."

We sat with it—not solving anything at the moment.

The next day, I left for the market, leaving Bradley in the apartment.

As I moved through the aisles, I felt unexpectedly emotional. I tossed things into the basket that didn't quite make sense together, ingredients for a meal without a plan. My thoughts were louder than the store, doubts slipping in where certainty had been all week.

On my walk home, my phone buzzed. It was Mom.

"Hi Mom." I shifted my tote on my shoulder.

"Heatherbug." Wind chimes clinked faintly in the background. Hearing her voice brought me comfort. "Have you been meditating every morning? You got that study I sent you, right?"

I smiled. "Yes, Mom. I saw it. I haven't exactly started my meditation journey yet." I stepped around a crack in the pavement. "But I do have some news."

"I knew it," she said immediately. "One of my tarot cards last week said you were going through a big shift."

"Well... I got an opportunity with Bloomingdale's. They want to showcase my line."

She gasped. "That's amazing. Your art is coming to life. I am so proud of you, bug."

"There's more." I slowed as I reached my block. "I ended things with Tripp."

A pause. "Don't be mad, but Tory told me."

I laughed softly. "Of course she did."

"Sweetie, I think he was dimming your light. You are so bright. You deserve to shine."

"Thanks, Mom."

I adjusted my bag and switched ears.

"I'm dating someone new. I guess he isn't new. I don't know if you remember Bradley.

"Oh my." I could practically hear her sitting up straighter. "The one from all those years ago?"

"That's the one."

"I had a feeling you were going to have some old sparks flame when you saw him at his concert.

"But it isn't easy. He's... quite famous."

"I've heard." She softened. "Honey, love will prevail as long as you both stay true to yourselves."

I stopped at my front steps and reached for my keys.

"Thanks for listening, Mom."

"Anytime, sweetie. And I am very happy that preppy pants is gone."

I laughed. "I just got home. I love you."

"Love you too, Heatherbug."

When I got back upstairs, Bradley was sitting on the couch with his guitar, his black notebook open on his knee. He was strumming softly, focused, like the world narrowed when he wrote.

"Hey, darlin'," he said, standing to take the grocery bags from my hands.

He helped put everything away, then turned to me, his expression gentler than usual. "I'm sorry we kind of got stuck in here all week."

"It's okay," I said, then hesitated. "How do you live with it?"

"With what?"

"All of it," I said. "The noise. The attention."

He leaned back against the counter. "It's still new. I try to drown it out. When I'm back in L.A., I'll keep a low profile. There are a lot of famous people around—I'm not that big of a deal."

I shook my head. "I think you're bigger than you know."

He crossed the room and pulled me into him, pressing a kiss to my cheek. "Come here."

His arms felt steady. Familiar already.

He glanced toward my bookshelf. "You've got board games," he said. "Should we start with checkers? Clue? Monopoly?"

"Checkers feels like a good two-person game."

"I was thinking the same thing."

We played game after game, sprawled on the floor, laughing and trading stories—childhood embarrassments, half-formed dreams, moments that had shaped us long before we ever found each other. It wasn't dramatic or profound. It was something better.

It was real.

Later, we climbed to the roof with a blanket and a bottle of wine poured into mismatched mugs. The city stretched below us, bright and alive. Bradley brought his guitar but didn't really play—just let his fingers wander across the strings.

I leaned back against his chest, his heartbeat steady beneath my shoulder blades.

"Another question for you," he said.

"Go for it."

"Will you officially be my girlfriend?"

I sat up and turned to face him. His tone shifted— quieter, serious. "I know being with me isn't easy. The lack of privacy. The distance. I know I'm asking a lot."

He held my gaze. "But I want you, Heather. And I don't have all the answers yet—but I want to figure them out with you. Whatever this becomes."

I couldn't help but feel the knots in my chest loosen. My heart fluttered. I wanted to be his more than anything; I'd wanted to be his since I was that girl back on that island. I was just terrified of all the noise that came with it.

I said in a low, careful voice, "I think I have always been your girl in some way."

With that, he leaned down and kissed me, pulling me into his arms.

Being with Bradley felt rare—extraordinary in the quietest way. The kind of thing you didn't fully understand until you were already standing inside it. It made me want to move carefully, to hold the moment like something fragile and valuable.

That awareness didn't comfort me the way I expected it to.

It scared me.

Because wanting him was easy. Falling for him felt natural—almost inevitable.

What scared me was the rest of it.

I'd already learned what it felt like to disappear inside someone else's life. To make myself smaller. To mistake silence for peace. I was smarter now. I knew myself better.

But the stakes were higher this time.

43

THE QUESTIONS WE LIVE FOR

HEATHER

Saturday, we didn't leave the apartment at all. He wrote a riff on my coffee table with a pen and a crumpled receipt. I paged through a stack of fashion sketches on the floor, pencil smudging the heel of my hand. He replayed the same chorus over and over, and I told him I loved it until he called me a menace and kissed my cheek.

The afternoon went syrupy and warm. We ended up in the shower, steam gathering fast enough to fog the mirror and bead along the tile, turning the small bathroom into its own little cocoon. Water pooled at our feet as we laughed ourselves breathless.

He drew a crooked heart in the haze before reaching past me and shutting off the spray. The water fell quiet, leaving only the sound of our breathing.

He stepped out first and grabbed my hand, guiding me with him onto the bath mat. Water trailed down our bodies, dripping in soft, steady rhythms against the tile.

Before I could reach for a towel, he turned me, gently facing the mirror, pressing my belly against the cool porcelain.

He kissed the back of my neck. My breath hitched, and I could feel his length grow against my ass. He reached down to feel if I was ready for him.

In the reflection, I caught us fully—damp hair clinging to my shoulders, his chest still slick and glistening, droplets sliding down the curve of his jaw. His hands were firm at my hips.

He looked up and met my eyes in the reflection—dark, focused, entirely present—and placed himself inside me.

Seeing us like that, flushed, unguarded, sent something slow and unwavering through me.

I leaned back into him, into the heat that hadn't faded, and let the moment pull us closer.

At dinner, we made pasta with whatever the fridge surrendered: cherry tomatoes collapsing in olive oil, basil rescued from the brink, Parmesan shaved thin with a vegetable peeler. He insisted on garlic bread with twice the garlic any sane person would use, then made me try it with my eyes closed. "Tell me this is the best Italian food you have ever had." He gave me a smug look when I opened my eyes.

"Yum, it might need a tad more garlic," I said through a snort.

He stared at me and huffed a laugh.

Later, when the dishes were drying in uneven stacks, we drifted into the living room. He stretched out on the couch, shoulder propped against the pillow, and nudged my foot with his.

He patted the space beside him. I sank down next to him without thinking, my pulse quickening at the quiet invitation.

"Okay, time for some questions," he said, lacing his

fingers behind his head. "Where do you want to live when you're old?"

"By water," I said. "Lake, ocean, river—doesn't matter. Somewhere the air smells like salt, fish, or dock wood."

It was the kind of answer I never would've given Tripp; he liked plans more than dreams. "Same question for you."

"Front porch," Bradley said. "Guitar, rocking chair, dog with a goofy name."

"What goofy name?"

"Gus," he said immediately. "Or Bucket."

"Bucket," I repeated, delighted. "That's awful."

He grinned at the ceiling. "What do you want besides work?"

I hesitated. Not because I didn't know, but because saying it out loud felt like opening a window I usually kept locked. "Something that feels everlasting," I said finally. "The feeling of... ease."

"Then that's what we make," he said, the words simple as breath, as if my fear of wanting things hadn't kept me cautious for years.

A part of me curled back at the thought—old reflex. I'd believed in something once, in someone, and watched it thin out until I barely recognized myself inside it. Tripp and I had always looked good on paper. I'd learned the hard way that paper wasn't the same as a pulse. And before that, when I was younger, I'd fallen for Bradley in a way that felt too big for the version of myself I was back then. Hope had always come with sharp edges in my world: my mother's two divorces before the third one finally held, my own engagement that flatlined long before the ring came off, the memory of being a girl on vacation who loved someone who couldn't stay.

The clock on my dresser ticked louder that night. His

suitcase by the door taunted me that the end was near. His flight was late morning; the driver would come at nine. I did the math I didn't want to do. He must've felt my body go tense because he rolled onto his side and tucked himself around me like he knew exactly which ghosts were circling.

"Hey," he murmured into my hair. "Don't go there yet."

"Where?"

"Tomorrow."

"I'm trying not to."

"Try with me."

He kissed the back of my neck in a line that felt like a smile and slid his palm down my arm, our fingers lacing. Tomorrow receded a little—polite, patient, waiting its turn.

Sunday dawned pale and too bright. I pulled on his sweatshirt like it could keep him here, like fabric had that kind of power. I made coffee slowly, stretching the pour as if time might stretch with it. He stood at the counter in a soft T-shirt, hair rebellious, eyes gentle. We ate eggs and toast like a ritual, each bite a bead on a string holding us together.

"Don't," I said when his gaze caught mine.

"I'm not," he said softly. "I'm just memorizing you."

I hated how much that undid me. This—whatever this was—felt too good, too big, too close to something teenage-me once believed in, and too close to the thing adult-me had learned to lose.

The suitcase wheels chirped against my uneven wood floor, and something in me flinched. But we still stood by the door together. He touched everything he'd borrowed from my life: the chipped mug, the blanket on the chair, the cheap fish-shaped bottle opener, the cork board of half-born dresses—pieces of me no one had bothered to see before him.

"Can I take something that smells like you?" he asked, shy in a way that could topple me if I let it.

I handed him the folded blanket. "It knows our secrets," I said.

Then he pressed something small into my hand. A guitar pick—black, edges worn, a tiny silver "B" scratched into the center.

"For luck," he said. "For when you need to remember this is real."

My voice cracked, "I will put it with the one you gave me in Punta Cana."

I slid it into my bra—there was nowhere closer to keep it. The look he gave me nearly canceled his flight.

"Say the thing," I said, not sure which thing until it came out. "Say the plan so I can hold it."

"I'll call when I land," he said. "I'll call before I sleep, and when I wake up, and when I get coffee, and when I write anything worth showing you. I'll tell Suzie I need more days like this. I'll send you pictures of Bucket when I find him."

"Gus," I corrected, my voice uneven.

"Gus," he agreed solemnly. "We'll do Chicago again. Or you'll come to California. We'll make both. We'll make something that's just ours. And we'll keep asking questions."

I nodded because speaking felt risky. Hope held in my heart.

He cupped my face, thumbs warm at my temples, and kissed me like an answer he'd been working on quietly for years. No cinematic dip, no sweeping music—just the kind of kiss that says *I'm here*, even when here is temporary.

We walked down the steps in silence. The air smelled like rain deciding what kind of day it wanted. There might've been cameras outside; maybe not. None of it mattered from the doorway.

"I'll see you soon, promise," he said.

"Soon," I echoed.

He lifted his bag and the blanket, then set them down to hug me again, tighter, like a man who understood memory and wanted to give me more than enough. I pressed my face to his chest, breathing him in.

"Go," I said. "Before I keep you."

"That is tempting," he murmured, smiling.

He paused in the doorway and looked at me like I was the last lyric he almost forgot but caught in time. Then he was gone, and the door clicked shut, and Lakeview thrummed to fill the space he left.

Back upstairs, I stood in the middle of my living room until the quiet rearranged itself. I smoothed the duvet—not for neatness, but for something to do. The clock ticked at the same stubborn pace. I made the bed, then unmade it slightly because his shape was still there, and I wasn't ready to erase it.

On the counter, a note:

Don't forget to eat the last of the nachos. :)

PS: That's the Way

A breadcrumb to our time together. To us.

I pressed the pick against my sternum, a cool coin of proof. I started a new list of questions on scrap paper and taped it to the fridge:

Dog name: Gus or Bucket?

Favorite season?
What color should our porch be?
Do you believe in luck?

When my phone buzzed, I didn't need to check the screen.

"Hey." His voice was thick as if the city had followed him into the car. "Question for you."

"Answer."

"When I'm old, and my hands stop working like they do now, will you cut up my food and still pretend I'm charming?"

"Obviously. But only if you admit Bucket is a terrible name."

He laughed, and warmth spread through my body.

"Deal," he said.

"Okay," I said softly.

We didn't say goodbye. We didn't need to. The week had given us a place to stand—enough for now.

I picked up my pencil again, shading the hem of a dress I might finish later.

From the window, I could hear the soft thunder of the L turning toward Southport and a breeze carrying the faint edge of the Lake.

I didn't move toward anything certain.

I just let the moment be what it was.

44

———

DECEMBER

BRADLEY

Christmas at Aunt Becky and Uncle Gary's always meant noise before you even got your coat off.

Tommy had taken over the armchair closest to the TV, one leg hooked over the other, beer balanced dangerously on the arm while he argued with Jared about whether the Bengals had been cursed or just poorly coached. Brett was pacing the length of the living room like he might personally fix the issue if given enough time. Jared hovered near the kitchen doorway, stealing food straight off serving trays and pretending not to notice Jamie swatting at him every time he passed.

Tommy's wife sat curled into the corner of the couch, their baby tucked against her chest, rocking gently while the room moved loud and fast around them. Every so often, Tommy glanced over, instinct sharp, even in the middle of whatever story he was telling, his voice dropping without him realizing it.

Aunt Becky floated between rooms, refilling drinks no one had asked for. My mom helped in the kitchen; she was laughing more easily than she used to. Jamie sat across from

Uncle Gary, sleeves pushed up, already halfway into a conversation about work she swore she wouldn't bring up. The house felt full.

By the time we said our goodbyes, the house was still loud behind us. Brett was halfway into another story. Jared was wrapping leftovers in foil like he planned to smuggle them out. Tommy stood in the doorway, bouncing the over-tired baby, jacket half on, promising he'd text when they got home. Aunt Becky kissed the baby goodnight.

Jamie and my mom walked out ahead of me, their breath puffing white into the cold. The car doors shut with a familiar thud, and just like that, everything quieted.

The drive back to our house was short. A few familiar turns. Streets I could take blindfolded. The one-story place we'd grown up in sat exactly the same way it always had—low and modest, lights on in the front room, the porch lamp casting that yellow cone onto the sidewalk.

Inside, my mom kicked off her shoes by the door. Jamie hung her coat on the rack.

We sat at the kitchen table instead of the living room. It was where everything real had always happened.

Jamie handed my mom her gift first. A stack of neatly wrapped boxes.

"Don't laugh," she said.

My mom opened a large box—pots and pans, solid and heavy, the kind meant to last years. She ran a hand over the lid of one, smiling.

"These are beautiful," she said. "You didn't need to—"

"Oh, stop," Jamie said with a tease. "Yours are from your wedding; it's time for an upgrade." Jamie took a sip of the tea Mom made. "I also set up an account for you on MATCH.com."

That got a laugh out of all three of us.

My mom reached for the bag she'd tucked under the counter and handed Jamie a small velvet box. Inside was a simple necklace—something she'd worn almost every day when we were kids.

"I think it belongs to you now," Mom said, tilting her head.

Jamie swallowed, nodding once as she clasped it around her neck.

Then my mom turned to me. She didn't wrap anything. Just reached into the drawer by the sink and pulled out a thin stack of papers—old, soft at the edges.

Lyrics.

My lyrics. Messy handwriting. Coffee stains. Songs I'd forgotten I'd ever written.

"You used to leave these everywhere," she said. "I kept them. Didn't know why. Just felt important."

My throat tightened. "Mom... "

She waved me off. "You always knew what you wanted to do. Even when you didn't know how."

I sat there for a moment, papers in my hands, in the house that held some sad memories but way more happy ones when it was just the three of us.

I slid my gift across the table next. A small box. My mom hesitated before opening it.

Inside was a key.

She frowned, looking up at me. "Bradley... "

"No more rent," I said quietly. "The bookstore's yours. You're the landlord now. Whatever you want to do with it— it's yours."

Her fingers closed around the key like she was scared she might drop it. "This is too much."

"It's not. You are the charm of that store."

She shook her head, eyes already glassy. "You didn't have to do this."

"You kept us standing on your own."

I didn't say my dad's name. I didn't have to.

She reached out, cupping my face. "You turned out strong," she said softly. "Both of you."

For once, it didn't feel like something I had to prove.

My mom wiped at her cheeks and smiled with pure joy.

Later, as Jamie cleared our mugs and my mom started tidying in that slow, unnecessary way that meant she didn't want the night to end yet, I stood and kissed her cheek.

"I'm leaving early," I said. "I want to see Heather before Europe."

She smiled, already knowing that was coming. "Go," she said. "You don't need permission anymore."

But I liked hearing it anyway.

The next morning, my mom drove me to the airport. The sky was still pale, the kind of light that makes everything feel unfinished. We didn't talk much in the car. The radio hummed low. I watched the streets I knew slip past the window and tried not to think too hard about what I was leaving or how much I was taking with me.

At the curb, she reached across the console and squeezed my arm.

"Text when you land," she said.

"I will."

She watched until I disappeared through the sliding doors, the way she always had.

The flight to O'Hare was quick, just long enough for anticipation to beat out a rhythm with my fingertips. As soon as I stepped into the terminal, the holiday decorations hit me. Garland wrapped around the banisters. Giant red bows. Lights strung overhead in lazy lines. It looked exactly like *Home Alone*.

I snapped a photo and sent it to Heather.

BRADLEY

What's your favorite Christmas movie? Can you guess mine?

HEATHER

Home Alone happens to be my favorite, too.

BRADLEY

Looks like we have plans.

HEATHER

In that case, I'll return my red lace getup.

BRADLEY

Don't tease a boy.

HEATHER

Let me know what door to pick you up at. I'm in the cell phone lot.

We'd agreed on small gifts, just things that meant something. I checked the zipper pocket of my bag, fingers brushing the edge of the box I'd tucked there. Still there. The thought settled me.

I texted her my door by baggage claim. When the sliding doors opened, a rush of cold cut through the terminal. I spotted her almost immediately. She sat behind the wheel of Nico's Mercedes, pulled up at the curb, hair twisted into a messy bun, cheeks flushed pink from the wind.

My heart did something ridiculous at the sight of her, like it forgot this wasn't our first reunion.

Uncle Gary and Aunt Becky had a cabin in Lake Geneva, Wisconsin—a summer rental that sat empty in winter. They'd offered it to us for a few days, and I couldn't think of a better way to spend the in-between of Christmas and New Year's.

The drive was just over an hour, highways thinning into back roads lined with bare trees. Heather kept one hand on the wheel, the other resting on the console where my fingers found hers. We talked about everything and nothing, the kind of chatter when two people didn't run out of things to talk about.

When we pulled up, the house looked like it had been dropped into a snow globe. White drifts banked against the porch, icicles hanging sharp from the gutters. The lake out front was frozen solid, glittering under the moonlight. I could picture how alive it must be in the summer—kids running barefoot, boats cutting through waves, grills smoking in the backyards. But tonight it was hushed, suspended in winter's stillness.

The garage sat tucked at the back. We carried bags through the side mudroom. The air inside was stale and icy, as if the walls had been holding their breath. Heather set the groceries on the counter and disappeared to crank on the heat. I exhaled into the silence, watching my breath cloud faintly.

The cabin groaned as the furnace kicked on, wood floors creaking like they were waking up after a long nap. A stack of logs sat by the fireplace, and I told Heather I'd get one going. Soon, sparks hissed and a fire caught, snapping and popping until the room glowed amber. Heather moved around the kitchen, unpacking groceries, sleeves pushed up, cheeks rosy. It felt absurdly natural, like we'd been doing this forever.

The cabin itself was simple. One bedroom downstairs, two more tucked beneath the eaves upstairs. The front windows faced the frozen lake, and I stood there a moment, staring out. *This is what peace looks like*, I thought.

The fire cracked behind me. Floorboards shifted as she crossed the room. I turned from the windows just as her hands wrapped around my chest.

She leaned in and kissed the back of my neck. My jaw tightened as her lips touched me.

I turned to face her. I slid one hand into her hair, taking a fistful, and wrapping the other around her waist. I pulled her in as close as I could and leaned down to meet her lips. I took her mouth hard. Our lips furiously collided, the need between us starting to grow at an intense rate.

I peppered her ear and neck with kisses, easing us down to the couch in front of the fire. Heat from the flames curled into the room as I peeled away winter layers until all that was left was a red lace G-string and matching bra. I grew so hard it almost hurt, hitting the restraint in my jeans.

She lifted my shirt over my head, rubbing her hands over me like windshield wipers, slow and deliberate. I tugged down one of the cups of her lace bra, exposing her pink nipple. I took it into my mouth, devouring it, feeling it harden under my tongue. I moved to the other side to give it equal attention. With one hand, I snapped the back of the bra free, and her breasts were bare.

She lowered her hands to my pants and unzipped me nice and slow, like unwrapping a present. My bulge sprang free, giving me relief. She tugged at my pants; I gave her a hand, and they were off.

She rubbed her hand over me in slow circles, leaving me

desperate with hunger. She slid my briefs down, and all that was left between us was the red G-string I planned to admire from behind the first chance I got.

She took me in her hand, moving slowly at first, then faster. I moved my hands to the top of her core, ready to slide a finger in. She stopped me, lifting one finger to her mouth, sliding it between her lips to demonstrate exactly what she planned to do.

Then she moved down and took me into her mouth in one smooth motion. I grabbed a fistful of her hair.

I could barely take it anymore.

When she came back up, I lost myself in the way she looked at me—like I wasn't just a man, but the *only* man. I held myself and stroked once, twice, trying to steady my breathing. She looked at me with yearning written all over her face.

I reached into my pocket and grabbed a condom, ripping it open with my teeth. I slid it on and moved her panties to the side before slipping inside her. She opened for me, and we both gasped as we merged.

I held her waist and bounced her up and down until I wanted a change of scenery. I lifted her and brought her to all fours, then knelt behind her, moved the tiny string, and slammed into her. The impact between us pulled moans from her lips, my name breaking at the end of them. I followed after, releasing, "Fuck," with a heavy sigh.

When I could form steps and words again, I went to the bathroom to take care of the condom.

As I came back, I admired her lying on a fuzzy blanket, the firelight flickering across her skin, making her look like a vixen.

I lay down next to her. One of her legs wrapped around me. Her hands slid over my shoulders, her fingers tangling in my hair as I kissed her forehead. Every brush of her body against mine sent sparks racing under my skin.

"I love you," I said quietly, the words coming from somewhere deeper than heat. "You're everything. Every song, every word—it's all you."

Her eyes softened, vulnerable in a way that undid me.

"I love you too, Bradley."

"You are smooth with words," she said softly, sitting up slightly to look me in the eye. "You make me feel like anything is possible."

I brushed a thumb along her jaw.

"It is," I said. "With you, it is."

The fire popped behind us, but nothing in me felt uncertain anymore.

45

HOME ALONE IN THE CABIN
BRADLEY

As Kevin from *Home Alone* began setting up booby traps on the screen, Heather curled into my chest, her legs tucked under mine, our fingers threaded together. The fire cracked behind us, light flickering across her face.

She turned toward me, chin resting on my sternum. "I think we're due for the question game."

"Oh yeah?" I brushed a strand of hair behind her ear. "You go first."

"Do you think chemistry is instant or built?"

I huffed a quiet laugh. "Ah, starting off deep, I see." I looked down at her. "It was instant with you."

Her eyes flickered—surprise, then something softer. "I like that answer."

"It's true." I tapped her nose lightly. "My turn. When you heard my song for the first time... did you know it was about you?"

She smiled slowly, like she'd been waiting for that. "I had a hunch. It felt like you were sending me a postcard."

"My plan worked."

"Sure did." She twirled her hair around her finger, gaze dropping for a second before lifting again. "Do you think you'll ever talk to your dad again?"

That one sat heavier.

"Honestly... no." I exhaled. "It took me years to take him off the pedestal I had him on. Then came resentment. Now I'm just trying to let it go." I swallowed. "He bailed when we were young. One day he was there, the next he wasn't. My mom carried everything after that."

She shifted closer without thinking, her hand flattening over my heart.

"How about you and your dad? What's the story?"

She stared at the fire for a beat. "Honestly? There isn't much of one. He works overseas. We talk from time to time. He shows his love in paychecks." A small shrug. "It's fine."

The way she said it told me it wasn't.

"It sounds like your mom's happy now," I said gently. "That guy Keith... he seemed like a keeper."

Her mouth curved faintly. "They're happy in their bubble of incense and sage." She hesitated. "You don't think we're doomed? Both coming from divorced parents?"

I tilted her chin so she had to look at me. "I don't. Our moms are strong enough to prove that."

She blinked.

Then her voice shifted, softer, careful. "I have to ask this... how long do you think you'll go on tour for?"

There it was.

"Not having a schedule worries me," she continued, eyes searching mine. "Your life is all over the map. And mine... isn't. I'm usually in Chicago. I like structure. I need routine. It's how I know where I am."

I nodded slowly. "My life doesn't offer much of that. Some tours last weeks. Some turn into months before you notice. Cities blur. Dates change. Sometimes you don't get to choose when you leave or when you're back."

She exhaled, her fingers tracing slow lines over my chest again. "That's the part that scares me. I don't want to feel like I'm fitting myself around someone else's chaos."

"I wouldn't want that either." I cupped the back of her neck. "I don't want you bending yourself into something that doesn't feel like you. I know what my life looks like from the outside. Hell, I know what it feels like from the inside."

She looked up at me, eyes still and vulnerable. "I just don't want to wake up one day realizing I waited for something that never settled."

"I hear that." My voice lowered. "I can't promise you a perfect rhythm. But I won't disappear into it. I don't want a life where I'm always coming and going and never really landing."

She studied me for a long moment, like she was deciding whether to trust what she saw.

"I want to picture it," she said finally. "Us. Even kids."

The word hung between us.

"Our kids would be very hairy. Lots of curls." I couldn't help it—I laughed softly, pressing my forehead to hers.

Her laugh slipped out, light but real, easing the tightness without erasing it.

We switched gears and finished the movie, Kevin finally reuniting with his mom in the most perfect snowfall. Heather wiped at her eyes quickly.

"You're crying," I teased.

"I'm not."

"You are."

She smacked my chest, smiling.

The next day blurred into reading books, cooking

together, making out in the kitchen like we were teenagers, showering with steam fogging the mirrors, and ending up on the rug by the fire while I strummed the guitar and she stretched out with her book. Pages rustled. Fire crackled. Music drifted through the room.

> *Forgot how much I loved you back then*
> *It's taken forever to remember. Again.*
> *Now I can't forget the Kerosene.*
> *When there's no fire to be seen.*

She lifted her head from her book, eyes glistening. "I like this tune. Did you just make it up?"

"Yep." I looked at her over the guitar. "You're dusted through all my writing."

♫♪

By evening, the weight of leaving hovered over us. It was our last night.

Time to exchange gifts.

We sat on the sofa, knees touching, fire low and golden. Heather went first, handing me a bag.

Inside was a framed drawing—me on stage with my guitar, the view from her eyes. The detail floored me. My throat tightened, my vision blurring.

"Heather... " My voice cracked as I looked at her. "This is the most thoughtful gift anyone has ever given me."

She searched my face, almost nervous. "So you like it?"

"More than like. I love it."

I handed her a small box, the bow slightly crushed from travel. "Sorry about the bow. TSA."

She opened it carefully. A black leather photo album.

Ticket stubs from my shows. Scraps of lyrics. Photos of cities and crowds. Pieces of us. On the last page, the Punta Cana ocean—the only image I'd kept from when we were kids.

On the back cover, engraved in simple script:

No matter the city, no matter the sound, every song I start finds its way back to you.

Her fingers traced the words slowly. Her eyes filled.

Silence stretched between us.

She looked up at me, voice barely above a whisper. "This is real, isn't it?"

"It is."

Her breath trembled. "I love you."

Something in my chest gave way.

"I love you too, Heather."

I pulled her into me, holding her tighter than I had all weekend, the fire flickering across the walls as if it were trying to memorize us too.

46

BETWEEN THE SEAMS
HEATHER

The cold hit me the second I stepped outside, sharp enough to make my eyes water. February in Chicago always found a way to sink straight into my bones, no matter how many layers I wore.

Today wasn't just another morning, though. My line had been selected to show at FashionBar's winter showcase, and I was one of the featured emerging designers. By ten a.m., the first shows would begin—models rotating through the space, editors and buyers taking their seats, the expectation building fast, and I couldn't let my cheeks become a blazing red when I got nervous.

Right now, it was just me and the final line I'd spent months perfecting. Every hem, every stitch, every sleepless night had led to this week. I pulled my scarf higher and picked up my pace. The city around me buzzed differently today, as if even the cabs and street vendors knew something electric was about to unfold.

Bradley had called in the middle of the night again—well after midnight here, but early morning in Italy. By the time I woke up, his voicemail was waiting, his voice comforting: *"Good luck today. Wish I could see you in the front row."* I replayed it twice on the walk to the studio, letting his words settle under my skin. A few minutes later, just as I fumbled for the keys, my phone buzzed again. A text lit the screen:

BRADLEY

You got this, darlin'.

It was mid-morning here, but already late afternoon there. By the time my show began, he'd be heading into his evening, and when I finally collapsed tonight, he'd be fast asleep. The six hours stretched between us like a chasm, making our lives feel just out of sync—close enough to touch, but never quite overlapping.

Inside the venue, the world shifted into a whirlwind. The sharp hiss of steamers filled the air, curling like smoke signals above racks of garments. Assistants darted between dressing areas, clipboards clutched to their chests. Models sat in long rows under glaring bulbs while makeup artists leaned in, brushes flashing, stylists tugging at hair with quick, practiced movements. Urgency ran through the room, every second wound tight.

"Lineup?" I asked Alena, already scanning the rack for a hem that looked off.

"All here," she called back, though her eyes looked frazzled. "Except model twelve—she's stuck in traffic."

There was always one.

I wove through the racks, running my fingers along the fabrics—silk that rippled under my touch, sequins that caught the light like bottled starlight. My designs. My life. I stopped to smooth the belt on look seven, then crouched to pin the hem of look ten myself, ignoring the sting in my already raw fingertips. When it was your name on the program, no task was beneath you.

"Can you please steam that sleeve again?" I said to one of the dressers hovering by the rack, pointing to a dress that had already been tended to twice. "I want it perfect."

The minutes bled together. I barked orders, checked seams, adjusted jewelry. A model complained her heels pinched; I swapped them for another pair without hesitation. Across the room, Nico was in his element, round brush in one hand, blow dryer in the other, coaxing sleek waves into place. "We're going to need more extensions over here," he called out, as he examined a model's hair under the lights. The line drew a ripple of laughter from the stylists nearby, but his focus never wavered. He caught my eye, gave me a reassuring smile, and kept working, his calm energy centering me as I pushed back into the chaos.

The air was misted with hairspray and nerves. A makeup artist brushed glitter across a model's eyelids, muttering, "Don't blink." Another tugged a curling iron through strands while balancing a phone under her chin. Assistants whispered the order of looks like prayers.

Tory slipped backstage for a moment, sneaking past security, and wrapped me in a hug that nearly knocked the wind out of me.

"You've got this," she whispered. "I am so proud of you."

Her voice strengthened me in a way nothing else could.

Tory squeezed my hand one last time, her smile trembling with pride. "Okay, I'd better get back to my seat. Marcus is waiting out there."

I nodded, reluctant to let her go, but she slipped back through the curtain, leaving me with the noise of blow dryers, the hiss of steamers, and the pounding of my own heartbeat.

Everything was coming together, or as best as I could hope. There was a bit of stress here and there, but it was time, and all I could do was surrender in the moment. I'd relax when it was over.

The lights dimmed, the bass thumped, and the first model stepped onto the runway. My heart pounded in rhythm with the music as the collection came alive under the spotlights. From the wings, I could see the crowd lean forward, cameras flashing, editors scribbling furiously into their programs.

Look one shimmered down the runway—an emerald silk slip dress cut on the bias, catching every ounce of light. Look two followed in sharp contrast: a tailored charcoal suit with a cinched waist, the kind of power dressing I'd dreamed of on the runway. Look three glided out in sequins —thousands of tiny glass beads stitched one by one by hands that weren't mine but might as well have been, given the hours I'd hovered over them.

The rhythm of the show carried me forward. Look seven —the one I'd fussed over backstage—earned an audible gasp from the crowd: a cream trench with exaggerated shoulders, belted tightly over a sheer underdress that whispered rebellion. Look ten, the one I'd pinned myself, flowed like water, the hem finally right.

I caught sight of Tory in the third row, her hand looped through Marcus's arm, eyes shining. They leaned forward with every look, Marcus whispering something in her ear that made her grin. Seeing them there anchored me, proof that I wasn't dreaming.

And then the finale: a black gown cut low at the back, with layers of chiffon that moved like smoke. When the model paused at the end of the runway, the cameras popped so furiously it felt like a lightning storm.

The applause was a tidal wave, roaring and crashing, drowning out even the bass. This was it. The dream. The thing I'd chased since I was twelve years old, sketching in the margins of my notebooks.

The stage manager nudged me forward, and I stepped into the lights. The roar grew louder, cheers and applause, and the surreal shimmer of flashes. I bowed once, twice, trying not to smile too hard. *Stay calm and cool, Heather.*

Backstage dissolved into champagne toasts and congratulations, Nico's hand clasping mine, voices tripping over themselves to praise me. Alena beamed. Stylists clinked glasses. Tory and Marcus barreled back in, wrapping me in another hug that made my eyes sting.

"Heather Brown?" I turned. A woman with a sharp black bob and a press badge swinging from her neck extended her hand. "I'm with *Chicago Style Magazine*. We'd love to feature you. Let's set up a time."

For a second, I forgot how to blink. *Chicago Style*. The word pulsed inside me like a drum. I managed to smile, to nod, to say something coherent. Inside, I was unraveling, the dream stretching bigger than I ever thought it could.

The Bloomingdale's team found me minutes later, offering hugs and promises of expanded orders. "You've outdone yourself," one of them said, her voice warm and certain. "We'll be placing more orders before the week is out."

It was everything I'd worked for. Everything I wanted. And yet—

Through it all, I kept reaching for my phone.

The first thing I wanted to do was call Bradley. To tell him everything. From the applause, the *Chicago Style* offer, the way Tory had nearly cried in the audience. To hear his voice.

I slipped into a corner, away from the cameras and champagne, and unlocked my phone. No new messages.

The ache crept back in, hollow and insistent that Bradley was missing... he was missing these big moments in my life.

I typed quickly.

HEATHER

This was incredible. I wish you could be here.

I hovered over send. He wouldn't see it until morning. By the time he read it, the glow of tonight would be dimmed, folded into yesterday.

Still, I hit send. Because what else could I do?

The applause still echoed in my ears, but the silence in my heart was louder.

47

———

UNSENT WORDS

HEATHER

The show didn't end so much as it spilled into the night.

By the time we'd wrangled garment bags back onto racks and hugged everyone twice, a black SUV line had formed outside the venue, headlights pooling across wet pavement. The February air snapped at my cheeks as the door opened and closed, opened and closed, people streaming out with the jittery relief that follows a good performance. I caught Tory's hand as we stepped into the cold, and we both laughed—because what else was there to do when your knees felt like gelatin and all your makeup had somehow stayed put?

"Public House?" she asked. Marcus and Nico were already there.

"Yes," I said with excitement.

Public House had been poured inside itself and shaken. Velvet chairs were packed with editors and stylists; models folded into corners like clean lines waiting their turn; the low lighting softened faces and edges alike. I practically floated to the banquette where Nico had already claimed a small territory—three low tables shoved together, guarded by his blow-dryer case like it was a VIP rope.

"There she is," he said, standing to kiss my cheek. His hands smelled like heat protectant and hairspray; it made me want to cry again for reasons I couldn't name. He tipped a flute of champagne toward me. "To our sensational gal."

I took the glass and the room blurred with the first sip— the way relief does when it finally has somewhere to go. People kept appearing, congratulating, pressing cold glass into my hands. The Bloomingdale's buyer leaned in to say they'd "circle back with expanded quantities" this week, which felt like a sentence composed solely to make my heart race.

I checked my phone: still nothing from Bradley. Of course there wasn't. It was around nine here, which made it three in the morning there. After a show, he'd be wired up in that high that always terrified him a little. I pictured him in a greenroom with too-bright lights and too many voices, or on a sidewalk with a hood pulled low, the world still fizzing around him. My chest lifted with the thought that he might be thinking of me right now, even if he couldn't reach me.

Nico slid in beside me, one knee on the bench, fanning out a section of a model's hair with his fingers the way some people shuffle cards. "We are going to need to use more round brushes," he said mildly to one of the junior stylists, as if he were remarking on the weather. I narrowed my eyes at him. "What?—I am giving free advice, and I'm right."

"You're always right about hair," I said. "Infuriating."

"Also right about you," he said, and his eyes softened. "You did it."

I laughed, shaking my head.

"To think I found you when you were still doing your own color from a box."

"Excuse me," I said, pressing a hand to my chest. "That is a lie. I have never dyed my hair from a box."

He arched a brow, smirking. "Well, your last stylist was using something that might as well have been. Cheap, brassy brand. I won't say more."

I swatted his arm, but I was smiling. His teasing cutting through the chaos without taking away from it.

Tory returned with Marcus and a plate of fries that glistened like jewelry and somehow tasted like salvation. She pressed her shoulder into mine, the kind of contact that sisters have. "Our girl," she said to Marcus, as if introducing me anew. "She took the city by the throat."

"Gently," I said. "And consensually."

We laughed. We ordered oysters because everyone said we should, and then I ate one and decided everyone is sometimes wrong. There were toasts and photos and hands; people saying "We need to talk next week," and "Your trench made me want to be a person who owns a trench," and "How did you get that hem to float?" I answered and smiled and hugged and felt like a balloon tied to a chair: aloft, but attached to something I couldn't see.

It didn't last. Highs never do. They flatten just enough that you can locate your phone again.

Still nothing from Bradley.

I slipped away. Past the velvet chairs and past an editor who'd corner me if I made eye contact, past a cluster of models whose legs went on so long they seemed like an optical illusion, past the bathroom line where two girls were saying how drunk they were. The service corridor by the restrooms was dim and quiet, smelling faintly of lemons and mop water.

I had no restraint at this point; I needed to call him.

He picked up on the second ring, and the relief was so sudden I had to press my palm flat to the wall.

"Hey, darlin'." His voice was close and rough with fatigue and whatever came right after a show. I could hear street noise, the echo of a door opening and closing, and someone laughing way too hard.

"Bradley... " I felt the distance the second I spoke. I tried to focus. "How was your show? You are in Brussels?"

"Yep, Brussels." His voice sounded relaxed. "The show was great. We went long. They don't cut you off like they do in the U.S." Then, softer, "But tell me everything. How did it go?"

"It was—" I closed my eyes. I wanted to pour the night into him, every light and gasp and the way Tory's hand shook when she hugged me. "It was everything. Better than anything. Chicago Style wants to—"

"Bradley?" A female voice came through. "Are you coming?"

I went still. He moved the phone, muffling it—"One second"—and the line shifted against a rush of chatter: a door propped open, footsteps on concrete. Then he was back.

"Sorry, people everywhere," he said, trying to sound casual, but it came out thin. "What were you saying?"

I couldn't unhear the voice. I couldn't stop my brain from arranging her into his night: hair, laugh, proximity.

"Who was that?" I asked, aiming for breezy and missing by a mile.

"What?"

"The girl."

"Oh." He exhaled, and his shoe scuffed—one of those telltale sounds that made me picture him looking at the ground. "Someone named Mandy."

"Mandy who?"

"Just—someone who loves the band." A too-long pause. "I guess a groupie."

I stared at the gray cinderblock wall, the lemon cleaner smell turning sour. "Okay."

"It's not like that," he said quickly, and for the first time tonight, his voice tilted, defensive. "We're at the hotel. People are hanging around. It's... nothing."

"Right." I smoothed my palm over the wall again, as if I could iron the moment flat. "Got it."

"Heather—"

"It's fine," I said, and we both knew it wasn't. "My night was pretty fucking great. I am going to get back to it; have a nice night with Mandy."

"Heat—"

I hung up before he could say my name again.

The corridor suddenly felt too cold. I stared at my reflection in the small metal plate on the wall, the stretch of my mouth, the way my eyes looked like someone else's. Then I pushed back into the noise and color and hands, the heat of the bar pressing close. If I couldn't share this with him, I would share it with strangers and friends and anyone who wanted to press a glass into my hand.

"Where did you go?" Tory asked, sliding me a fresh champagne. Her eyes sharpened, reading me the way only sisters can read anything.

"Just air," I lied. "I needed air."

She didn't push. She tucked herself into my side and lifted her glass. "Okay, let's celebrate you some more."

I drank more. It hit fast. Champagne always did. I

asked for something stronger because it felt like a kind of decision, a way to turn the volume down on everything that had just turned up. The room tilted; our laughter rose. Someone's playlist slid into a song I loved from seven years ago, the kind that makes you think you're still the age you were when you loved it. Nico started a story about a blow dryer catching fire in Paris, and by the end of it, we were all crying, laughing, napkins pressed to our eyes.

I decided, with the force that only a certain kind of tipsy grants, to be okay. To be more than okay. To be the kind of woman who could drink champagne in a velvet chair and ignore a word like "groupie" as if it were a typo. I danced in place on a banquette, shoes dangling from my fingers, one arm looped around Tory's neck. Marcus took a photo of us and promised to delete it. *He won't delete it*, I thought, and I didn't care.

When we finally spilled out onto the sidewalk, the air was cold enough to make us gasp. Doors swung. I waved too much. I hugged everyone too tightly. Tory kissed my forehead like a benediction. We got home, somehow, the way you always get home when you're held up by a night and a city and the kind of friends and sister who make sure you make it.

Morning punished me for it.

I woke in a tangle of sheets and blankets with mascara in the shape of rain. The inside of my mouth tasted like if metal had feelings. The ceiling fan drew slow circles, a metronome for regret. I reached for my phone instinctively and blinked in the light.

No messages. No missed calls.

Just the photo Marcus sent at two a.m. of me kissing my sketchbook like it was a person.

"What a creep," I whispered to the ceiling, though I wasn't sure which of us I meant.

I showered with my eyes closed and ate toast so dry it felt medicinal, and then scrolled through a hundred small digital versions of last night: stories, tags, a clip of look seven set to a song I didn't recognize. My name sat under them in small letters, a caption that made my stomach flip. People were talking. People with blue checks, people with hearts in their bios, and people who wouldn't remember by Wednesday. Somewhere in Belgium, he was asleep. Or awake. Or both, if you counted the way musicians nap through the afternoon like cats.

I didn't have the luxury. By noon, I was back in the studio, hair twisted into a bun that still smelled faintly of champagne, notebook in one hand, espresso in the other. Buyers had already emailed asking for look sheets, *Chicago Style* wanted to confirm Tuesday, and my team was buzzing about the possibility of a second delivery window if we could scale production. My head pounded, my heart felt bruised, but the work didn't wait. Fashion never waits.

By late afternoon, the exhaustion caught me by the hair and pulled. I finally went home and closed the curtains and got into bed with the intention of just closing my eyes for ten minutes, which is how adults lie to themselves. I slept like I hadn't in weeks—hard and immediate. When my phone finally vibrated against the nightstand, it took me three tries to open it.

"Hello," I choked out, my voice smaller than I meant it to be.

"Hi, how was the rest of your night?" Bradley asked, his tone gentle, like he was afraid of the answer.

"It was the best night of my life," I said, the words surprising me in their nakedness, as if they'd been waiting at the back of my throat and used the first open door to get out. "And I couldn't even celebrate it with you."

A beat. Street noise, a horn, the scrape of a shoe. "You knew this was my life," he said, softer than it read, and maybe too tired to steer around the truth to make it pretty.

"I believed you when you said we could do this," I whispered, hating how small I sounded.

"We can," he said quickly, his voice shifting, urgent now, like he could hear the cliff in mine. "I'm not saying we're over. I'm not— Heather, I don't want to tie you down. You deserve to enjoy this. Your career is about to catch fire. I just think we need to... " He trailed off, searching. "Take the pressure off. Grow. So when we're together for real, it lasts."

The words coming out of his mouth were breaking me.

"So we should see other people?" I hated how my voice made me sound like a fourteen-year-old.

"I'm not saying that. I'm saying let's not destroy this by making it carry more than it can right now."

Something in me recoiled—at the metaphor, maybe, or at the carefulness of it. I wanted the ugly truth over polished caution. I wanted to be fought for, even if fighting for me meant losing sleep and stepping outside of loud rooms to say my name without looking at his shoes.

In the background, a female voice again, "Bradley?"

It was gentler this time. Not close to the phone, but not far. A door opened or closed. He inhaled.

"Well," I said. I watched my reflection in the black screen of the turned-off TV, my mouth still making shapes I recognized as mine. "Seems like you have to go."

"Heather, wait—" he said, the words catching, genuine. "It's just—"

"I know," I said, and I meant it, which somehow made it worse. "It's your life. Sounds like Mandy needs you."

Silence pressed in. My throat burned. And before I could stop myself, the words broke free, sharp and aching, "I left my fiancé because of you. I believed every single thing you said. I have to go."

"Please, Heath—"

This time, I hung up before my voice could do the thing where it breaks and keeps breaking.

The room was very quiet. Outside, somewhere below my window, a car alarm hiccuped itself into silence. I lay on my back and stared at the ceiling and waited for the kind of grief that makes you want to run or call or scream, but what came was smaller and sharper—an ache like a new tooth cutting through. I thumbed open my phone and typed out a dozen sentences I deleted. The only one that stayed was the one I didn't send.

HEATHER

I'm wrecked.

I set the phone face down. In the morning, I told myself I would get up, take a meeting, and answer emails with sentences that ended in periods. I would say "Tuesday works," "Thank you for coming," and "We're thrilled to increase quantities on those sizes." I would be the version of myself who could carry triumph without asking it to carry me back.

Tonight, I let the quiet have me. I lay in my bed and cried until there were no more tears. I commanded my body to take several deep breaths till my heart slowed down and finally matched the rhythm, and I fell into a dark slumber.

A few days later, I woke up with pain, regret, hurt, and

anger braided through me. It sat heavily in my chest. I reached for my phone.

A missed call from mom. She was at a retreat in Arizona.

I sat up in bed and called her back.

"Hi, Mom."

"Heatherbug—what is wrong?"

"Nothing. I'm fine."

"Bug, I thought you would be elated after your show. I am deeply sorry I couldn't make it."

"Mom, don't worry about it. How's the retreat?"

"I am worried. I can feel it. I'll focus my next practice on you."

"Mom, I swear I'm fine," I said through clenched teeth.

"If you don't feel like sharing, that's okay. But I hope you celebrated. Tory sent beautiful photos of you girls. You should be proud. Whatever is weighing on you, take a step back. Remember the blessing that just happened."

A tear slipped down my cheek.

"I'll try."

"I am here whenever you're ready to talk. In the meantime, namaste, Heatherbug."

I heard a knock at my door before it opened.

Tory looked at me and made a little frown face.

"You look like you need a hug." She walked across the room and sat on my bed, then wrapped herself around me, small but fierce.

"Thank you for always being here," I whispered.

"I'm going out with Joel later. Want me to cancel?"

"No. Go. I will be okay."

I forced myself to shower. When I got out, I checked my phone and had one missed call from Bradley.

My stomach dropped.

I called him back, still in my towel. I had to hear his voice.

He answered after a few rings.

"Hey." His voice sounded far away.

My heart started pounding. "Bradley."

"Are you okay?" Concern threaded through his voice.

"I don't think so." The truth spilled out before I could stop it. "I'm sorry for how I acted. But I don't know if I'm cut out for this."

"Heather... I know what I'm asking of you is a lot."

"You have been honest. And I am being honest with myself and you; I won't feel like part of your life unless I give up mine and travel with you, but I would only be Bradley Hart's girlfriend. I would lose myself."

"You're right." He exhaled slowly. "Heather, I don't know how to give you what you deserve."

The words stabbed my heart.

"I want to say we'll get through this," I whispered. "But right now I'm not sure. I don't like this version of myself. I should have been basking in my moment."

"You should have. I am so proud of you. And I'm sorry I wasn't there. I think... we need to let things be. For a while."

"I don't want that."

"I don't either." His voice softened. "But I don't want to hurt you. This is my life right now."

Each sentence landed heavy.

"You can call me anytime," he added.

I knew I wouldn't.

"Okay. I have to go. I'll miss you."

"Heather... I am so sorry for ever hurting you. I love you."

The words caught in my throat.

"I have to go," I said instead.

I hung up.

The silence in my room felt enormous. I pulled my knees to my chest and wrapped my arms around them, holding tight like I could keep myself from splitting open.

It felt like my heart was bleeding out slowly.

I stayed that way until exhaustion dragged me sideways into my pillow, praying sleep would blur the edges of everything.

48

FOUR LEAVES

HEATHER

March in Chicago was a trickster. One day, it dangled the possibility of spring, the air almost warm, sunlight slanting against glass in a way that made you think coats could be packed away. The next day, it snapped you back to winter with gray skies and rain that soaked your shoes in seconds. Today was the latter—rain drumming against the windows of my apartment, the city smeared into watercolor shapes beyond the glass. It matched my mood too perfectly.

The weeks since FashionBar had blurred together into a series of emails, fittings, and meetings. *Chicago Style* had run the feature, my designs splashed across their digital cover, a handful of quotes attached that I barely remembered saying. Bloomingdale's had doubled their order, and two other buyers had reached out about possible collaborations. By any measurable standard, my career was thriving. And yet, all I felt was hollow.

Bradley had called. He had texted. Messages that still lit up my phone, polite, patient, careful.

BRADLEY

How are you?

Thinking of you.

Call me when you can.

I miss you.

I hadn't answered a single one. Was it childish? Yes. But...

At first, it was because I couldn't. My chest was too raw from that last conversation, the sound of the woman's voice in the background, his too-careful words about "taking pressure off." But as the days passed, silence became a habit, and habits harden faster than you think. Each time his name flashed on my screen, my thumb hovered. Each time, I pressed decline.

He didn't push for long. He let me keep the space. That was maybe the hardest part.

By the end of the first week, Tory had asked if I was okay. By the second, Nico stopped by my work and brought coffee without comment. By the third, the rain came in sheets, the city dull with it, and I realized I hadn't really laughed since the night of the afterparty.

Despite the rain, Chicago was still a city designed for walking, and it didn't stop me from heading out. As I walked, the weather continuing to mimic my mood, I passed a shelter.

It was just a storefront I usually walked past without noticing, tucked between a laundromat and a café that burned their espresso beans half the time. A handmade sign was taped to the window:

Adopt. Don't Shop.

Below it, a series of Polaroids—dogs with wide eyes, cats curled like commas. I didn't know why I stopped. Maybe because the rain was coming down harder, and I needed cover. Maybe because something in me was tired of only surviving.

Inside, the air smelled faintly of bleach and kibble. A volunteer in a sweatshirt smiled as I shook out my umbrella.

"Looking for anyone in particular?" she asked.

"I... don't know." My voice sounded strange in the quiet. "Just looking."

The rows of cages filled with soft noises—purring, scratching, the occasional bark. I moved slowly, rain still dripping from my coat. Then I started walking toward the cages lined with cats.

There was one in particular that was perched on a fleece blanket in the middle row, gray-and-white fur patchy at the tips, green eyes locked on mine like she'd been waiting. Her paws were tucked neatly under her chest, but her gaze was direct, unflinching.

"That's Clover," the volunteer said when she noticed me stop. "Two years old. Sweet as can be. Came in from a family that couldn't keep her."

"Clover," I repeated, tasting it. The name landed gently, like a feather settling on my tongue.

I crouched, pressing my fingers lightly to the bars. Clover stretched one paw forward, pressing it against the metal in silent recognition. My throat tightened unexpectedly.

"I had a cat growing up—Mookie," I said, half to the volunteer, half to myself. "I loved her. She used to sleep on my sketchbooks and knock over my markers if I ignored her for too long." A laugh slipped out, small and sad at once.

"Sounds like you aren't new to this," she said, shifting a stack of forms on the counter.

It was ridiculous. I had fittings tomorrow, sketches due, and a buyer call to prepare for. My apartment wasn't set up for a pet, my schedule wasn't forgiving, and my heart wasn't level. And yet I couldn't make myself stand up.

I thought of Mookie, how her purr could settle me when nothing else could. Losing her had left a space I never really filled. Maybe that was what this was about. Not starting over. Just... filling the quiet with something that wouldn't leave.

Clover tilted her head, green eyes unblinking, like she knew.

"Can I hold her?" I asked.

The volunteer hesitated only a second before coming around the back of the cage. She opened the latch carefully, murmuring "kitty kitty" as she scooped Clover up. When she placed her in my arms, Clover melted against me as if she'd been waiting for this exact moment.

And just like that, something inside me loosened.

The volunteer handed me the paperwork, her pen already clipped to the top. My name looked shaky as I wrote it, like my hand hadn't quite caught up to what my heart had decided. I skimmed the questions, signing where I was told, not really absorbing the words. Occupation. Address. Phone number. The sections were a blur.

A few minutes later, Clover was in a cardboard carrier with air holes punched along the sides, the blanket she'd been curled on tucked inside with her. She gave a single meow as the volunteer closed the top, as if she already knew she belonged to me.

By the time I stepped back onto the wet street, I was drenched, my hair sticking to my cheeks, the box in my grip.

Clover shifted inside, the faint sound of her paws scratching the cardboard, and something about it stilled my thoughts.

When I got home, Tory was already there, curled on the couch, watching some reality show.

The second she spotted the carrier, she squealed. "Who is this?"

I set the box on the rug, my throat tight with something between nerves and relief. "I did something dumb today."

She was already crouching, peeking through the holes. "You did not."

"I did," I insisted, though my voice wavered. "This is me officially starting my single life with cats."

"Oh, stop," Tory said, reaching in. She lifted Clover out carefully, pressing her against her chest. Clover melted instantly, her purr so loud it filled the room. Tory's grin spread wide as she kissed the top of Clover's head. "I love her. She's perfect."

I watched as Clover tucked herself into the crook of Tory's arm like she'd been here all along. For a second, I almost believed that was true.

Joel's name lit up Tory's phone, where it buzzed on the coffee table. She sighed, kissed Clover one more time, and handed her to me. "You two bond. I've got to take this."

Clover settled into my lap, paws kneading against my sweater, purr rumbling. I leaned back into the couch cushions, exhaustion sliding through me like a wave.

From the doorway, Tory called, "Want to go out with us tonight?"

I shook my head, stroking Clover's fur. "No. I'm staying in. Maybe I'll start knitting."

Tory rolled her eyes at me.

The apartment went quiet once her footsteps faded down the hall. Rain tapped against the windows, persistent and endless, but it didn't feel quite as heavy. Clover curled tighter against me, warm and certain, her eyes blinking slowly as if to say she'd chosen me too.

I rested my cheek against her soft fur, whispering, "It's just you and me now."

She purred louder, and I let myself believe I might be okay.

49

WHEN THE MUSIC DIES

BRADLEY

London should have felt like the summit.

The O2 venue was alive before the doors even opened; a buzz was in the building, in the walls, like the place itself was vibrating. Final night of the tour. Four months of buses, planes, dressing rooms that all smelled faintly of sweat and fried food, and now here we were—thousands of people waiting on the other side of the curtain. Any other year, I would have been buzzing.

Instead, I felt nothing.

Soundcheck passed in a blur. My hands knew where to go, my throat did its job, but it was muscle memory, not joy. Josh plucked a few notes from behind his bass, grinning. "Last show, man. Don't hold back."

I nodded back, but the truth was, I'd been holding back all spring. Not onstage—that part I could get lost in and feel the music—but everywhere else it was questionable.

My phone sat facedown on the amp case. If I flipped it, I knew what I'd see: nothing. Or worse, a reminder of the last message I'd sent that went unanswered. The silence had stretched since February. Three months without her voice, three months of messages disappearing into a void. Each day it cut a little deeper, like water carving stone.

Suzie found me pacing the corridor, cables and gaffer tape underfoot. "Save the brooding for later," she called, her voice carrying the way it always did when she needed thirty people to listen at once. "Go eat something. Last show."

"I'm good," I muttered.

She narrowed her eyes. "You're not. But you can get through ninety minutes."

That was the job. Ninety minutes of songs for people who didn't know or care that my chest was caving in. I could do that. I'd been doing it since February.

Back in the dressing room, I flipped my phone over. The last stack of messages stared back at me.

BRADLEY

Thinking of you.

How's your day?

I'm proud of you.

No pressure. I just miss you.

No texts. No photos. No questions. No replies. Nothing.

I rubbed a hand over my face, hearing again that night, replaying it in my head.

Not one specific moment, *all of it.*

The noise behind me. The chaos. The cameras. The way my world always sounded like it was moving at full speed. I'd gotten used to it. I forgot how loud it must feel on the other end of the line.

It wasn't about one girl, one tabloid. It wasn't about anything happening. It was about the world I lived in, and how little of it she felt part of.

It was me.

The way I sounded distracted. The way I didn't stop everything and make her feel like she was the only thing that mattered. Her fashion show should have felt sacred. I should have carved out time that wasn't squeezed between soundcheck and a hundred people pulling at me. I should have made it feel like I was standing right beside her, even if I couldn't be.

Instead, I let it feel like just another night on tour.

And then, because I couldn't stop myself from making it worse, I'd muttered something about not wanting to tie her down. The second it was out, I hated myself for it. I wasn't trying to give her the idea we couldn't get through a rough patch, but that's exactly what I'd done. Hearing her call me from a place of such elation, after a night of everything she wanted and more, and me not there to help her celebrate, felt all too familiar, and I didn't want to picture her waiting for me, just like my mom had for my father, as all this good was happening around her.

But listening to her go quiet on the other end of the phone, I heard something I didn't want to recognize. Distance.

Not from miles. From decisions.

I made them every day without thinking—tours, press, appearances—and she wasn't part of them. I didn't know how to include her in something that already moved faster than I could control.

I said what I said, without explaining myself. She'd gone silent after that, and I hadn't figured out how to bring her back.

"Doors in thirty," Suzie called from the hallway. Her lanyard smacked against her hip as she leaned in the doorway, taking inventory of me the way she did with amps and flight cases. "If anyone's going to have a crisis, do it now. I've got a laminated schedule for everything else."

"I'm fine," I lied.

She stepped inside, shut the door with her foot, and lowered her voice. "You look like you've been sleeping on gravel."

"Bus mattresses are basically gravel."

"Bradley."

I met her eyes. She didn't flinch. Suzie never flinched. "She hasn't answered since February," I said, the words coming out like I'd been carrying them in my teeth. "It's getting... hard to keep pretending it doesn't matter."

"It matters," she said. "Pretending it doesn't just makes the fall longer." She tipped her chin at the phone. "You tried again?"

"Every way I know how." I set the phone down. "I'll try again when I'm back in the States. In person."

"Good," she said. "Show first. Heart surgery later."

I huffed a laugh. It wasn't humor, exactly, but it kept my soul from locking.

Out on the deck, the room buzzed like a hive. The O2 was one of those places that holds sound in a way that makes you feel both tiny and enormous. Our tech ran through the last checks. Josh slid past me, bass over his shoulder, and rapped his knuckles twice against the body like he was knocking on wood. "Last one," he said, mostly to himself. He grinned at me and was gone.

When the house lights dropped, the roar came up like the weather. I walked out into it and did what I was built to do. I let the routine carry me—count in, downbeat, first line. The band locked in tight around me. People sang words we wrote in a basement like they were scripture. I could feel the heat off the front row, the little tremor the subs give you in your ribcage. I moved through it the way you move through muscle memory, not joy.

Halfway in, I asked for the lights to fall and stepped forward into a single spot. The chatter in my head went quiet in that cone of white. I thumbed the neck of the guitar and felt the satin of the worn wood under my hand.

"This one's new," I said. "For someone who is always on my mind."

I didn't say her name. I didn't have to. It was in the first chord, the way I let it ring too long. It was in the line I wrote on a coach seat somewhere between Hamburg and Prague, the one about phones lighting up like beacons and still not finding their mark. It was in the pause before the chorus, where my throat always caught, and I had to force the note out anyway.

The arena did that strange, generous thing giant rooms sometimes do: they let a quiet song be quiet. In the back, I saw phones lower. In the pit, a girl closed her eyes and leaned her head against the barrier like she was praying. I wasn't thinking about God. I was thinking about a living room in Chicago where a cat I'd only seen on Heather's Instagram was probably asleep on a sofa I'd sat on once, the woman I loved somewhere inside not answering a phone with my name on it.

The last chord faded. The sound came back like a tide—long, heavy, huge. I nodded, stepped out of the spot, and let the machine of the show take me the rest of the way. Sweat. Lights. Words I could sing half-conscious. Hands reaching, confetti bursting at the end like an apology for everything the songs had asked for.

Then it was done.

Backstage was steam and wet hair and the metallic smell of beer cans opened too fast. A guitar tech got doused in champagne and swore cheerfully. Someone bear-hugged me, then someone else. Pete whooped, rain of paper still floating down out on the floor. "London!" he yelled to no one and everyone, grinning like his face might split. "We're going home."

Home. The word echoed around my ribs.

I showered, put a hoodie on over skin that hadn't cooled yet, and found the road case I always ended up on when there was nothing left to do but feel whatever's left. Suzie materialized with a bottle of water and that look that said she was trying to calculate the exact amount of managing a human heart requires.

"How's your oxygen?" she asked, handing me the bottle.

"Thin at this altitude."

"Mm." She nudged the phone with her toe. "You going to try?"

I turned it over in my hands. The draft thread was right where I left it, the last three messages stacked above the blinking cursor like little nameless tombstones. I typed:

> Can I come see you?

I stared at it. My thumb hovered. My chest did that stupid throb it does when a choice is the size of a fingertip. I backspaced. Typed:

> I wrote you something tonight. I want to play it for you.

Another blink. Another minute I couldn't get back. I backspaced again and set the phone face down.

"I want to tell her in person," I said. "I want her to hear me tell her, not see it in a message she can ignore."

"Then be in front of her face as soon as you can," Suzie

said. "Not in a dramatic rom-com way. In a functional adult way. Knock on the door at a normal hour. Use your words."

"Copy," I said. "Functional adult."

She studied me. "Also, sleep. We're wheels up at ten. If you try to fix your life on thirty minutes of unconsciousness and two granola bars, I'm not responsible for the choices you make."

I nodded.

"And Bradley?" she said.

"Yeah?"

"The Mandy thing?" She lifted a brow.

"Nothing," I said. "Less than nothing. I didn't touch her. I didn't want to. It was bad wording at the worst moment. Heather heard what she heard."

"Then lead with that," Suzie said. "Own the word, not the rumor."

She peeled off to wrangle load-out. I sat there a minute longer with the bottle sweating in my hand and the music still replaying in the walls. I thought about a thing I'd said to her months ago—how I didn't want to tie her down. I meant *I want you to fly.* I should've said *I want to learn how to fly next to you.* That was the thing about phrases: once you let them into the air, they behaved how they wanted.

On my way to the bus, the night felt wet and cool. A cluster of fans waited at the barricade, determined and tender, holding markers and sleeves and hope. I signed what was held out to me, took a picture with a kid whose hands shook so hard I had to steady his phone for him. A girl in a denim jacket said, "Your songs got me through," voice quivering like a plucked string. I said, "You got me through, too," and I meant it, because these nights were the only time the silence didn't feel like it was winning.

The bus smelled like coffee and detergent and the end of

a long thing. Bunks ran down one side like little coffins. Somebody's jacket was wadded in a corner. Josh was still buzzing, telling a story to the drum tech, hands carving shapes in the air. I nodded at them and pulled back the thin curtain to my bunk.

Ceiling six inches from my nose. The hum of the generator. The half-life of adrenaline shaking out in my hands. I lay there and watched the plywood above me and tried to count backward from a hundred. It worked until it didn't.

I pulled out my notepad and wrote lyrics, thinking about the one who kept choosing me whether I wanted it or not. I added a line I'd been circling for weeks:

If you open the door, I'll leave the whole road outside

When I read it back, it sounded raw and human. Good. I didn't want polished. I wanted true.

On the next page, I wrote:

June. Go to her. Knock. Don't apologize with poetry. Apologize with facts.

Then, because I was apparently an idiot who wanted responsibility, I grabbed my phone, opened the browser, and typed *dogs good on tour?* The results were not in my favor. Half the articles were smiling pit bulls in bandanas; the other half were warnings about schedules, noise, and stress. I could hear Suzie's voice in my head—*"Start with a plant."* I closed the phone and pictured a leash hanging by my front door anyway. Wanting something solid didn't make me ridiculous. It made me honest.

The bus lurched as we rolled out. London blurred by in streaks of sodium light and wet glass. I let the motion do what it always did—rock the thoughts' sharp edges to a dull ache. Out of the small window, buildings thinned, then tilted toward the motorway. I told myself the distance between here and Heathrow was the same kind of distance I'd been measuring for months; the difference now was that it was closing.

I must've slept because when I opened my eyes, the sky was hinting at morning and the bus was still. The venue's smell had been replaced by diesel and damp. We piled out in hoodies and hats, a little tribe of people who'd learned how to move together before we learned anything else. Suzie shepherded us through check-in with the competence of six air traffic controllers. My guitar went into a case I trusted more than I trusted most humans. Security took my water and gave me nothing in return. Normal travel things. Good to have something to complain about that wasn't the size of my own heart.

At the gate, I sat with my hood up and watched planes taxi like obedient beasts. Every few minutes, my hand went to my pocket, the reflex so ingrained it felt like its own heartbeat. I didn't pull the phone out. Not yet. I wanted to land in Chicago with something in me other than fear.

Suzie dropped into the seat beside me, then handed me a packet of almonds like a nurse with a shot. "Eat," she said.

"You going to push hydration next?"

"Always." She leaned back. "What's the plan?"

"Find her," I said. "Not in a dramatic way. Just—find her. Tell her the thing I should've told her months ago. That Mandy was nothing. I chose the worst word. That I can do better at this than I've done. That I want to try."

"And if she says no?"

I let the question sit there. I watched a plane lift and disappear into the low, pearled light over the runway. "Then I'll hear it with my own ears and stop living inside a question," I said. "And then I'll figure out how to sing without missing her every third word."

"That's the first sensible thing you've said in weeks," she said, which, from Suzie, was basically a standing ovation.

We boarded. We were in first class; I took the window seat and pressed my forehead to the cool plastic, trying not to think about how many hours sat between me and the city where my entire life either still was or wasn't. The engines wound up. The wings flexed. London dropped away in cut-up pieces—roads, slate roofs, a river like a scar.

I closed my eyes and pictured her door. Not the empty screen. Not the messages that never came. The actual door. The wood grain. The paint chipped near the bottom where someone once kicked at it, impatient. I pictured my hand knocking. I pictured Clover, the gray-and-white cat from the photo I'd stared at for too long the night I saw it on Instagram, sitting on the back of the couch, watching with those green eyes like she knew how to weigh a man.

I pictured Heather opening the door, and I didn't let myself write the expression on her face. That part wasn't mine to script. Mine was three sentences: *I'm sorry I said the wrong thing. Mandy was nobody. I've only wanted you.* And then a question, I hadn't earned yet: *Can we talk?*

Somewhere over the Atlantic, the plane leveled, and the cabin dimmed into the artificial night they create on daytime flights. I let my head fall back, finally, and the months of holding everything together let go a fraction. I slept an hour that felt like a minute and dreamed about standing in a doorway with my hands empty and the right words in my mouth.

When I woke, the map showed a tiny plane icon over a cartoon ocean with a line arcing toward Los Angeles. June was close enough to name. The summer dates waited out there in July like dominoes, but none of that mattered yet. There was one door between me and the rest of my life.

Home first. Then her.

That was the whole plan.

50

FORGIVE

HEATHER

June in Chicago had arrived with that unmistakable shift—everything suddenly became fuller, brighter, alive. The trees along the lakefront were lush and deep green again, and you could almost taste summer lingering on the breeze, mixing with the smell of caramel popcorn from a vendor's cart and the last trace of blooming lilacs. The sun broke through wide, drifting clouds, warming the tops of my shoulders as I walked the path. Children laughed at a nearby park, a saxophonist's notes carried over from a nearby bench, and couples stretched out on picnic blankets across the grass with rosé bottles and dog-eared paperbacks.

I breathed it all in and felt, for the first time in a long time, that I was in a better place. Bloomingdale's asked me to do another capsule. Several boutique stores from Coast to Coast added some of my pieces to their stores. I still couldn't quite believe it. It was the kind of accomplishment I had once thought about, too afraid to dream out loud. I had beaten my own expectations, and it felt like headway into a life I wasn't sure I deserved.

The one thing missing was love. But who needed love when I had a career on fire, an adorable cat waiting at home, and the two constants who had never failed me—my sister and my best friend?

I had just been telling Nico all of this, and he nodded, squinting at me over his sunglasses.

"I'd have to agree with that, girl. You were getting dangerously depressing there for a bit. I'm glad Tory and I don't have to mend you back together."

"Gee, thanks, best friend."

He smirked. "I'm only kidding. Being in love with your first love, who just happens to be a rock star? It had to come with some drama. But don't you think you cut him loose a little too soon? Tory told me he tried to reach out several times."

"Are you on my side or his?" I asked, half joking.

"Always yours. But I'm double checking. You know your heart was broken when you were young. And this Mandy girl—are we even sure he cheated on you with her? I mean, yeah, we saw those European tabloid shots Marcus so graciously dug up for you, but that doesn't mean anything."

I stopped walking for a moment, the words sticking to my ribs.

Because part of me already knew that. And part of me was afraid of what it meant if he was right.

I knew I'd been harsh with Bradley. I'd left my fiancé within minutes, jumped headfirst into a relationship with Bradley, started a new job, and tried to reinvent myself all at once. The thought of wrecking things with Bradley on top of all that change had been too much. I couldn't bear it. So I had cut him loose.

It felt like survival at the time. It didn't feel brave now.

"Let's get ice cream," I said, breaking the heaviness and glancing at a shop ahead.

"No can do, baby girl. You get some. I can't. Actually, I have news."

"You can't be pregnant, or you'd already be all over the ice cream situation."

Nico's contagious laugh spilled out as he grabbed my arm.

"Marcus and I are moving in together. And—we're getting married. I want you to be my maid of honor."

I stopped dead in my tracks, turning to him. A tear rolled down my cheek before I even realized it.

"This is the most amazing news," I said, hugging him hard. "Is that why you're banning ice cream?"

"I have to be skinny when I say yes to the dress."

We both laughed.

"You're going to be a stunning bride. And Marcus too," I teased. "When are you thinking?"

We drifted toward the door, and I was still determined to get my scoop. The moment the bell chimed, the smell of fresh sweets wrapped around us.

"Well, we're thinking Napa. End of summer." He looked at me carefully, like he was waiting for my reaction.

"Wow—that's soon. But amazing." I turned toward the shopkeeper. "Strawberry, single scoop, please."

"We're getting older, and we want to adopt soon."

"Oh, Nico. That's the most fantastic news." Joy and ache twisted together in my chest, impossible to separate.

"We also want you to be our stylist for our matching tuxes."

I thanked the shopkeeper, then took a lick of my spoon, grinning. "I am so beyond honored."

We left the shop and walked until we reached his block, the late-afternoon sun catching on the brightly painted facades and big bay windows lining his street. After long goodbyes and promises to start planning, I turned back toward Lakeview, deciding against the bus or the Red Line. It was not far, but a walk up Halsted and over toward Fletcher felt right for a Saturday this beautiful.

My feet would ache later, but the neighborhood pulled me forward, rainbow flags snapping in the breeze and patios filling with people easing into the early evening.

On the way, I stopped at a flower shop, letting the buckets of tulips and roses pull me in. I chose a bunch that looked like spring itself had spilled out of them. Afterward, I stopped in a convenience store to grab a bottle of wine and a new nail color.

The thought of sinking into my couch with a glass of wine, Clover curled against me, and losing myself in a sketch while listening to Janis Joplin, then taking a break to paint my nails the color of "Bubble Bath," sent a little thrill through me. Saturday night was mine alone. Tory was with Joel this weekend. I had the place to myself.

I headed home, and when I turned the corner, there he was—sitting on my steps, baseball cap tugged low like he was trying to disappear. I stopped short, my breath catching in my throat. For a split second, I wondered if my heart had finally started inventing things.

"Bradley… " My voice carried his name in a hush.

He stood up, towering even though his shoulders were slouched. "Heather."

Seeing him there, waiting, made my heart pound in a way no success ever had.

"How long have you been here?"

"Ten minutes. Maybe… okay, three hours."

"Oh my God, why didn't you call?"

"You haven't answered my calls. Or texts." There was no accusation in his voice. Just truth.

Heat crept into my cheeks. I knew I had been petty, letting pride steer the whole thing. At my age, I should have been better than a slow fade.

I swallowed. "I know. I'm sorry." My voice felt weak. I had a thousand things I wanted to say, but the words were stuck inside me. "Want to go inside so we can talk?"

"Yes. I'd like that."

My fingers fumbled with the key until he gently took the flowers and magazine from my arms. "Here, allow me."

We climbed the three flights of stairs together, silence thick between us. At my door, I managed the lock, my pulse thundering.

Inside, I set the flowers and magazine on the couch while Bradley pulled off his cap and dragged a hand through his hair. He looked tired in that soft, end-of-the-road way—like someone who'd finally stopped running—but his green grassy-colored eyes still sparked, and that familiar, boyish curve of his mouth undid me just as easily as it ever had.

"Something to drink?" I asked. My voice still sounding off pitch.

I hated that he could still do this to me—knock me off balance without even touching me.

"That'd be great." He shifted, resting his hip against the counter, watching me with an ease that made me feel suddenly overly aware of everything I was doing.

"Water? Wine? Beer?" I asked, stalling. I could feel the heat creeping up my neck, the faint sheen of nerves at my temples.

"Water's fine."

I poured him a glass and set it in front of him on the counter. He drank right away, watching me as I trimmed the flower stems and arranged them in a vase, buying myself time.

My hands needed something to do before they reached for him on instinct.

It was ridiculous, really. I'd faced buyers and deadlines and rooms full of strangers without blinking. But Bradley, standing there in my kitchen, felt like a test I hadn't studied for. Every small movement—the scrape of the glass on the counter, the quiet shift of his weight—pulled at me. I told myself to breathe, to settle, but my body didn't listen. It already knew what my heart was trying not to say.

I broke the silence before it could stretch any tighter.

"What brings you here?"

"You," he said simply.

The word landed heavier than it should have. My chest tightened, breath catching before I could stop it.

"I owe you an apology," he continued. "I shouldn't have put us on hold. I thought I was doing the right thing— giving you space during your big moment. I didn't want to be a distraction." He shook his head once, quiet regret in the movement. "I thought pulling back would make it easier for you."

Easier. The irony almost made me laugh.

I leaned beside him, close enough now to feel the warmth of his leg against mine, every part of me aware of his proximity. Before I could say anything, Clover padded out of the bedroom, tail flicking as she assessed the situation.

"Clover?" Bradley asked softly, surprise softening his voice. "I stalked you on Instagram," he admitted with a faint smile. "She was the only personal piece."

I smiled despite myself, watching her circle his ankles like she'd already decided he belonged here.

"She's been my healing buddy."

Bradley's gaze lifted back to mine, something unreadable passing between us. The room suddenly felt smaller, quieter. Like whatever I said next mattered more than I was ready for.

"Heather, I'm so sorry."

This time, he looked directly at me.

His shoulders were slightly rounded, his jaw tight, eyes searching—as if he needed me to see that he meant it.

"Bradley, I'm sorry too. I shouldn't have ignored you or let jealousy swallow me. The thought of you hurting me again felt harder than just ending it. Or so I thought."

He exhaled, shoulders dipping as if a weight finally slipped free. I had never seen him look so open, so unguarded.

"I know," he said quietly. "But I should never have left you wondering where you stood with me. The truth is... I stepped back because I convinced myself you deserved stability, and I belong to a rhythm that never slows down. So instead of being present, I pulled away."

He was honest without any excuses.

"I do not want to keep repeating that pattern," Bradley continued. "And something has to shift. I talked to my team. I am cutting back on touring after this summer. No overseas runs in the winter. I want to be here. I want to build something *real* with you, and I cannot do that from two continents away."

The certainty in his voice felt different from anything he had said before. This was not a grand gesture. This was a decision he had already made.

He watched my expression carefully. "I want a life that

does not pull me away from the people I love. I want a life that includes you."

A slow warmth moved through me, the sensation of something inside me finally letting itself believe him.

"I should have told you this months ago," he added. "Maybe we would not have broken apart the way we did."

I felt my own truth rising, impossible to ignore.

"I did the same thing," I admitted. "When things got hard, I withdrew. I thought ending it first would hurt less. It never did."

My voice softened. "And I never made space for your world either. I never even made it to Los Angeles to see your place. I think I was afraid it would make everything too real. But I want to see it. I want to show up for you."

His eyes gentle in a way I had missed for months. "Then we meet in the middle. Not you folding into my life, not me disappearing from yours. We build something that belongs to both of us."

He took my hand and held it against his chest. "I love you, Heather. But love works only if we choose it every day."

"This time," I whispered, "I will choose you. Fully."

He took a breath. "I don't want silence to be our pattern anymore. If I'm overwhelmed or exhausted, I'll tell you. I won't disappear; I won't retreat to hotel rooms without you knowing why. I want you in the parts of my life I used to keep to myself."

Something in me softened.

"And I won't run when I get scared," I said. "If something feels off, I'll say it. I won't punish you with silence or pretend I'm fine when I'm not. If we're apart, we stay connected. We talk. No disappearing acts from either of us."

A faint smile pulled at his mouth. "A rule, then?"

"A rule," I agreed.

"If I am traveling, we make time. Real time. Not rushed FaceTimes between rehearsals. And when I'm home," he added, brushing his fingers along my cheek, "I'm actually home. Fully. With you."

And that—finally—felt like change. Real, lived-in change.

He reached over, his thumb brushing a tear I hadn't realized had fallen.

"I know things were tough. We were barely speaking. I didn't know how to fix it. But Mandy is nobody. She was clinging around. I should have only been congratulating you, not making you doubt me."

I let out a small cry that felt like a release.

Clover stretched at our feet, and Bradley bent to scoop her up. To my shock, she melted right into his arms, purring.

"She likes you," I whispered.

We both laughed, and something inside me unbuttoned. The pain in my heart was slowly coming out.

"I think we need to get her a friend. Bucket," he teased.

I smiled. "You mean Gus."

Then his voice grew rougher, deeper. "I love you, Heather Brown. I've loved you since Punta Cana, and I'll love you always—no matter how much time goes by without us speaking."

Tears blurred my vision. "I love you, Bradley Hart. I'll never ignore you again."

His lips crushed mine, desperate and sure, and all at once I was in his arms again. His hands slid to my waist, pulling me tight, the kiss deepening until I couldn't breathe for wanting him.

"Things won't be easy," he whispered against my mouth, "but we'll grow together. If you can hang on to this rock-and-roll life, I'll do everything I can to show up for you."

Before I could answer, his mouth found my neck, kissing the tender spot beneath my ear, sending a shiver racing down my spine. My body trembled, ready, aching.

"Bradley... " My voice broke into a plea.

He didn't hesitate. In one swift movement, he picked me up, my legs instinctively wrapping around his waist. He carried me down the short hall to my bedroom, kissing me the whole way, pausing only to murmur how much he'd missed me.

By the time he laid me on the bed, my heart was pounding. My hands tangled in his hair, my body arching toward his without thought. His mouth traced my collarbone, my shoulder, every kiss unhurried and deliberate. He took his time, moving lower, until I was holding onto him, breath breaking apart, soft sounds slipping free as he moved with his lips. Slow. Precise. Rhythm that left me shaking.

When he came back up, he kissed me deeply, then paused, just enough to look at me. He reached toward the edge of the bed, toward his jeans.

I caught his hands and pulled them back to me, my head shaking once.

"I want to feel all of you."

He searched my face. "Are you sure?"

I nodded. He cradled my head and kissed me again, deeper this time, until there was nothing but the press of our mouths, the pull of our bodies. We moved together until there was no space left—skin to skin, breath to breath.

When he pushed inside me, I couldn't hold back my gasp. My mouth fell open, my eyes locked with his, something widening and settling all at once. He moved slowly, fully and the connection between us felt complete—fingers interlaced, bodies finding their rhythm, in sync, everything else falling away.

His grip tightened, my body answered and the sound we made felt shared, one release into another.

This wasn't just passion, this was us choosing each other —our chance to begin again, woven together like a horizon we could finally see.

51

LOVE THAT FINDS YOU

BRADLEY

I hadn't let her out of my arms all night.

The blinds leaked pale morning light across Heather's sheets, and she was still tucked against me, her hair spilling across the pillow. Her chest rose and fell in a rhythm that almost convinced me this was a dream. After months of waking up in hotel rooms and tour buses, the quiet of her apartment felt unreal.

But it wasn't. It was her. *Us.*

And the truth hit me harder than I expected: I felt at home for the first time in years.

For the first time in too long, I didn't have to think about what was next in the calendar—the next show, the next stop. No call sheets, flights, or soundchecks. Just her, warm against me, exactly where she belonged. The simplicity of it —her legs tangled with mine, her fingers curled lightly against my side—made something inside me settle, like I'd finally found a place to put down what I'd been carrying.

And I wasn't going to mess this up again.

In the stillness, she shifted just slightly, a soft sigh drifting from her lips. I let my fingers trace slow lines along her back, memorizing the shape of her, the quiet, the way morning light painted her skin gold. I had forgotten what it felt like to wake up next to someone you didn't want to leave. Someone you didn't want to lose.

We stayed in bed for hours. Talking, not talking, kissing until laughter broke between us, until the need to touch her outweighed every other instinct I had.

Her mouth was soft under mine, her skin warmer still, and soon the covers were sliding off us, the sunlight spreading across her shoulder. I rolled over her, but Heather pushed me back with a grin that said she had other plans.

She kissed down my chest slowly, deliberately, her hands pressing into my sides, leaving heat in their wake. I hissed through my teeth when her mouth found me, the world shrinking to nothing but the feel of her. I buried a hand in her hair, every muscle tightening as she took her time, as if she knew exactly how close I was to unraveling.

"Jesus, Heather," I groaned, the words slipping out unfiltered.

When I couldn't take it anymore, I pulled her up to me, kissed her hard, and flipped her beneath me. The rest was a blur of heat and breathless whispers—her laugh breaking when I pressed my mouth to the spot under her jaw, her nails dragging down my back, my name on her lips as we came together.

When it was over, I stayed inside the circle of her arms, my forehead pressed to hers, both of us breathing hard. Her hair was damp, and her little curls framed her face.

This wasn't just sex. It was a vow. A second chance. And I wasn't letting it go.

She fell asleep for a bit, curled into my chest, and I didn't move. Couldn't. I just watched her. The way her lips parted slightly. The way her lashes brushed her cheeks. The way her hand kept resting over my heart.

I thought about all the mornings I'd had without her—waking up in strange beds, strange cities, rooms with no connection except the next show on the calendar. None of it mattered. Not like this.

And maybe that was the thing I'd been afraid to admit: I didn't want that life anymore if she wasn't in it.

By late afternoon, I left for an hour to grab my things from the hotel. I'd kept them there just in case she had turned me away. A small suitcase and my guitar. I carried them through her front door like they belonged there.

Heather looked up from the couch when I came in, a faint smile on her face. She didn't say anything, but she didn't need to. She shifted over an inch so I'd have a place next to her.

Later, while she tapped at her laptop at the kitchen table, I strummed on the couch.

I adjusted my grip on the guitar and murmured into the strings:

> *"Girl with the midnight curls and a cat named*
>   *Clover,*
> *I left for a minute, but I'm not starting over... "*

Heather looked up from her screen and smiled at me across the room; it felt like music had never mattered more.

She made the place feel lighter. Safer. Mine in a way I had never expected.

Later that night, we cooked whatever we could cobble together from the fridge and pantry. The verdict: banana pancakes with a side of sunny side up eggs.

"Breakfast for dinner. My favorite," Heather said, flipping the pancakes with a flourish.

I snuck up behind her, slid my arms around her waist, and pressed a kiss to her cheek.

"Careful," she laughed, tilting her head away. "I might burn these if I don't pay attention."

"I like mine crispy," I murmured, kissing her again—this time lingering.

She tried to glare at me, spatula in hand, but her smile betrayed her. "Then don't complain when you get the dark ones."

I tightened my hold and kissed the curve of her neck, breathing her in. "Deal."

Cooking with her felt like something married people did, something solid and ordinary and perfect. It settled something in me I didn't even know needed settling.

After dinner, we curled up on the couch, the cat stretched between us like a referee. Heather's hair was still damp from her shower, curling against her shoulders.

"Question game," she said suddenly, tilting her head toward me.

I chuckled, setting my guitar aside. "You're on."

She grinned. "Okay, what's the first thing you thought when you saw me yesterday?"

The answer was out before I could think to guard it. "That I was an idiot for ever letting you go."

Her lips parted, eyes soft, and for a moment she didn't say anything. Then she leaned in and kissed me, slow and sure, as if she was letting me know she agreed.

I pulled back just enough to look at her. "Okay, my turn. What did you think when you saw me again? A bit of a stalker?"

Her smile faltered, just for a second, before it softened.

She reached for my hand, her thumb brushing across my knuckles.

"That I should have never ignored you," she stated earnestly. "That I missed you more than I wanted to admit."

The words hit me harder than I expected, low and deep. I bent to kiss her before she could see how completely it broke me open.

After we made love right there on the couch, I held her close, both of us coming down from the high. It wasn't just heat this time—it was raw, vulnerable, like we'd stripped away everything that had come between us and started over.

When she finally pulled the blanket across us and curled into my side, her eyes drifted shut almost instantly. I brushed a kiss across her temple, the steady rise and fall of her breath anchoring me more than anything ever had.

I looked around her apartment, her books stacked on the coffee table, her sneakers by the door, her cat staring at me from the ottoman, and I felt at peace—*home*.

Music had always been my compass, my calling, my magic. But the real magic was here, asleep against me— proof that every note had been leading me back to her.

And this time, I wasn't going anywhere.

This life with her, what we could be, and the life I finally wanted. The life that had her at the center.

52

TO THE GROOM AND GROOM
HEATHER

A FEW MONTHS LATER

Nico was wrestling with his cufflink when I found him. His hands trembled just enough to make the silver slip against the buttonhole.

"Hold still," I said, brushing his fingers away. I guided the cufflink through the fabric and fastened it with a click. "There. Crisis averted."

He exhaled, half laugh, half nerves. "You've saved me three times today. First the boutonniere, then the flower girl's meltdown, now this. If I fall apart during the vows—"

"You won't," I cut in, pressing the folded tissue I'd tucked in my clutch into his hand. "But if you do, at least you'll look polished doing it."

Nico chuckled, though his eyes were already damp. I squeezed his arm, letting the pressure steady him. From down the corridor, the planner's voice rang: "Five minutes!"

The quartet's tuning drifted faintly from the glass-walled hall, notes stretching thin and sweet. I could imagine the guests shifting in their seats, leaning forward, waiting for the first glimpse of the grooms.

I hadn't had much chance to stop and take anything in yet—the garlands of magnolia leaves spilling down the aisle, the scent of eucalyptus and roses filling the air—but now, standing with Nico, it all hit me at once.

And so did the truth that had been circling me for days: Bradley was here.

His summer tour had ended just last week, and for the first time in months, there was no suitcase waiting by the door, no countdown to his next flight. We'd had whole days together, mornings that slid lazily into afternoons, nights that belonged only to us. We'd survived stretches of weeks apart, calls from hotel rooms, grainy FaceTimes in different time zones, quick weekends squeezed between rehearsals. But this was different. This was him home. With me.

And tonight, as maid of honor at Nico's wedding, I felt like we were both stepping into steadier seasons. Not just Marcus and Nico, but Bradley and me, too.

The glass-walled hall glowed as Nico and I stepped inside. Candles lined the aisle, their flames flickering against polished wood. Magnolias and eucalyptus garlands spilled in lush swags, bowls of ivory roses and plum dahlias catching the light. Beyond the altar, the Atlantic stretched dark and endless, the last streaks of sunset gilding the horizon.

Joel stood across from us beside Marcus, tall and confident in his best man suit. His hand clapped Marcus's shoulder once before he stepped aside.

Marcus's whole face broke open when Nico came into view. His smile wasn't polite—it was raw, unguarded, like sunlight breaking after rain. His shoulders eased, his whole body leaning toward Nico.

Beside me, Nico's breath hitched, but when Marcus reached for his hand, everything settled.

Their vows were unpolished and perfect. Marcus stumbled, muttered a curse that made the crowd laugh, then got back on track. Nico's voice cracked halfway through, and Marcus brushed his cheek with his thumb until the words found their way out again. There was no polish, no performance—just truth, thick and bright, filling every corner of the room.

When the officiant declared them husbands, the cheer that rose shook the rafters. Marcus swept Nico into a kiss so bold the string quartet scrambled for their notes. Applause thundered, laughter rang out, and Joel's booming whistle joined the noise as he clapped hard enough to make Marcus grin mid-kiss.

I clutched my bouquet tighter, blinking back tears I couldn't stop. From the front row, Bradley caught my gaze. His smile was quiet, certain, the kind that promised forever.

The ceremony spilled into hugs and congratulations, champagne flutes clinking as servers carried trays of sparkling glasses through the crowd. Doors to the deck opened, letting in the sharp salt air and the low crash of waves against the shore.

I slipped back into maid-of-honor motion: ushering Nico's grandmother toward the fire, re-pinning a boutonniere that had gone rogue, saving Marcus from being cornered by three overzealous cousins with cameras. Joel was busy too—half best man, half brother, keeping Marcus's nerves from unraveling under the weight of everyone's attention.

Tory found me near the escort table, her cheeks pink, her champagne glass already half empty. Her dress shimmered in the firelight, and her hair had been swept into a knot that looked like effort disguised as ease.

"You look incredible," I said, hugging her quickly before someone flagged me down again.

"So do you. And you look... happy." Her gaze flicked past me to Bradley across the room, standing with Ben, laughing, a flute of champagne dangling from his hand.

"I am," I admitted.

She hesitated only a moment before saying, "Then I should tell you—Joel and I are moving in together. We're getting a place after the holidays."

"Tory... my baby sister, I am so thrilled for you."

Her happiness filled me with joy.

"I'm over the moon for you," I said, pulling her into another hug.

She squeezed me back. "And I'm happy for you. You've got Bradley. We're both finally... settling into something real, you know?"

I glanced back at Bradley, who was already watching me from across the room, a faint smile on his face. "We really are."

♫♪

The reception hall smelled of rosemary and butter. Long farmhouse tables were draped in ivory linen, adorned with taper candles glowing between bowls of flowers. Servers carried platters of roasted chicken and steaming risotto; laughter spilled louder with every glass poured.

Joel gave his toast first, standing tall at the head table. "As Marcus's brother, I can confirm he's been a pain in my ass since birth," he began, earning a roar of laughter. He softened as he spoke of Nico, how he'd never seen his brother so sure of anything. "So here's to the one thing Marcus got right without me correcting him—Nico."

Applause thundered, Marcus flipping Joel off before hugging him tight.

Then it was my turn. My knees wobbled as I stood, champagne flute trembling in my hand. Nico's eyes met mine, wide and damp, Marcus's hand anchored firmly over his.

"I've known Nico through so many chapters," I began, voice clear despite the lump in my throat. "But this—this is the chapter he was always meant to write. With Marcus, he laughs louder, shines brighter, lives freer. Together, they remind us what love should be—not perfect, not easy, but compromise, honest, and worth every stumble along the way."

I caught Bradley's gaze across the room, and the words pressed deeper, landing on me as much as them.

"To Marcus and Nico," I finished, raising my glass.

The room echoed it back, voices bright and sure, glasses clinking until the rafters shook.

The band cranked up the energy after dinner, and the first blaring horns of Van Morrison's "Domino" burst through the speakers. The room erupted—guests whooping, stomping, clapping to the beat.

Bradley was in front of me in an instant, hand outstretched, grin boyish and wide.

"Dance with me."

I laughed, letting him tug me into the crowd. The horns were brassy and wild, the rhythm infectious, the floor vibrating under the stomp of feet. He spun me once, caught me back against his chest, and I was breathless, laughing into his collar.

Around us, Marcus and Nico glowed in the center of the

floor, Joel and Tory twirling nearby, laughter bursting from them both.

I leaned closer. "So—Tory told me she and Joel are moving in together."

Bradley nodded, pulling me tighter. "I've heard," he said simply. Then his voice dropped lower, thoughtful. "And it kind of got me thinking... everyone's settling down. What do you think about me coming to Chicago more full-time? Us getting a place together. Bigger. Room for Clover and maybe Bucket."

I laughed, the sound half joy, half disbelief. "Gus," I corrected, grinning up at him. "It's Gus."

His smile widened, boyish and unguarded, and he pressed his forehead to mine as the horns of "Domino" soared. The chorus crashed, the room clapped and shouted, but all I felt was him.

53

CHRISTMAS WITH A HEART
HEATHER

DECEMBER

The boxes were still stacked like a miniature skyline against the loft's brick wall, but I didn't care. We'd only moved in a week ago, and most of our dishes were still wrapped in newspaper, but there was no way I was letting December pass without a tree.

"Priorities," I told Bradley as he wrestled the six-foot fir through the door.

He shot me a mock glare, grunting as the branches scraped the frame. "You know, most people unpack before they deck the halls."

"Most people don't have me," I countered, holding the base steady while he straightened the trunk.

Gus immediately tried to dive nose-first into the pine needles, his golden tail sweeping boxes like a wrecking ball. I scooped him up before he toppled the entire tree, his warm puppy body wriggling against my chest.

"Curious boy," I muttered, kissing the top of his head.

Clover, unimpressed as ever, gave us all a regal glance from her perch on the windowsill.

We strung lights and ornaments in between bursts of laughter. Bradley untangled strands of bulbs like he was wrestling a boa constrictor, swearing under his breath until I rescued him. I hung ornaments I'd carted from my old apartment—delicate glass stars, snowflakes, angels. He added a few from a box his mom gave him, including a tiny guitar that looked exactly like one of his Martins.

When I placed the last ornament, Bradley slid an arm around my waist and leaned back with me to admire the glow. The tree cast warm light across the open loft, bouncing off the tall windows and making the brick walls feel softer. For the first time, it felt less like a warehouse full of cardboard and more like a home.

"Not bad for a week in," he murmured.

"Not bad at all," I agreed.

The rest of the day blurred with unpacking—Bradley cursing at Ikea instructions, Gus running off with socks from half-open suitcases, me reorganizing the kitchen twice before admitting defeat. By the time the sun dropped, we were sweaty, hungry, and still stepping over piles of flattened boxes.

We ordered Chinese and ate right out of the boxes, cross-legged on the floor, as we stole bites from each other's orange chicken and chicken fried rice.

By the time we made it to bed, I could barely keep my eyes open. Gus settled into his crate with a groan, and Clover curled in her round little bed.

Bradley leaned back against the pillows, hair damp from the shower, looking unfairly good for someone who'd just unpacked all day. "Okay," he said, his grin mischievous. "Questions."

I groaned, sliding under the blanket. "Now? I was hoping for sleep."

"Just one each."

I sighed dramatically. "Fine. You first."

His eyes softened, even as his smile stayed boyish. "Will you be my girl forever?"

I blinked, my laugh catching in my throat. "That's your question?"

But then he reached into the nightstand and pulled out a small velvet box. Inside was a ring—antique, simple, with a delicate setting that looked like it had lived a hundred stories before finding its way here.

My hand flew to my mouth. "Bradley…"

He held it out, voice steady. "Music gave me everything I thought I wanted. But what it really gave me was you. And I don't want to spend another day wondering if you'll be here when I come back from the road. I want you. Always."

Tears pricked my eyes, spilling before I could stop them. I laughed through them, nodding too fast. "Yes. Of course, yes."

He slid the ring onto my finger, and seeing it there— solid, certain—made my chest ache with joy.

"One more question." I laughed and nodded, still in disbelief.

"How about we get married in Punta Cana, New year's? Keep it small?"

"I love that idea, toes in the sand. Surrounded by all the people we love."

"I thought we agreed on small."

"You know, the core people." I looked at the ring, then rolled over toward Bradley. He pulled me on top of him, and we kissed until the world narrowed to just us, until Gus shifted in his crate with a sleepy sigh, until Clover stretched in her bed like she was satisfied the night was complete.

I curled into Bradley's chest, the ring pressing softly against my skin. It felt like the note we left hanging all those years ago finally found its way back to us.

THE END

Chapter 1
Meredith

I told myself it was for the best.

The thing is, I don't fall for people. I don't let it get that far. Once was enough—and I promised myself I'd never do it again.

So I should've known better than to get involved with a sexy surfer who lived halfway across the country. The kind of man who made everything feel easy until it wasn't. Evan and I were a slow-motion train wreck from the start. Distance, timing, too many ghosts between us. Two people raised on divorce trying to prove we weren't built the same way.

The subway jolted, pulling me back to the present. I was two stops from my East Village loft when my phone buzzed —Natalie. My older sister.

I let it go to voicemail. There was no way I could reach my pocket without ending up in the lap of the sixty-something-year-old man beside me, who was holding a cat carrier that smelled faintly of tuna.

When the train screeched to a stop, I climbed the stairs and stepped into one of those rare spring days that make New York feel almost kind. The kind where you can actually feel the vitamin D soaking in, the sun kissing your skin in the most perfect way, and you know summer is just around the corner.

My stop left me a few blocks from home. I passed a café that knew my order, a record shop that never seemed open when I had time, and a mural that always changed but somehow stayed the same.

My building was a narrow walk-up on East Ninth, rent-controlled and stubbornly standing against time. My corner loft had the same mismatched decor I'd pieced together over the years, plus a few of Natalie's "finds" to make it look less tragic. Like the brass lamp that gave off the softest glow next to my forest-green reading chair—the one place I could breathe.

That's where I dropped my bag and called her back.

"Hey, Mer," she said, her voice muffled as a door clicked shut behind her.

"Hello my loving sister, you called earlier."

"I was checking to see if you really can't make it for the Fourth this year. We rented a lake house in Coeur d'Alene— plenty of room for you."

"I already told you—Jack's got a new boyfriend, so his all-white party in the Hamptons has to be extra. It's our thing."

"Last year, we were your thing."

"Last summer was different."

"I know," Natalie said softly. "I really thought you two were going to be it."

What she said stuck in a place I didn't want to touch.

My natural reaction was just to bury every piece of him.

I'd spent the past year convincing myself I was fine. That what happened with Evan was just a mistake. That I didn't need anyone. I'm best alone.

And then, as if the universe were listening and wanted to test me, my phone buzzed again.

Evan's name lit up the screen.

ACKNOWLEDGMENTS

I have always been infatuated with musicians. We rarely get to truly see their love stories, only fragments through lyrics, interviews, or the occasional glimpse on social media. Every time I attend a concert I love, I leave transformed. The music reaches something deep in my soul, and for those few hours, I become completely carefree.

I have to thank my husband, who first started bringing me to live shows. Somehow, every time we stand in a crowd and let the music get under our ribs and beat in our chests, we rediscover each other.

My goal with this book was to capture a bit of that magic, to take readers behind the scenes and into Bradley's world. I knew the perfect girl for him would be another artist, someone who finds passion and joy in creating.

I kept thinking, how wild would it be to meet your true love when you are young and on a trip?

To make that believable, I had to backdate the timeline. It was much harder to find people in 2001. I wanted the story to feel authentic. I worried that setting part of the book in 2016 might bring some pushback, but Bradley and Heather needed to reconnect in their early thirties.

Having lived in Chicago during my twenties, I was able to immerse myself again in that season of life, The Hangge Uppe, riding the El, the city streets, revisiting old hotspots in my memory.

It is always my intention to be as real and raw as possible

through my characters' eyes. Stories come to life through letters and words stitched together on a page.

As always, there are so many people to thank when bringing a book into the world.

To start, my dream team.

Bree Sleater, you not only read this book early, you read chapters as I wrote them, showing up for this story in real time. You were in the trenches with me, helping me work through scenes and even nail one of my spiciest moments. I am forever grateful for your support, your honesty, and the way you poured into this book with me.

Jess Pajda, you used your magic to build an incredible content and ARC team and created so much momentum around this book. You spent countless hours organizing, promoting, and bringing this story into the hands of readers across the country. I am so appreciative for everything you poured into this.

Autumn Morgan, you have been such a steady and important part of this journey. From refining the editing and formatting to creating beautiful digital pieces, your care and attention to detail shine through in everything you do. You keep everything running so smoothly, and I am incredibly grateful for you.

You all are the reason this book has reached so many readers. Thank you, truly.

To my editors, thank you for your patience.

Sara Oestreich, you pushed me to dig deep into Heather and Bradley's emotional layers and helped shape them into the love they ultimately found. You believed I would finish this even when I wanted to toss the manuscript out the window.

Liza Illuzzi, you always swoop in and save me. Your calm energy and sharp eye are unmatched.

To my beta readers, this book carries your fingerprints in more ways than I can count. You caught the details I missed, asked the questions that mattered, and pushed me to make this story stronger, clearer, and more honest.

Amy Barnhisel, Kristy Cropper, Jessica Walton, Dee Whetton, and Allison Moffett, thank you for showing up for this story and for me. I am so grateful for each of you.

And to Laura Low, Kristin Pokrass, Vanessa Frias, and Nancy Purcell, thank you for reading this story in its earliest stages and believing in me.

To Jimi Purse, I do not even know where to begin. Thank you for taking the time to speak with me and walk me through your world. The way you described life on stage, the moments backstage, and the weight music carries shaped Bradley in ways I could not have created on my own. You did not just share your experience, you wrote three songs for him. You brought him to life in a way I will never forget.

To my content and ARC team, holy cow. I do not know how I got so lucky. Thank you for reading this story and taking a chance on me. You are shining stars in the indie world, and I am endlessly grateful for you.

To my daughters, thank you for being so patient when I worked endless weekend hours. Thank you for checking in and asking how many chapters I had left. You have my whole heart.

To my husband, whom I met when I was fifteen, I suppose we had our own second chance romance. Our story began in those teenage years, and though there was always something there, it took thirteen years to truly begin. I got so lucky with you. You are the sound to my heart. (I know so cheesy but, sometimes I have to be.) I love you!

And finally, to my readers, thank you for choosing this

book and for spending time with Bradley and Heather. Your messages, posts, and comments mean more than you know. I savor every one of them.

If this story stayed with you, one of the most meaningful ways you can support it is by leaving a review. Even a few words makes a difference and helps indie authors like me continue telling the stories we love.

From the bottom of my heart, thank you.

Some stories stay with us long after the last page, like a song we never stop hearing.

ABOUT THE AUTHOR

Jillian Marie Feulner is a writer, reader, and mom to three daughters who inspire much of the heart in her stories. She lives for cozy mornings with tea, sun-soaked beach days with her girls, and quiet evenings at home with a good book —and her husband, who's always cheering her on.

She writes about love, longing, and the unexpected turns that make life beautiful. When she's not writing, you'll likely find her in her happy place: Coronado, with sand between her toes and story ideas swirling.

CONTENT WARNING

- On-page sex
- Emotional neglect from a partner
- Depictions of emotional abuse and controlling behaviors from a partner
- References to divorce and absentee fathers
- Emotional cheating
- Non-marital infidelity (kissing only)

P*lease evaluate what you can handle and prioritize your mental health.*

This story features emotional abuse from a partner and childhood trauma from parental abandonment and emotional immaturity.

It also features emotional cheating and physical infidelity (kissing and cuddling).

These can be triggering for survivors; however, this is still a romance at its core, and there is a healing journey to be made. If you do decide to continue reading, you can take comfort in knowing that you're not alone. I'm here with you. And the story does contain a Happily Ever After.